THE LOVESICK WOMEN OF
THE EMERGENCY WARD

Pam is on the brink of realizing her dream of power at Chandler Medical Center, only to find herself back in the arms of a doctor who could turn it into a nightmare.

Lisa has one last chance to break the hold that drugs have on her body and that a diabolically domineering dealer has on her flesh.

Avon discovers that wearing her white uniform will not make people in power forget the color of her skin.

Rosa is torn between her determination to be a perfect doctor and her desires as a woman.

Meredith can deal with patients' mental disorders but not her own guilt about her heritage.

This is Chandler Medical Center, where contagious scandal stalks the corridors in crisp and spotless uniforms and hides behind a medical mask. . . .

THE NURSES

THE NURSES

Tyler Cortland

A SIGNET BOOK

SIGNET
Published by the Penguin Group
Penguin Books USA Inc., 375 Hudson Street,
New York, New York 10014, U.S.A.
Penguin Books Ltd, 27 Wrights Lane,
London W8 5TZ, England
Penguin Books Australia Ltd, Ringwood,
Victoria, Australia
Penguin Books Canada Ltd, 10 Alcorn Avenue,
Toronto, Ontario, Canada M4V 3B2
Penguin Books (N.Z.) Ltd, 182–190 Wairau Road,
Auckland 10, New Zealand

Penguin Books Ltd, Registered Offices:
Harmondsworth, Middlesex, England

First published by Signet, an imprint of Dutton Signet,
a division of Penguin Books USA Inc.

First Printing, January, 1996
10 9 8 7 6 5 4 3 2 1

Printed in the United States of America

PUBLISHER'S NOTE
This is a work of fiction. Names, characters, places, and incidents either are
the product of the author's imagination or are used fictitiously, and any resem-
blance to actual persons, living or dead, events, or locales is entirely
coincidental.

BOOKS ARE AVAILABLE AT QUANTITY DISCOUNTS WHEN USED TO PROMOTE PROD-
UCTS OR SERVICES. FOR INFORMATION PLEASE WRITE TO PREMIUM MARKETING DIVI-
SION, PENGUIN BOOKS USA INC., 375 HUDSON STREET, NEW YORK, NEW YORK 10014.

If you purchased this book without a cover you should be aware that this book
is stolen property. It was reported as "unsold and destroyed" to the publisher
and neither the author nor the publisher has received any payment for this
"stripped book."

This book is dedicated to:

Mark Waldman, for his encouragement,
support and caring;
Ron Patzer, for the gift of Mark Waldman;
Mark Lirman, for his many hours adjusting
and repairing my computer;
Ron Francis, for his technical advice
and proofreading;

and

in memory of
Melissa, a pit/lab girl, who should have
had a happier life

STAFF OF CHANDLER MEDICAL CENTER

Dr. Josh Allister New York radiologist; dated Allison and now engaged to Margaret

Dr. Richard Bell former chief of staff; suffering from Bell's Palsy

Dr. Leroy Carter wisecracking anesthesiologist

Avon Dupree, R.N. witty black nurse from Chicago who didn't think Chandler Springs would be quite so racist

Dr. Meredith Fischer CMC's head of psychiatry and new Chief of Staff who has to confront her own past before she can move into her future

Carrie Harper, L.V.N. barely making it through the one-year licensed nursing program, she cried her way through training and changed her name to get this job

Dr. Ellis Johnston the perfectionist head of surgery

Vicki Kantera, R.N. former music prodigy who gave up her career and ended up in Chandler Springs

Dr. Marcus Laurence former hospital administrator, a Yankee who couldn't keep his hands off Pam

Dr. Catherine McCormack endocrinologist

Dr. Sara McNamara compassionate pediatrician

Dr. William Martin greedy radiologist

Dr. Cole Morgan good ol' boy chief of ER for CMC, finally married to his high school sweetheart, Sophie, and rightful father of Lisa

Sophie Drummond Morgan, R.N. harried head of nursing, and married to her high school sweetheart, Cole

Sean O'Neill, Ph.D. Irish psychologist; boyfriend to Meredith

Pam Roberts, R.N. a new nurse with a secret score to settle

Nelson St. Clair mysterious and sleazy new administrator

Dr. Rosa Sanchez feisty but dedicated cardiologist

Jennifer Stauton, R.N. having been through Vietnam and Houston's trauma center, Ben Taub, she wants to put her past behind her

Dr. Ken Stevens CMC's head of OB/GYN

Dr. Patrick Thompson Ellis' partner, specializes in surgery of the limbs

Dr. Tyler Van Fleet donut-loving pathologist, neighbor to Ellis

THE RESIDENTS OF CHANDLER SPRINGS

Emma Chandler matriarch of Chandler Springs hiding a secret past

Allison Chandler her beautiful but spoiled granddaughter

Margaret Chandler Allison's disfigured sister

Lisa Drummond Sophie and Cole's troubled daughter

Amy Johnston Ellis' teen daughter

Hillary Johnston Ellis Johnston's bitter and unbalanced wife

Will Johnston Ellis' young son growing up too fast

Salty Larson shifty land developer

Coral May McQuade Jacob McQuade's second wife and ex-cocktail waitress

Jacob McQuade, deceased Allison and Margaret's maternal grandfather

Karin Martin Bill Martin's long-suffering wife

Randy Ogelby Pam's nasty baby brother

Ophelia Thompson daughter of Patrick Thompson and girlfriend to Will

Frank Willis Sophie's one-time boyfriend and bigoted chief of police for Chandler Springs

THE VISITORS TO CHANDLER SPRINGS

Julius Ciss old man in the plane crash

George Dupree Avon's younger and favorite brother, who visits her on vacation

Nancy Hoffner young pianist from the plane crash

Dr. Ari Mendelson grandson to Julius Ciss; friend to Meredith Fischer

Angel (Stauton) orphaned Asian infant from plane crash

Ian Williams Vietnam pilot who turned to drink and now flies charters instead of copters

CHAPTER 1

Not many people flew on Christmas Eve, but those who did were usually able to get special-rate tickets. A bargain. Maybe.

While the mechanics did their routine safety check, Flight 441, an eleven-seater Beech Super King Air 200, was shown as being fully booked. Being a low-wing twin turboprop, it could cruise at 329 mph, while holding a ceiling of nearly 33,000 feet, which should have been enough for the majority of weather conditions.

Pilot Ian Williams felt confident of his skills and of the weather, so confident that he drank "a few for the road." After all, it *was* Christmas Eve. Bad enough he had to work and wouldn't see his daughters until late the next day.

William Hobby Airport, smack dab in the center of Houston, was usually bustling with people. But not tonight. Ian looked around from his stool. Tonight, only the bar, one restaurant, and one bookshop were open.

"Weather ceiling's awfully low," the bartender commented. "You sure they're still having you fly?"

"Yeah." Ian gulped his gin and tonic. "The company wants every dollar it can get—and then some. Besides, I can probably fly over it. Give them a nice velvety ride." He rode his hand down the old-fashioned, polished counter. His hand seemed to shake ever so slightly with the effect of the drinks.

The bartender shrugged his shoulders as the P.A. announced the flight. They were headed first to Corpus Christi and then on up to Dallas before returning to Houston.

"Gotta run. Thanks for the Christmas cheer. Check you next time around."

"You do that."

Gingerly the plane started its climb as the tower gave permission to leave the runway. The power edged up a little too slowly for comfort. The wet weather had probably driven the humidity up. Ian should have checked before climbing in, but he had to fly this route no matter what. Besides, he'd been late filing his flight plan and the company didn't like tardiness. Not where the FAA was concerned.

Not many planes out tonight. In fact, damn few. Ian wished he had called the company. Should have stood up to them. Should have told them it was a no go, but he wanted the cash, too. After all, a little overtime went a long way to pay those alimony checks, not to mention Christmas gifts for the girls.

Turbulence began almost immediately. A little rockin' and rollin' never hurt anybody. Besides, it wasn't like they were serving gourmet here. It wasn't like they were serving anything at all. What a comedown from the 747s he'd flown for United, or even the B-52s in 'Nam. But, hey, all that was history. He had his application in to the Concorde people. Imagine flying *twice* the speed of sound. With a record like his, how could they turn him down? But now the rollercoaster ride started again. Speed bumps in the sky, he called it.

He spoke into the mike, but it had stopped functioning, again. He remembered he hadn't told the mechanic that it had refused to come on before. Well, whatever. Ian's voice being plenty loud, in a plane this size—there were few extra amenities and no flight attendants to serve coffee or tea—he shouted over the noise of the engines.

"Everyone needs to keep their seat belts on for the whole flight." Then he pointed toward the exit doors in case of emergency. Shit. They shoulda had one of the gals come on board just to do that.

In his twenty years of flying, some even in 'Nam, he'd never used the emergency exits. Never had to. Never planned to.

Besides, they were only going over to Corpus Christi. A mere hop and skip. By the time he jumped, Ian thought, he'd be in Dallas and then back to Houston.

Ian glanced back at his passengers: A bearded old man in a black hat swayed a bit as if trying to keep the plane on course, an Asian girl of about five going to Dallas for adoption. He shook his head. Some people were desperate for babies, no matter what the color. And then there was Nancy Hoffner, the celebrated pianist. He didn't know about hands, but her legs were something to stare at.

Keep your cool, Ian. A beauty such as that probably has a dozen or so swarming around her. Still, he wouldn't mind being the thirteenth. A baker's dozen.

The plane rocked. "Jesus!" he cursed. It was worse than the Matterhorn ride at Disney. The winds clocked at 300 mph. He pulled the throttle, trying to climb above the storm, but the craft couldn't gear up to full power.

He checked the fuel mixture and then tried to throttle again. Everything was set at maximum. This Beech was an old gal. The company should have retired her before this, but they wanted to squeeze every last cent out of their machines.

Everyone knew control worsened with increased humidity, but he hadn't expected it to be this bad. Temperature and humidity played key factors in making density altitude a problem, but usually it was easier to fly in the cool weather.

Ian tugged at the throttle, pulling it back farther. If this baby wanted a fight, then he'd just take her all the way. No one was getting the best of Ian Williams.

Hail hit hard, huge balls glancing off his windshield. Good thing the instrument panel worked, because he couldn't see a blasted thing. He pulled the throttle harder than he'd ever done before. All the way to the top. Not even the fear of the stick breaking off in his hand stopped him. Ian became only vaguely aware of the engine noise above the sound of his own heartbeat. "Come on, baby. You can do it, girl."

Sweat beaded his temples. He tried listening harder. The engine was gone! He'd lost control of the right propeller. Iced over.

"Jesus!" Ian wiped his brow with one hand as the other reached for the radio. This altitude made him dizzy. Maybe he'd best head down a bit.

He remembered his flight trainer saying, "The higher you get, the higher you get." He'd only had two drinks. A mere pittance of alcohol, yet it was acting on him as if he'd had five or six. Who would have thought that? "Jesus H," was all he could say as he clicked on the radio.

Static. Just static. He wiped his brow again.

Well, he'd dealt with one engine before. Third day out of Cam Rahn Bay. The gooks had gotten one of his engines. He'd handled that just fine. He'd handle this one fine, too.

Ian tried the radio one more time as he glanced

around. "Beech zero-zero-four-niner to tower. Anyone copy?"

In a fog bank now, he'd no idea where he was or if he was still on course. The compass spun crazily. Too much goddamn electrical stuff in the air.

Suddenly, he felt the plane falling as if the air and the winds stopped. Just like that time in 'Nam when his parachute stuck shut. *Jeez.*

He glanced in his mirror. The engine was working. *The left engine was working,* he repeated to himself. Must have hit a downdraft. Damn! All he needed now was a wind shear. Mouth dry, he attempted following the winds down and pulling the plane back up. No big thing, usually—but now the damn throttle wouldn't move.

As the plane continued its fall, Ian realized his attempts were fruitless.

Sweat poured from his brow as he swallowed and prayed harder than ever before.

No matter what he did, crashing was inevitable.

It was well past midnight. Everyone was at Emma Chandler's spectacular annual Christmas party at the Circle C, just outside the town the old matriarch ruled, Chandler Springs. She was queen of her own private court. Her holiday galas almost always proved a success. *Except for tonight,* Emma's granddaughter Margaret thought. Tonight Nana had let the snake out of the can.

To put it mildly, the local medical center's chief radiologist, Dr. William Martin, seen by many as an overpriced adulterer, had not been pleased with Nana's announcement that Dr. Meredith Fischer, Chandler Springs's psychiatrist, would be the new chief of staff when Dr. Richard Bell retired at the end of the year. Bill had been so positive Emma would reward him with the vacated position that he had already ordered his new cards. Emma ruled the hospital just as she did the town and her ranch, didn't she? He should have just sucked up to her more.

It would have been an even crueler joke on Bill if Dr. Bell had been convinced to reconsider keeping his position yet another year, as he had so many times in the past. But the Parkinsonian symptoms of uneven gait, drooling, stuttering, and especially the palsied limbs made it impossible for Bell to continue on either as a physician or as chief of staff. Not even his associate, Dr. Bob Tilton, who was nearly as infirm as Bell himself, could have taken on the job.

What dug even deeper under Bill Martin's thick skin was that Emma Chandler handed the reins of power over to a woman—a woman like Meredith Fischer! What the hell did a psychiatrist know about running a hospital?

It's not that Bill had anything he could pin against Meredith; it was just something about her that never seemed right. Maybe she had gone into psychiatry so she could shrink herself. Imagine dating a man nearly half her age. How old was she? Probably in her late forties. Bill snorted. The Irish lout, Sean O'Neill, chemical dependency psychologist, could be no more than thirty, with about as much sense as a ten-year-old.

Bill gulped his martini and poured another while his wife, Karin, made a tight frown.

"We'll just see how long she lasts," he said, ignoring his wife. "A woman like that can't handle the stresses and pressures. Not the way I can." He mumbled more to himself than to Karin.

"How could Emma have done this to you?" Long-suffering Karin whispered to him, watching her husband down his third martini. "I thought it was all arranged. Bill, uh, maybe you should talk with her."

"Yeah, I'll tell you what was arranged. Joshua Allister and his New York buddies. You think *I* don't know that the great thoracic surgeon Ellis Johnston sucks up to him because he's going to be a Chandler? In fact, that's what they're all doing. Stupid jerks. That's what was arranged. Now that Joshua, the medical center's *finest* radiologist, has wormed his way back into Emma's good graces by announcing his engagement to the ugly sister tonight, he's in for keeps—"

"Bill!" Karin hissed. Josh's fiancée, Margaret stood within earshot of them, and Karin hoped she hadn't heard.

"I don't give a damn!" He shook Karin's hand off and raised his voice a little. "I'm going to show them a thing or two." He stared goggle-eyed for a moment, looking at Pam Roberts in her low-cut dress. The little two-bit whore! He would love to just take her now. Right here on this floor and . . . all right, so she was Emma's grand-niece, but who was she to hide all her secrets from him? He'd make her pay for that. Beg for mercy.

His head pounded with anger. Who the hell was she to have made an ass out of him? Why had she decided to play with him? He clenched the stem of the glass. With only a touch more pressure, it would break in half, just like he wanted to break her? Why the hell hadn't she said something to him?

How could she be a Chandler and not tell him! How?

By God, Bill Martin did not like being made a fool of. *He'd make her pay for that. Beg for mercy. Yeah.* He gulped down most of his martini and grimaced, thinking of all those stolen moments—in the nurses station, the linen closet, the empty bed, the floor of the medication room, and of course, her apartment. They'd done it all—everywhere.

His mouth became tighter. So why the fuck hadn't she trusted him with this? God, what a waste of a chance! After all, he had trusted her with the knowledge that . . . well, never mind. It didn't matter now what he had told her, only what she hadn't told him. He was in control of this game and that's the way it would stay.

Why, if he'd known that she was Emma's niece, he would have been on his hands and knees immediately. A slight smile parted his lips as he thought of her sparse blond hairs peeking out of her string panties as she walked on her hands and knees. Bill Martin flushed. If only he had known. That last time . . . no, she wouldn't hold it against him. After all, she'd been asking for it. Just like the whore always did.

He could have made such use of their relationship in achieving what he wanted from the old dame. Bill wanted to cry. It was all her damn fault. If Pamela had told him that she was related to the Chandlers. . . . Well, he knew certainly that Dr. Fischer, with her yapping mind, would never have received the honor, which was to have been his. All Pammy would have had to do is put a good word into Auntie Em for him.

And why was it that Emma was just *now* announcing her relationship? What the hell was the girl's game?

Yeah. He'd have a word with her, too. But those words would be in private.

Unaware that the almost empty glass he'd placed on a table had fallen, Bill mowed through the crowd, blundering into a band member, knocking over a tray of capers and cheddar cheese. His face reddened in anger even as he continued thinking about the insult.

Joshua stood in the exact center of the room, right under the Waterford chandelier. Bill reached his "partner" in two uneasy steps and grabbed Joshua's shoulder, spinning him around.

Bill yanked the glass from the surprised Joshua's hand, spilling some of the drink on the man's tux. "Do I say congratulations, *Dr.* Allister? You have the prize catch. Should be worth a sweet penny or two. Maybe now you can stop making such a fool of yourself in radiology and let the big boys practice the way it's *supposed* to be done."

Recognizing that Bill Martin was drunk, Josh decided not to say anything. It wasn't his fault that the majority of the physicians at Chandler Medical Center—CMC—sent him all their patients. Bill had mixed his own cement, especially when he'd performed the sloppy lymphogram on Jacob McQuade and then had the gall to cover it up, making it seem as if Ellis Johnston, their best thoracic surgeon, had made the fatal error that resulted in Jacob's death.

Maybe if Bill had admitted his culpability, the rest of the staff would have understood. Everyone made mistakes, but not everyone buried evidence of their mistakes in the back files. Had Joshua not found the original report, Ellis might still be fighting the lawsuit.

"Not talking?" Bill said with a sneer. "Must be the cream of satisfaction, *Dr.* Allister." He turned to glance at Pam for a long moment. She knew what he'd— they'd—been planning. It had been Pam's idea for him to start his own outpatient clinic, rivaling the costs and expertise of CMC. And that was just what he intended on doing.

Of course, Pam wanted Bill to leave Karin and marry her. He hadn't thought about that until now; until he had learned that Pam was really part of the Chandler family. Might just be the little feather for his cap. He grinned leeringly in her direction. He'd just have to do something about Karin, that's all.

Then he turned his attention back to the matter at

hand. "Answer me, Allister, or I'm really gonna get angry."

Coolly, Josh pried his glass out of Bill Martin's hand and placed it carefully on the table behind him. "I think you're drunk, Dr. Martin. I also think you're already furious about not getting the chief of staff position. But you'll get over it."

"Hell, I will!" With two beefy hands the radiologist shoved Joshua Allister to the floor.

For a brief moment Josh lay there, rubbing his jaw, and then struggled to his feet. He stood with his fiancée, Margaret, at his side.

"Bill!" Karin ran to her husband.

"You stay out of this. You don't know anything. All you want to do is stay home and raise those damn Appaloosas. They're more important to you than I am. Even the boys complain."

"Bill, the boys don't live with us anymore. Remember? College? Grad school?" She grabbed his arm. "Come on. Let's go home."

"Leave off me, woman. I'm tired of your nagging." With the same strength he'd used on Josh, he pushed Karin to the ground. The onlookers who'd gathered around quickly moved to give him space, gasping at Bill Martin's actions.

Meredith bent to help Karin up.

"I understand. It's not your fault," Karin said.

Meredith frowned and glanced from Karin to Bill and then to Sean, whom she'd recently gotten back together with. "I'm more concerned about you than I am about him. Is he like this a lot?" She handed Karin some tissues to wipe the blood from her nose.

Karin shrugged. "Bill is Bill."

"And you. You stay out of this!" Bill turned his wrath to the new chief of staff. "I don't know what you did to con the Chandlers, Meredith, but believe me, you'll pay. All of you will."

Sean stepped forward just in case he had to defend Meredith's honor.

The whole room had their fingers on some imaginary but very real VCR pause button. Muffled sounds filtered in from the dining area, where the servants placed last-minute preparations on the buffet table.

Bill's eyes darted from one "enemy" to another. Enough said. He roughly grabbed his wife's arm and dragged her from the party.

The long pause continued. It was as if someone had forgotten to push the VCR's play button.

Then suddenly Meredith took Sean into the middle of the makeshift dance floor, where Josh and Bill had scuffled not minutes before.

Naturally and busily, everyone began speaking and moving at once. The band returned to the string quartet exactly where they had left off.

Within seconds, only the principal players were still thinking about the events of the past few minutes.

It had been expected that Bill Martin would be unhappy. Almost everyone knew he'd been buttering Emma up for this promotion. Now it was all in the past.

Emma herself wondered why he hadn't just come up to talk to her as she had hoped he would—in a civilized fashion. Obviously, the alcohol had gotten to him, and just like Meredith, Emma couldn't help wondering how much abuse Karin took. She, too, had noticed Karin's weight loss and sallow complexion.

Emma wanted to believe Karin's present physical problems resulted from the aftereffects of her previous near brush with death. But even when she tried bringing the subject up, the radiologist's wife had said that everything was fine.

No matter how many times Meredith or Emma spoke with Karin, Mrs. Martin refused to believe that her fall down the hospital steps two months ago, which had resulted in a broken leg, had been deliberately planned.

Maybe Meredith or Emma might have been willing to accept the fall as "an accident" even though their instincts told them it was not. But then while she'd been recovering from the fall, how was it that an overdose of heparin, a drug not even prescribed to Karin, had found its way into her IV line?

Karin had at least admitted that she felt lucky her physician, Rosa Sanchez, had chosen that night to check in on her. Staff member or not, Bill Martin would surely have sued the hospital if his wife had died. Unless, of course, they could prove that he had had a hand in her death.

Although Karin's leg remained in a cast, she had been released weeks ago by Rosa Sanchez, the director of cardiology, whom Emma had recruited from UCLA. Dr. Sanchez had pronounced Karin free of the excess heparin that had overwhelmed her body. But maybe not quite. Why else would Karin's nose bleed so quickly?

Emma pressed her lips together. She did not tolerate abuse from her men. Nor did she tolerate it among any of her workers, ranch hands to physicians included. She wanted this occurrence investigated. If warranted, she would ask Bill Martin, despite his longevity on staff and despite his radiology department being the only real moneymaker for the hospital, to leave. As to his displeasure over Meredith Fischer's appointment as chief of staff over him, Emma shrugged. If Bill wanted the job, short of killing the psychiatrist, the radiologist would have to force Meredith into quitting.

Like the queen mother she was, Emma motioned for Pam to come sit by her on the podium. Emma had noticed her new niece's look of surprise when the girl had been called onto the podium. Probably she wondered how Emma had discovered who she really was, but Emma wasn't going to tell her that Meredith had been the one to investigate because she'd been jealous of the girl's relationship with Seth.

Emma didn't care about that and neither would the girl. That young'un was strong and she was smart. Not that her Allison and Margaret weren't smart, too, but they were softer, more pampered. Emma could see in the girl's face and in her eyes that the girl was just like her. It wouldn't take Pamela long to discover anything she wanted, even the fact that Emma'd phoned her lawyer to come for a bit of champagne and to meet the newest Chandler heir and maybe sign a paper or two.

But Emma had more surprises in stock for the one who was a spitting image of herself. It still choked her up to think that her oldest sister, Dottie, had thought of her, Emma, on her deathbed and sent Pam to her.

"Come on over, Pamela." Emma again patted the Italian leather bench next to her. She smiled fondly at her grand-niece. Her heart burst with pride, almost like it did when she'd birthed Tommy. This was a girl after Emma's heart. One she could mold properly. And she was going to make sure that her new niece lacked nothing.

Most of the staff knew that Pam had been seen in Bill's company more than once. If Emma's grand-niece was going to travel in the company of married men, the older woman felt there might be a thing or two the girl ought to know.

*   *   *

Rain continued to pelt the ground, coming down like bullets, while the wind whipped up, swaying the few scraggly trees as if isolated beach dancers.

Margaret stepped onto the patio for some air. She had never liked parties and this one in particular. But for Nana's sake she always attended. Of course, tonight had been special since she and Josh announced their engagement. She loved him so very much. Did he really love her the same? The same as he had loved her sister, Allison, when the pair had been dating?

How could he even compare the two? Even with her crutches, Allison was so much prettier and livelier than Margaret was. Allison would make a perfect physician's wife—always entertaining and making sure her husband had the best of everything.

Were the rumors being whispered around actually true—that he was marrying Margaret only for the Chandler money? She didn't want to believe it, yet she felt so frightened. If only Grandpa Jacob were still alive. She'd be able to talk to him, and he'd cut right through her cow pies.

Margaret's hand automatically darted to her face. Even though the laser surgery fixing her burn scars had been done nearly six months ago, Margaret still thought of herself as the ugly duckling. Allison's poise and beauty made her the one who wowed the crowds with her knowledge of style and fashion.

Margaret felt she owed a great debt to her Beverly Hills' friend Katherine White, wife of the movie magnate Nathan White. If it hadn't been for Katherine's nagging, Margaret would still probably not have owned half of the rich and fashionable clothes she did. While she hoped Katherine and Nate would come for the ceremony, she secretly wished Katherine would help her select her wedding gown.

The French doors opened behind her. The band played "Pachebel," one of Nana's favorites. Margaret's too. When Emma Chandler gave a party, she spared no expense.

The wind gusted in her face. Margaret turned to see who was crazy enough to join her in the rain.

It was Raoul, her head *vaquero* from the Rocking M, the ranch Grandpa Jacob McQuade had left Allison and her. Jacob had always hired Mexicans because he believed the land was originally theirs. Upon Grandpa's death, she and Allison had kept everyone who had been with Grandpa. If it worked, why change it?

She watched Raoul tilt back his head to drink in drops of rain. Obviously he was more drunk than he realized. She would have to make sure that he didn't drive home. With his six kids to feed, she didn't want to add their names to the list of her already growing responsibilities. But of course she would. The workers had no insurance. They had nothing but what Jacob McQuade and now the Chandler sisters had to offer them. But going over the books, as she had often done for her grandfather, Margaret had made sure that even the oldest employees received a pension. It was important, she thought, that they knew they were appreciated.

Her mind wandered to the house she and Josh would build out there. Everything, even this storm tonight, seemed unreal. It was too bad the original ranch house had burned down, but that was Coral May's doing.

Grandpa's second wife, Coral May, had been a lounge singer and waitress in Richmond before she'd met Jacob. Nana called her white trash and hated dealing with her. While Coral May's West Texas twang was definitely irksome, she apparently meant well. Margaret tried to keep that in mind. She felt sure that Grandpa had enjoyed his final years with her.

If only . . . No, Margaret, she told herself firmly, "*if only*" *will not bring Grandpa back.* Nor would it bring back the house. Coral May had been so insistent on a gazebo with lights that Margaret had finally given in. Hoping it would keep the woman from taking the easement water headed for the lower ranches.

But giving in to Coral May had proved the worst move Margaret could have made. The older woman didn't know anything about safety hazards and probably didn't care, so long as it all "looked pretty."

Once the house had burned down, Allison and Margaret had two choices. To rebuild for Coral May—but that would have been difficult, considering the adjuster offered only $150,000. The other option was to trade with her, taking the land and finding her a house in the city.

As a wedding present, Allison had agreed that Margaret could trade her half of their fashionable spa for the area encompassing the former ranch house. It was there that Margaret and Josh would start their dreams.

Margaret wondered how Allison survived with *that* woman. But her sister said that Coral May's hostessing in the lounge had helped her mingle with the people, bringing them in. Maybe the fire was a good thing after all. Nana always said that "God didn't close one door without opening another."

"*¡Dios Mio!*" Raoul cried out, pointing to the northern sky at what looked to be a meteorite streaking down. "A sign from Jesus, no?" He blinked rapidly as if he could not believe it. "Maybe we will have three wise men and a babe. Yes?"

Margaret cursed her new contacts as she peered into the darkness, trying to determine what had fallen and where. "No, Raoul, I don't think so. It looks more to me like something's on fire and it seems to be near the Rocking M."

Turning quickly, Margaret darted through the ballroom and up the double marble stairs to her room. She switched on her CB, changing frequencies, listening as she shimmied out of her formal gown and back into her comfy jeans, boots, and sweater.

As her frustration mounted, she heard the news: An eleven-seater Beech had crashlanded in Rocking M's northern field, and there just might be survivors.

CHAPTER 2

Ian Williams first regained consciousness as hail and rain pelted him. He was no longer inside the plane. Having been thrown through the windshield as the tiny commuter exploded on impact with the trees, Ian was vaguely aware of aches all over. He tried moving, but without much success. He didn't have to see the stickiness surrounding him to know it was his own blood.

The pilot shivered from more than just the cold. He was staring Old Man Death right in the face. And he wasn't ready to go.

Damn, why hadn't he filed that flight plan?

Thoughts of his daughters, his ex, and even the time in 'Nam circled his mind like so many "injuns" waiting their turn to scalp him or help him. He wasn't sure which anymore.

Stretching his head as far back as he could without excruciating pain, Ian blinked and then stared at part of the fuselage, its ragged edges like a cracked champagne bottle after a christening.

And what of the other passengers? Had all ten of them perished in the crash?

As if in answer to his question, a child's cry pierced the howl of the winds. The Asian kid. He tried moving again, but it was no use. Whatever had fallen on him had him pretty well pinned down. He'd just have to wait for whatever would happen.

Ian closed his eyes and wondered about the kid's condition. Was she dying like him? Was anyone else there with her? He tried to think of the pianist; her long, lovely legs curled around the seat edge. Oh, God! He hoped they weren't all dead.

Would anyone think to search for them? A stabbing pain filled his body as he sucked in a mouthful of hail.

His lips curled upward in a vague smile. He'd always told his mom that Texas would be the death of him yet.

Inside the plane, Angel Lee, the five-year-old Chinese girl, continued wailing. She was probably more banged up than hurt, but there was a huge cut on the side of her face.

"Come here, darling." The old man spoke soothingly to the child, stretching out his free hand. Weakness flooded him. Every movement devoured his energy and sapped his strength. His right arm felt numb and he knew blood covered his new suit. How much had he lost? Whatever it was, it was far too much.

But he was here, alive for the moment, and so was she. The only two who seemed to have regained consciousness.

Had the pilot been able to call for help? Did anyone know they were here?

"Mama!" the girl wailed.

Despite the effort it cost him, Julius Ciss took hold of the Asian girl and rocked her frail body with his one arm. "Hush. Hush." His voice, husky from the pain. "Shall I sing you a song from Russia? One my mother sang to me."

Angel glanced up at him. Her huge brown eyes brimmed with tears. She sniffled and sobbed, but quieted some. Fingers in her mouth, she rested her matted, blood-streaked head against his shoulder and began rocking back and forth.

"Shah. Shah. That's good. Yes. We will sing the song and then you and I, we will say the Shema." The Shema was said by every practicing Jew at least three times daily, but most Jews only recited the prayer when they faced times of danger or when life seemed nearly at end. *So? What better time to say it than now?* Julius thought.

The little girl looked up at him. "*Shema?*" she repeated.

"Yes, *kinderlach,* my little one. The Shema. So God will protect and watch over you, too." Julius leaned over. After kissing the child's brow, tasting the saltiness of her blood, he began humming the Russian lullaby which his mother had often sung. Angel's eyes slowly closed. Julius, too, wanted to close his. But not yet.

With a fervency he didn't know he had, the old man sang out, "Here, O, Israel, our Lord is God, our Lord is One." He repeated the verse in Hebrew. Then and only then did he allow his eyes to shut. A coldness enveloped him. He felt her warmth as his own ebbed away.

Pam had stood in a robotic trance during the battle between Josh and Bill. Stupid man. She was glad now that she hadn't married Bill Martin. And that she had avoided him asking her.

How could he alienate all these people and treat his wife that way in front of them? Didn't he ever consider the consequences of his actions? Good thing she saw this beforehand.

Even though she didn't much like Emma Chandler, she had to admit that her great-aunt was right about Bill Martin. He was someone to be avoided. In fact, association with him could just ruin any new plans Pam might develop.

Who'd told Emma? Not Randy. He might be a bastard, but it wouldn't have helped her younger brother any to have 'fessed on her. And that boy only did what he thought would profit him. She knew Bill hadn't known, nor had any of the other medics. And she'd been so careful in covering her tracks when she put the drugs in Lisa Drummond's drawer. No, it couldn't be that.

So how? Or rather, who? And what else did this spy know about her? Pam didn't trust Emma's sudden change of heart or her "love for Granny Dottie." No, this Emma was a sly one. Pam was gonna be on her tiptoes, watching for cracks in this sugar cookie. Determined not to let any of this upset her but still stunned by the fact that her secret had been uncovered, Pam took a fresh pitcher of martinis from the waiter and headed toward the patio, a bit bemused by Margaret Chandler's mad dash upstairs.

Margaret's face had been flushed. Maybe Joshua Allister had suggested the pair make love before marriage. Taking another swallow, Pam emitted a harsh, short laugh. Those two sisters were so opposite. Margaret such a prude, and Allison . . . well, everyone knew Allison was a whore.

Pam tipped the pitcher of martinis and filled her glass again. She had to admit, when Auntie Em threw a party, she went all out. Well, maybe Pam would do the same. One day.

The ice swirled around in her drink as she stepped onto the covered portico. She had almost expected to see Joshua Allister here. But he was nowhere in sight. Drat! She would have taught him a thing or two about what being with a woman was all about.

Seeing what had transpired with Bill, Pam was sorrier now that she hadn't made a stronger play for this New Yorker. But like one of those damn Texas hurricanes, Allison had spun him around and around so that he could see nothing but her in the center.

Still, Pam couldn't help wondering. If she'd told Josh that she was part of the Chandler clan . . . but no. That would have spoiled all her plans. As it was, the plans she had made had melted like the ice sculpture in the entryway. She wasn't quite sure what to do with the runoff.

They're destroyed already, Pamela. You have to give up.

"No. No. That can't be. Revenge. I must avenge Granny Dottie. I . . ."

Pam realized she was talking—no, arguing—aloud with herself. Quickly she glanced around, worried that someone had heard. She watched while the stupid Mexican foreman from the Rocking M made a fool of himself with one of the housemaids. She could hear Allison talking to someone, but she wasn't sure where her "cousin" was or who she was with. She drained the last of the martini in her glass.

From what Aunt Em had just hinted, after the sisters Pamela Roberts was the next heir in line to the Chandler fortune. Hum. Something interesting might come of that. Pam knew then that good ideas never disappeared, they just took different shapes.

Inside, Joshua frantically searched the crowd for Margaret. He knew his fiancée had been upset by that incident with Bill Martin and had been especially hurt by Bill's comments to Karin. Everything had happened so fast that Josh hadn't had time to reassure her then, and he needed to do so now. His poor Margaret had such a fragile ego. Joshua blamed both her grandmother, Emma Chandler, and her sister, Allison, for that. Because of the accident that had scarred her face, Margaret had spent her life hiding from the public eye.

And even now, following the surgery that had taken most of keloid tissue away, she couldn't seem to get accustomed to the idea that she was beautiful, not only to him, but to others as well.

"Have you seen Margaret?" Joshua asked Ellis.

The thoracic surgeon shook his head, a worried look on his face. "But Hillary might have. Though I doubt you'll get much of an answer from her. She's been up there trying to sing with the band for nearly an hour now."

Joshua frowned. "What's she on?"

Ellis nodded. "Haldol five milligrams b.i.d. and ten milligrams at night. I would have thought that would slow her down. But look"—he motioned to his obviously drunk wife dancing up a storm on the band stage all by herself—"she's not even dancing with the music, Allister." He shook his head again. "I tried to make sure she didn't get any alcohol, but I think she must have picked up some when I wasn't looking. She doesn't believe anything is wrong with her."

"They seldom do." Joshua nodded. How terrible it must be for Ellis, especially with his well-known family here in Texas, and for the kids. "Amy and Will come with you tonight?"

Ellis shook his head. "Amy's still recovering from that dermoid cyst, and Will took a baby-sitting job with Ty's bunch." He motioned to the Van Fleets across the room. He had never liked Ty much, even though they were neighbors. Not until the pathologist had stood by him during the lawsuit crisis did Ellis and Ty become friends.

Josh glanced up, watching the performance onstage. Some inner voice appeared to be propelling Hillary Johnston into wild twisting and stomping without any real rhythm. "Looks like her meds need to be reevaluated. Maybe Meredith can help you with that. Maybe . . ." He turned, astonished to see his fiancée dressed as though she was headed for a roundup rather than dancing on Christmas Eve.

Margaret had returned to the room wearing her warmest sheepskin coat, thick jeans, boots, and cap. "A plane's down," she announced. "Somewhere in or to the immediate north of the Rocking M. There may be survivors. Who's coming in the copter with me?"

The whole room froze, similar to the Martin-Allister scene. Only this time it was different.

Meredith stepped forward. "I guess this is my first job as the new chief of staff for CMC." She paused to look around and take count of which doctors were still there and which ones she would have to call in from their homes. "Margaret, did your source say how many?"

"Eleven-seater Beechcraft. Pilot neglected to file a flight plan, so there's no telling how many passengers."

Meredith pressed her lips together and nodded. "Rosa, why don't you go with Ellis—"

"No-o!" Hillary came swinging down from the stage like Jane fighting for Tarzan. "No! You cannot go with that woman." She turned on Margaret, beating at her with her fists. "You're in on this, too. I thought you of all the Chandlers would understand how it is to be betrayed, Margaret. But no-o. You're just encouraging them like the rest. I don't believe that there's any plane crash. I don't believe Ellis is needed. He *is* my husband and he *is* staying with me. He *will* not fly off with *that* woman." She pointed a red-manicured nail at Rosa. "I won't have it. Do you hear me?"

She flung away from Margaret then and launched herself at a surprised waiter, removing a clean serving knife from his tray.

Meredith whispered something to Emma Chandler, who nodded and hurried off.

Ellis was only dimly aware of something else happening, but he couldn't ask any questions. His main effort had to be focused on his wife before she did something stupid.

"Hillary! Put that down. Now. Before you hurt someone."

She glared at her husband. "Don't be such a wimp, Ellis. Afraid of a little blood?" Her words were slurred, but she swung the large knife like an extension of her arm, flashing it through the air. Suddenly her left wrist flowed red. "Like that, Ellis." She grinned at him. "You're a surgeon. What's wrong with a little blood?"

Ellis took a step toward her.

"No. You don't come near me. I know. You and she have been planning this." For a fraction of a second her eyes darted toward Rosa. "When were you going to kill me? And how? Poison? Make it seem like I had a cyst just like your daughter."

"Amy is your daughter, too, Hillary."

"Ha! You've done a neat trick. Turning her, Will, and everyone else in this town against me."

Ellis sighed. "Hillary, you know that's not true." His voice sounded soft. Soothing. He took another step forward, not taking his eyes off his wife, yet noting Joshua and Meredith closing in behind. In her hands Meredith carried a syringe. Ellis didn't want to know what was in it or how Meredith had come to have it. He only wanted Hillary safe.

Margaret gave Meredith a pleading look. Time was wasting. They had to get to the downed plane.

Meredith nodded curtly. Having done only outpatient work and with very few of them depressed medical patients, Meredith could only hope she was doing the right thing. It had been years since she worked the state hospital. And that had been the last time she'd done a take-down. Her eyes met Joshua's. He was ready.

Hillary waved the knife again, making it look as if she were going after Ellis. Only at the final moment did she swing it aside. Her right wrist now flowed red. "Fooled you. But you're not going to fool me, Ellis. I know what's happening."

"No one ever said you were a fool, Hillary. You're my wife. I love you."

"Like hell." She broke down sobbing as Joshua made his move, wrapping her in his arms, forming a human straitjacket. Ellis grabbed the knife, then took his wife's feet.

Hellcat Hillary fought as Meredith injected two milligrams of Ativan into her exposed upper arm.

"Ah—yee." Wildly Hillary scanned the room, screaming. "Don't you see, everyone? They're trying to kill me. That's what they want. That's what—"

"Come on, Hillary. We're going to lie down a bit," Meredith said, dropping the used syringe onto a nearby plate and supporting Hillary's head.

"Hillary! Behave. There *is* a plane crash. Margaret wouldn't say so otherwise," Ellis tried reasoning, but it was hopeless.

She struggled, yanking at Josh's grasp, biting his arm through his tux sleeve.

"Hillary, stop it! I am going to help those who may need me—" Ellis started.

"And I don't? What about—"

Emma hurried in. "I have a room ready." She beckoned to Josh, Ellis, and Meredith as they carried Hillary in the three-man take-down. Ellis' wife would probably trash Emma's lovely blue room before the tranquilizer worked, but it was the nearest bedroom with a lock on the door.

Ellis hurried along, reassuring his wife. "Hillary. I

love you. I am not going to be with Rosa. I am going to help the injured."

"Don't lie to me, Ellis Gary Johnston!" his wife shouted as she squirmed and twisted, attempting to kick free.

Ellis only sighed. To Margaret and Rosa, standing by the outer door, he gave a sad smile. "Meredith and I will be there momentarily."

"No, you will not!" Hillary ranted. One arm free, she raked Josh's face with her fingernails. Blood from her cuts smeared over his white shirt.

"Hillary! Stop this! As soon as you've calmed down some, I'll dress your wounds," Joshua commanded. He held her down. "Ellis, get out of here! You, too, Meredith."

"Help! Rape!" Hillary shrieked, kicking harder as Meredith and Ellis fled the room.

"Too bad we don't have any leathers," Meredith shouted above the noise as the pair ran for the helicopter. She referred to the restraints they'd often used at State. "Maybe this will be an incentive for Emma to let me have a psychiatric wing."

Back at the house, Joshua slipped out of Hillary's room and winced as he heard one of the lamps near the bed crash against the wall. With the help of some of the servants, Hillary had been tied with some sheets. But it didn't look as if that was going to hold her. He only hoped the Ativan took effect soon. And for the first time in a while, he was glad he'd chosen such a calm field like radiology.

"Mrs. Chandler—Emma, perhaps we can start making some coffee. I have a feeling we're going to need it," Joshua said.

CHAPTER 3

With the high-wind velocity, Margaret was surprised that she could even land the helicopter. It took considerable skill and all the strength she could muster. She touched down close to the crash site. Any closer and she'd be inside the body of the plane itself.

She waited anxiously until the three physicians left the helicopter and were safely away from the whirling blades. From her position in the cockpit, she could see at least three injured or dead on the snow, and probably more inside.

A quick overview of the situation told her that she was right in having alerted the company. Nana would have to forgive the breakup of her annual Christmas party. Even Nana knew saving a life took precedent.

Over the static, Margaret instructed the medicopters with the exact latitude and longitude of the crash site.

"Roger," Margaret acknowledged the message from Hobby. Crews would be coming from Texas Medical, as well as from her own Chandler Medical Center. Naturally, Nana wanted all the casualties for CMC, and probably most of them would end up there, but there were some things that CMC was not equipped to handle. Besides, it wasn't the welfare of the hospital that concerned Margaret.

Lights flashed sporadically in the distance telling her

that it would be at least an hour before help arrived by land.

She waited a moment more to see if anyone needed last-minute assistance, and then decided it was time to recruit the other physicians still left at her grandmother's.

Fighting the hail, which still pelted the windshield, Margaret stretched her arm out the window and gave the flight signal as she rose again, higher and higher until from below the whirling blades melted into the sounds of the storm.

Ian shivered awake. A foggy dream state surrounded him. Helicopters? Then he remembered where he was. The sounds of the storm masqueraded as helicopter blades. *Like 'Nam,* he thought. *Just like 'Nam.* When he'd been wounded and his buddies came out searching for him despite the gooks and their incessant fire.

But his buddies weren't here in Texas with him on this Godforsaken plain. He was in Texas, all by his lonesome.

Ian tried moving his hands. Either the bitter cold had frozen them or they were one more part of him already dying. Whatever the reason, he felt nothing.

How much longer would it be before Charon took him over the river Styx?

The child cried again. His little girl. No, not his little girl. The *gook* kid. He thought again about 'Nam. Maybe it might have been his kid—at one time.

Ian felt sorry almost as soon as the thought came to him. Not like the five-year-old Asian had had anything to do with 'Nam or with Ian himself. He was just in one hell of a crappy mood.

The crying came again. But with it was another sound. He had to be hallucinating. It couldn't be a woman's voice. Impossible. Unless maybe it was one of the passengers? That piano girl? Hoffner?

Naw, he thought, with a crash like they'd just experienced, everyone probably died instantly. But what about him? He had survived, hadn't he?

He tried glancing back toward the remnants of the plane. *Good luck seein', fella,* he told himself. Even if his vision had been clear, even if he'd been able to crane his neck back, the hail and snow made everything a white blur.

The wind increased its force. He felt like one of those comic strips when the water comes pouring out of the holes just ripped through the character. Only this was no comic strip and what poured out from him was blood.

The lights appeared first in the northeast. They attracted his attention, but only momentarily. He wondered if he hallucinated them, coming closer and bigger. And when they seemed to disappear, he knew he had.

No one would be fool enough to come out on a night like this. Not unless they were getting double pay, he thought ironically. Would the company pay his girls? He certainly didn't want that bitch of an ex getting her hands on his hunk of cash, no matter how small it might be.

Ian tried recalling if he'd written a will. But all he remembered was the thing he and Cheri had first signed, agreeing to donate each other's parts.

The thought made him sick. But he supposed if he could help someone else . . . maybe he could still live on. Watch over the kids through someone else's eyes. Wouldn't that be a hoot!

From the corner of his eye, he saw lights again. This time they seemed to be coming from the left. The plane? Was it on fire?

Tears froze in Ian's eyes. He knew if anyone there had survived the crash, most likely they wouldn't survive the flames. His heart broke. If he did survive this, he would have to live with the deaths. Why hadn't he just refused the trek? Why?

Numbness faded into unconsciousness until he heard the voices again. Nearby. Could someone have really come?

Despite the searing pain, he inched his head around. It *was* a helicopter! He hadn't imagined it. But surely . . . He watched, mesmerized as a dark-haired angel wearing a white sequined gown floated toward him. This wasn't how Ian Williams had expected death. He had to be dreaming.

The angel, or whatever she was, continued to advance like one of those slow-motion replays. He blinked his eyes again.

She was still there.

And then . . . suddenly she was next to him.

"Hello. You must be—"

"Ian Williams," he choked out. "The pilot." If she was an angel, why didn't she know? He couldn't keep his eyes off her. If he looked away for a millisecond, she'd disappear.

He wasn't sure if he was floating up to her or she was floating down to him. Still in slow motion, she leaned down, touching his brow. "We're here to take care of you."

"We?" Ian inhaled. Frozen air stabbed his lungs. "There're more angels?"

She laughed and glanced down at her now blood-stained white dress. "I'm Dr. Rosa Sanchez from Chandler Medical Center. One of our board members heard about the downed plane on her CB—and here we are."

She paused, looking up as the air gusted and the

storm suddenly worsened. With her teeth, she ripped open an antishock blanket.

Ian hadn't even seen her carrying anything. He closed his eyes. Help was here. That was all he needed to know.

Rosa covered the pilot with the light thermal cloth. Obviously he'd lost quite a bit of blood and was in a red or critical condition. With a sigh, she stood and wondered if he'd survive the trip back to the hospital.

The doctor, herself shivering, thought about putting one of those blankets around her bare shoulders. But they didn't have enough to go around for the injured. She would manage as she always had.

"Ellis, come help me with the pilot." Luckily, her voice carried over the wind. "Let's get him into some shelter." She nodded toward the cockpit of the plane, which had been blown separate of the body.

The thoracic surgeon hurried over. He studied the situation a moment. "You're sure, Rosa?"

Moving an injured man was always a difficult call to make and especially on a night like this. If they left him here, even with the blanket he'd probably go into hypothermia, if he hadn't done so already. And if they moved him, they might cause more damage, invisible to the naked eye, but life threatening nonetheless: internal damage, like puncturing a lung or allowing a broken bone to spear a kidney. But without X rays to know what damage he'd already suffered, they were playing Russian roulette.

Rosa nodded. She laid her professional judgment on the line and called the shot. It would be she who would face the consequences if she decided wrong.

Ellis inhaled a frozen breath before nodding and then, as a practiced team, the pair gently lifted the patient.

Ellis didn't envy Rosa the decision. But it wouldn't be the first time she had called it, and it wouldn't be the last for him, either. The trouble now was that the Good Samaritan law had been repealed for medical personnel: You were damned if you did and damned if you didn't. Either way, a person you stopped to assist could sue you for not doing enough or being overzealous.

Once they had placed the pilot in a section somewhat sheltered from the winds, Rosa and Ellis hurried to find the other victims who were still in and outside the plane.

Hillary took another half hour before she calmed, falling into a trancelike sleep.

Sadly, Emma noted that she had been right about the room.

The good Mrs. Johnston had not only turned the mattress upside down and off the bed, but had ripped a hole in the center of it as well. Did she think by attacking the mattress she could tunnel out of the room? Emma shook her head as the ambulance from the Houston Psychiatric Center drove off with Hillary. She knew that Ellis or his family would make good on the damage Hillary had done physically, but she wondered if the damage Hillary was doing mentally to her children could be halted.

Even though Meredith had been a psychiatrist for nearly twenty years now, and had participated in the several crises which had faced the town in the past year, this was the first time she had actually ever worked triage.

However, as the new chief of staff, Meredith felt it was her responsibility to be here—at least for a short time—to assess the situation. So here she was. Right in the middle of the guts and gore, deciding who would go in for treatment first and who would stay until last, either because it was thought they could wait, or it was felt certain that nothing would help them.

Ever thankful for the efficient Rosa and Ellis assisting her, Meredith knew now why she'd gone into psychiatry. It was a lot less messier—usually.

Watching as Margaret rose back into the sky, Meredith decided that as soon as Cole came, she would head back to the hospital. Thus far, she had counted five injured and that didn't even include those in the plane.

Maybe it was time she checked inside.

Gingerly, she climbed over the broken glass, shreds of metal—once part of the fuselage, and through the uneven gap where the door had been. The jagged edges of the metal reminded her of a monster's mouth, with sharp teeth ready to destroy anyone daring forth.

She stepped inside what remained of the plane, smelling the damp red blood seeping from the boy at her feet.

Meredith leaned over. A mere teenager. With a crew cut and spikes. Artfully torn jeans in today's style. A leather jacket, with his broken arm busting through. The ornate cross he'd worn had been flung up in his face, gouging out one eye. It was all Meredith could do to keep her dinner from joining the bloody mess on the floor.

Even in this dim light, Meredith could see the expression of pure panic on his face. No doubt about him being dead. She bent down to feel for a pulse anyway, just in case. Because of the freezing temperature, rigor mortis would no doubt be delayed. The irregular hole in the young man's side showed where he and the remains of the door had met.

There was nothing more she could do for him now.

She hesitated a moment, and then closing his eyes as best she could, Meredith moved the body out of the way while she proceeded farther in.

She passed two more bodies, heads at such odd angles that they probably died instantly. Her fingers gripped tightly on the once white head portion of the lounge chairs.

Had anyone inside survived?

The whimpering moans of a child brought her to the back of the plane where an elderly Caucasian gentleman hugged a young Asian girl. The tail of the plane had smashed apart and those in this section were also exposed to the freezing winds.

Undecided on whom to check first, Meredith turned to the young woman seated next to this strange pair.

She recognized the girl as Nancy Hoffner, the concert pianist. Meredith and Seth had been making plans to hear Nancy perform. Now they probably never would.

Gently, Meredith examined the girl's upper torso, resting her fingers briefly on the girl's neck. At least, Nancy Hoffner still had a viable carotid pulse. The fact that she moaned when Meredith touched her gave the doctor some hope. Pain was one of the last sensations to be felt and was often used as a neurological test to see how far into unconsciousness a patient had fallen. Those that responded to a moderate amount of pain were given good chances of emerging from their comas.

Meredith looked down at the girl's hands. The left one looked crushed between the seat and the window. The psychiatrist frowned as she attempted moving the seat. By herself, Meredith didn't have the strength. Besides she didn't want to cause more injury than already was present.

She'd wait for the medicopters to come with their equipment and even then, she'd want Patrick Thompson, Ellis's partner, to check everything out before they did anything. While Ellis concentrated his finery on the heart, lungs and throat, his partner did most of the general surgery, but liked to think he specialized in hands and the outward appearances.

It had been a long time since Meredith had been called upon to diagnose anything but psychiatric disorders, but she was pretty certain Nancy's other hand had suffered a green fracture of the wrist. But even here, the girl's pulse was still strong. She only hoped that the girl had enough guts to survive and go on.

Meredith bit her lower lip. She knew these temperamental types. Her younger brother, Danny, was the stereotypical model. When he'd been attacked in the throat by the gang of thugs, his promising singing career had halted, dead-ended. The injury to his vocal cords was so great that no one thought her brother would ever sing again and all the glorious contacts and contracts he'd made faded one by one.

Danny, once outgoing and bright, became a depressed shell of the person she had known. The only thing he lived for was revenge on those men who'd once attacked him, and others similar to them. Now instead of finding joy in his life, her brother only hated. His whole being burned in anger.

She hoped Nancy wouldn't be like that. But it was touchy, especially when one's whole family puts their hopes and dreams on "the career"—just like Meredith's mother had done with Danny.

The girl would probably come through physically, but whether she would play again was another matter. It would take all of Meredith's expertise, when the time came, to tell Nancy Hoffner of the suspected prognosis. If the girl played the piano again after this injury, it would be a miracle.

Meredith did her best to splint the wrist with a length of broken vinyl from the plane's wall. Not exactly the neatest job, but it would serve for the moment.

Above she heard the sound of the copter. It was too soon for Margaret to have returned, so she could only assume that the medics had come from Houston.

This girl would be among the first to go back. But she didn't know about the old man and the baby.

She moved across the aisle to the pair, being careful not to hit her head on the jagged metal.

Edging in next to the little girl, Meredith pushed back the dark blood-streaked hair. A huge gash showed the meaty part of the brain. Carefully, she unwrapped the old man's bloody arm from around the little girl.

"Mommy! Mommy."

"Shh . . ." Meredith put her finger to the girl's lips. "It's all right, honey. You're fine. We're going to take you to your mommy."

Somehow it surprised Meredith that the child spoke English. And quickly she chided herself for such a thought, reminding herself that the girl could very well be American. Since she'd come to Texas ten years ago trying to escape her own past, she hadn't seen many Asians. Probably just as well, since they wouldn't have blended in very easily in a town like Chandler Springs. At least, not like she had fitted in.

No one knew Meredith's history and she was going to keep it like that.

Taking a large gauze roll from her jacket pocket, Meredith began wrapping the child's head. The blood soaked through even as she continued placing the soft white fabric around the cranial split. No doubt Cole would order her into surgery the moment they arrived at the hospital.

But the old man, though he still had a pulse, didn't look as if he'd survive.

She quickly glanced at his wound. There was something very familiar about his face, but she couldn't place it. Did she know him from somewhere before? She didn't think so. But there would be time to play geography later on. Right now, she had to see about getting him stitched up.

Where were Rosa and Ellis? Where was Margaret with the others? In that moment it felt as quiet and silent as it had ever felt, and Meredith shivered.

No matter what happened, she was all alone.

She told herself her racing heart was merely because she felt ill equipped to deal with emergencies like this very one. From now on, Meredith decided, she'd let the medical experts handle it. She'd stick to the mind.

Yanking open one of the antishock blankets Ellis had given her, she placed it over the pair.

Then, tearing off the sleeve of a man's jacket, she tried stemming the arterial bleeding. It amazed Meredith that she still remembered how. When you were away from a practice for a long time, you couldn't always get back on the bike and ride immediately.

Meredith tore the tape with her teeth and fastened the gauze as she began checking his other wounds. He hadn't lost that much from his arm, so she knew there had to be internal bleeding.

Palpating his chest, she heard a definite sigh.

The fact that he responded to such slight pain was a good sign.

She shown her flashlight into his eyes, checking for pupil dilation and brain damage, just as she'd done with the girl. The old man's pupils contracted with the light. Another good sign.

It was then that she noticed the white-fringed garment he wore under his shirt. *Tzitsits?* Not here in Texas of all places. Frozen by memories of her past, Meredith stared at the garment, which most religious

Jewish men wore commemorating the 613 commandments given to them by God.

Forgetting where she was, Meredith momentarily
touched the fringe and recalled playing with her grandfather's while sitting on his lap. *Sabtah*. That's what
she had called him. *Sabtah*. Grandfather in Hebrew.
Tears came to Meredith's eyes. Quickly she brushed
them away.

Meredith moved back a moment, taking a deep breath
to steady herself. Her head bent uncomfortably low
under the broken roof of the plane. She ached to
stretch, to get out from here, but she felt frozen to the
blood-soaked rug and continued to stare at this man
who might very well be from her past. Even the beard
was straggly like *Sabtah*'s had been.

Her mother had turned her back on the family when
they had refused to acknowledge her father, a German
Lutheran. Many had thought that Gayle (Gitel) had
quite a bit of nerve marrying one of *them*, especially
in the aftermath of World War II. But there was no
accounting for love and especially no accounting for
Meredith's mother.

CHAPTER 4

It didn't surprise Margaret to find the party had broken up. She ran into the foyer, nearly colliding with Joshua, who had the remains of a turkey sandwich in his left hand.

"How does it look out there?"

Margaret shook her head. "They need Cole and Patrick, that's for sure. If you want to come with me, I'll drop them and take you and Meredith to the hospital."

"I'm going with you, too," Pam said, gulping down steaming black coffee. "How many wounded are there?" Pam's eyes roamed over Josh's body, like a steak she wanted to devour.

"Too many." Margaret eyed her new cousin distrustfully. Had Nana noticed what Pam was trying to do?

The petite nurse turned to grab her jacket, paused, and waited patiently for Joshua.

Emma Chandler's hand reached out instead. "Do you really think it's wise, Pam? After all . . ."

Margaret had never much liked this girl. That and the fact that Pam had kept her relationship to them a secret for all these months made Margaret suspicious. What was Pam's agenda? Her heart beat uncomfortably as she glanced at Josh again.

Margaret desperately wanted to feel confident that Josh wasn't flattered by the girl's attention, and yet she studied her fiancé for any signs that he might be eager to take what Pam offered. Margaret breathed a sigh of relief when Joshua appeared not to notice Pam's blatant stares and yet . . . Margaret felt uneasy shivers go through her.

After the rumors she'd been hearing about Pam and Bill Martin, Margaret's instincts told her that this fair-weather cousin was probably behind some of Josh's troubles with his "partner," the infamous Dr. Martin.

Margaret looked to her nana, to her sister, and then back again to her cousin. She couldn't ever recall a time when her grandmother had tried keeping her or Allison from helping out. Of course, no one could ever stop Allison, but it seemed strange that Nana would be so much more concerned about this girl, who might not even really be kin.

Was Nana being taken in by Pam?

"It's perfectly fine, Aunt Em." Pam's voice wavered with the drinks she'd consumed that evening. She snatched her fur wrap from the hands of her great-aunt.

Had that been hostility Margaret heard in her tone? She hoped her cousin was just a poor drunk. Whatever the reason, no one got away with an attitude like that in front of Nana. Maybe it was just Pam's disappointment that Josh hadn't taken the bait.

She and everyone else waited for Emma Chandler's reply, but to their amazement, the matriarch said nothing.

Margaret decided then and there that she was going to find out everything she could about this sudden relation of theirs. She knew Allison would help. Her sister didn't seem to care much for Pamela Roberts, either.

This story about some great-aunt from the Ozarks couldn't be real. Even she, Margaret, the practical one, doubted such a thing. Maybe Nana really did have a sister named Dotty, but just maybe this Pam wasn't really her granddaughter.

Sounds of the wind outside, lashing furiously against the trees, brought Margaret back to reality. She had to get out there again before the winds made it impossible to move around.

"Well, we have some injured folks out there. Are we going or not?" Margaret asked. She glanced at Josh, Cole, and then at Pam. Then without another word she hurried outside.

The waiting helicopter shimmied in the strong winds. "After that bronco ride, this shouldn't be too hard for you, Cole," Margaret teased as the tall Texan attempted to step inside the craft. She was referring to the CMC annual rodeo.

The last one they'd had, Cole had gone out flying. Only Ellis Johnston, playing the clown, had been able to distract the bull from goring them both.

"You'd think by now I could handle this stuff, but I can't." Cole Morgan gave Margaret one of those smiles that had won the hearts of all of Chandler Springs High School girls, including Sophie Drummond's. Even so, it had taken Sophie nearly fifteen years to admit her feelings and finally marry him.

Margaret revved up the motor. Why was Cole hesitating in getting on board? It was freezing outside and the extra wind force being blown up by the propellers wasn't helping. She glanced around, impatient to be airborne again. "What's holding us up?" she shouted back at Cole.

He glanced around at his wife standing in the doorway.

"Sophie. She can't find Lisa. Doesn't want to go without her."

Cursing to herself, Margaret shook her head. Lisa

Drummond Morgan was a headstrong teenager who had three times nearly died from drug overdoses and still did not appreciate the new father—her real father—that she had.

After a hurried conference between husband and wife, Sophie hurried up. Her husband put his arm around her shoulder.

Cole leaned into the pilot's seat. "Margaret, why don't you take Pam, Josh, and Sophie? I'll go find Lisa."

"Cole . . ." his wife protested, looking up at him.

"Sophie, she'll probably listen to me better than she will you. Besides, we have our share of doctors at the site. We don't have enough nurses there. I'll hop in the car and rush back to the hospital." He kissed her brow. "Be there before you, I'll wager."

The chubby blond nurse had to admit that Cole was right. Not about the crash site but about Lisa. *Their* daughter, Lisa, whom Sophie had raised as a single mother for nearly fifteen years. The girl had been one trial after another to her. For a long time Sophie would tell no one who Lisa's true father had been. And everyone had always assumed it was John Drummond, the man she eloped with.

But now that she had found Cole again and had told him that Lisa was really his, it felt so much better just to let him play the heavy.

"All right," Sophie said with a sigh. "I'll just stay at the crash site a moment to assist with the triage. Then I'll meet you at the ER."

"Carry on, nurse." Cole grinned, using the British comedy slang. He kissed his wife once more, still not believing the good fortune he had in finding her again as he gave her a boost up into the rolling bird.

He waited a moment until the copter rose above the tree branches. With the storm clouds thickly surrounding the house, it was almost impossible to see any farther.

Then he turned back to the house and hoped that he could find his daughter, Lisa, before she did something rash.

Cole Morgan returned to the now silent house. The band had already packed up, leaving the stage empty of all but a few loose sheets of music and some streamers.

With a sigh, he realized that other lives were at stake and he couldn't waste any more time searching for her right now. Raoul had said he'd seen her here at the stables, but if she was present, she wasn't showing herself. Emma Chandler would send her back home when she found her, *if* she found her.

The nagging worry that she might be doing drugs again had to be pushed down in favor of the emergencies that would soon need his full attention. He couldn't justify staying at the Chandler mansion any longer.

Was Meredith at the hospital yet? Was she taking charge of the triage team and wondering where he was? She was capable as a psychiatrist, but as with every specialist, she had gotten rusty in medical procedures she didn't often perform.

No one had even thought about notifying Bill Martin, even though he was the senior radiologist. Certainly not after the scene he'd made that evening. His animosity toward both Dr. Joshua Allister, his former partner, and Dr. Meredith Fischer was all too clear.

In a crisis such as this, it was imperative that everyone keep calm and coordinate with the team. No one, not even the great Bill Martin, who believed he could do anything but who had done very little med-surg in the past years, could be counted on to perform the whole job by himself. And knowing of his volatile temper, she could not even rely on him for the X rays.

Aware of her new responsibilities, Meredith used the radio and called into the hospital. Relieved to be returning to the hospital, she quickly hopped into the copter, squeezing in next to Josh.

Back at Chandler Medical Center's Emergency Room, Dr. Sara McNamara, head of pediatrics, had begun organizing the triage.

As soon as Meredith had told her that a child was involved, Sara knew she was going to be needed. While Meredith accompanied Margaret to investigate the crash site, Sara had driven over straight from Emma's party with her son, John, a Down's syndrome boy who helped in the mailroom.

And until Meredith or Cole arrived, Sara was the senior doctor available.

She put John to work stamping the admission forms and running errands while she began calling those who had not been at the Christmas party.

Knowing how much John idolized Cole Morgan, even buying a black Stetson hat like the emergency doctor, Sara reasoned that he was unlikely to get in the physician's way.

It was decided that Rosa, Ellis, and Pam would remain at the crash site until the medi-copters arrived, which would be momentarily.

Flashlight in hand, Pam Rogers moved toward the human hand she saw stretching out over the ice. She felt the freezing muck sloshing over her lace slippers, and cursed her dedication to nursing. She'd paid more for these than for any other shoes she'd ever owned. But she comforted herself with the fact that now, as a result of Emma Chandler's announcement, she had the money to buy a dozen pairs just like these. Even so, the waste of good shoes upset her, especially since she hadn't had many shoes growing up.

Maybe it had something to do with the five martinis she'd had, or maybe it was just time to think of home. Whatever it was, the chill of the marshlands reminded Pam of her home in the Ozarks, especially on the winter nights when they had no heat, and the many Christmas Eves when they had no presents to give out.

Raising the Overby brood had fallen to her as the eldest. Pam's present to herself at those times was just being glad that she could keep herself and "the kids," her eight brothers and sisters, alive. Times like holidays she most resented her ma for having run off, and her pa for his licorin' and brawlin'. Why, she could count on her fingers the number of times Pappy'd spent time with them and not in the courthouse. Even fewer than they saw Ma.

But not for long. Pam was fourteen when she'd had enough of Randy's backtalking her and the others not minding her. And so she just took off. "Survival of the fittest," Granny Dottie had once said. Probably from one of those scandal sheets Granny always read.

It had been hard at first. Pam never much liked doing "it," but if working on her back was the only way she could survive, well, then she'd play their game and right them one up. She soon found out just how to please a man and make the most of his desire. And she knew one day it would serve her right nicely.

"Pam, what are you doing?"

"Oh, Dr. Johnston!" Pam started, and quickly brought herself back to the present.

"I need help over here."

Nodding, Pam quickly hurried over to him, and they wrestled yet another plane victim from the mud. She didn't have to take his pulse to know that he'd been dead a good hour or more. Just that wide-open stare into the nothingness beyond told her. She was surprised that Ellis Johnston couldn't see that. Why in tarnation hadn't she gone ahead to medical school? Then she really could have made some money for herself, not just what she'd get from Great-aunt Emma.

She watched the surgeon, carefully wondering if maybe he was intoxicated. No, he seemed more nervous than intoxicated.

She glanced over at Rosa Sanchez and quickly lowered her eyes as the Mexican American doctor looked her way. Maybe there really was something between Rosa and Ellis. And just maybe Hillary needed to know.

It was another five minutes before the first of the medi-copters landed and took on the first three victims determined to most need the care. Quickly, the second copter was loaded with the second three. A third helicopter picked up the remaining staff. The bodies of the dead would be dealt with after emergency care had been given to those who needed it.

CHAPTER 5

After almost five minutes of searching, Cole gave up looking for his daughter. It bugged him that she could just disappear like that without telling anyone. He only hoped she wasn't in more trouble.

If only he had been around earlier to help her. Well, actually, he had. Only Sophie hadn't told him Lisa was his until recently. And for a while there, it looked like she and Frank Willis, Chandler Springs' police chief, were planning to marry.

Cole's rodeo stunt, which nearly killed him, made Sophie realize how much she truly still loved him. Only then did he learn that the young Sophie, foolishly worried that Cole, her high school sweetheart and the father of the child she carried, would give up his medical career if she had told him about the baby. And she had run off to marry the first man who would give her his name.

Well, that was past now. He hadn't been part of Lisa's life, except indirectly, and now he'd jumped in at the deep end. Somehow the three of them—Cole, Sophie, and Lisa—would adjust.

Everyone who remained was assisting in the kitchen, getting ready to take coffee and food out to the crash.

"Lisa?" he called out, pushing past the swinging door through the butler pantry and into the massive ballroom, a room that could have housed Sophie's whole home before he had married her.

His leg injury from the rodeo still bothered him. Absentmindedly, he massaged his knee. *"¿Raoul, ha visto a mi hija, Lisa?"*

Even after years of living in this small Texas town, Cole's Spanish was still rusty, but he tried using it whenever he spoke with any of the Mexicans. His father, much like Jacob McQuade, had always taught him that it showed respect.

The Mexican shrugged. "No, *Señor*. The last I see her she was going there." Raoul pointed toward the stables.

Cole frowned. What had made Lisa go there? He didn't want to think the worst and yet . . . it was hard not to, ever since the last time she had become involved with her drug-dealing boyfriend and she had overdosed.

Mindful of his obligation to the hospital and the emergency gathering there, he hurried toward the stables.

CHAPTER 6

From his car phone, Cole connected with Margaret's radio.

From the helicopter's transmitter, Meredith described some of the patients' conditions to Cole. The little girl's fractured skull worried her, and so did the old man's status. His blood pressure was high and still climbing, and she feared that he had damaged his kidneys as well as the other obvious wounds.

Trying to keep as cool as she could, she described the injuries with the clinical awareness of a first-year medical student, but Cole said nothing as he quickly took notes on his dash notepad. Then he called the hospital, giving orders to those nurses already there, telling them what he might need for preparation.

His wheels screeching to a halt, Cole flew in the emergency room doors and nodded to Sara as he quickly prepared himself. The ETA for the other doctors was five minutes, and for the patients and the medi-copters it would be ten to twenty. He only hoped that considering it was Christmas Eve, the medi-copters were fully loaded with oxygen and drugs.

Now back at CMC, both Meredith and Sophie were getting finger cramps dialing everyone they could think of—including nurses like Jennifer Stauton and Avon

Dupree, who'd left the hospital only hours ago after working doubles.

Sophie hated having them called back, but with the shortage of nurses in such an emergency she could do nothing else. She had also called in Wendy, the nurse who'd been a nervous wreck since being stuck with the needle from an AIDS patient.

With misgivings about asking Carrie Harper, the LVN she'd recently hired, Sophie continued calling. There were at least six wounded coming in, and Sophie was going to need all the help she could muster.

Even Margaret, who'd just arrived, was now running for the doctors, doing errands to ready the emergency department. She would be assisting her radiologist fiancé, Joshua McAllister.

And though now officially a trustee of the hospital, having been nominated to the position by her great-aunt only this evening, Pam Roberts was in the ER. The rush of adrenaline sparked Pam into high gear— as it did so many of the nurses who fought against death. To Pam, saving a life or seeing it end was all the same. But the power. No one could deny the power it gave you. And when, like Pam, you'd felt powerless all your life, such a rush was heady.

Pam relished and devoured all the power she found here. Everything and anything would be helpful in her fight against the great Emma Chandler, formerly Emma Toms of Tanner's Gap, Kentucky. Maybe in another life the wealthy Chandler mistress might think again when her kin needed help; maybe she'd think about it now, before the end of this life. Pam smiled. Yes, she would see that old Auntie Em did just that.

Meredith finished her calls and turned to see what else she could do. Even though she had M.D. after her name, she felt hopelessly lost in this milieu. And as

CMC's out-patient psychiatrist, she had assisted only two other times in an emergency.

"Jennifer, what else do we need to do?" She handed the surgical nurse, Jennifer Stauton, a list which included chairing the press conference down at the bottom. It didn't seem like a high priority, but as a communicator, this was supposed to be her specialty. The least she could do was keep reporters out of the way.

"What do I say?" she asked the nurse. While many doctors might have a problem taking advice from an R.N., Meredith wasn't one of them.

The news media had begun gathering in force, crowding into the hospital: everyone from the local *Chandler's Chatter* and Houston dailies, to the press associations, and television stations. Several times Meredith had to order them out of the lobby so that any friends or family and the local FAA could get through.

"No comment." Jennifer smiled. "You'll do fine."

Meredith nodded. Jennifer was right. There was nothing to worry about.

Jennifer herself had every reason to hate the press.

For nearly four years, right after nursing school graduation, Jennifer had worked the war fields in Vietnam, experiencing her share of the casualties. On her return to Houston, Jennifer, who obviously hadn't seen enough trauma in her life, had signed on at Ben Taub, Houston's charity hospital. One would think that after all that, CMC, even assisting Ellis Johnston in the OR, would be a slow dance for cool, proficient Jennifer. But the blond nurse apparently liked it here.

Certainly, there had been plenty of emergencies this past year—the overturned school bus, the factory explosion, and the bar destruction—to keep one's awareness up. Though Meredith wondered if Jennifer really had to do anything.

Sounds of the medi-copter landing told Meredith that the first load of injured had arrived.

She hurried to the door to greet them. Part of her hoped and prayed the old man had made it; part of her hoped he hadn't.

The gurneys rolled in. Three of them. As the techs raced in, two patients had hanging IVs of sugar water, which would help replenish their lost body fluids. Something crucial, especially with burn victims.

Quickly Cole assessed them. Even though Ellis and Rosa, now in the surgical suits, had coded them according to what they felt were the survival chances of each, Cole tried his damnedest to not be swayed by others' judgments, deciding on his own. And then he went with Ellis and Rosa.

It was hard being objective, especially since even in the few minutes traveling from the crash site to the hospital, a patient's condition could change for the better or the worse—and usually it was the worse. Cole always hated having to decide whom to work on first, who of the injured benefited by the quickest use of medical treatment.

Those who needed minimal assistance would be on the next copter. A third copter would bring those injured but deemed so critically wounded that there were high odds against them surviving. Those already dead, of course, came in last.

But these first three were the ones Cole and his workers had to fight for. Even then their survival was not guaranteed. He always blamed himself if one of the early arrivals died. He always wondered: If he had worked on them first, would they have made it? And he never knew.

Cole moved quickly, scrubbing up so that he could

stitch some of the more minor wounds before he shipped them into the OR.

"Dr. Fischer." He called the psychiatrist over. "Would you find Dr. Allister and tell him I need a lateral and supine X ray of the cervical spine and the pulmonary area for Mr. Ciss?" He indicated the pressure bandage, which Rosa or Ellis had applied as they tried stopping the profuse bleeding from the artery. "The right clavicle area, too."

He hated using Meredith as a messenger girl. It seemed so sexist, and yet Meredith was the first to admit that her med-surg skills were rusty. Cole was sure, judging from some of the injured, that Meredith's ability as a psychiatrist would come in handy later.

The chief of staff nodded, tight-lipped.

She rolled the old man away from Cole so that he could take care of the Asian girl next.

"Please, miss. You are a nurse or doctor?" Mr. Ciss asked.

"Doctor," Meredith answered quickly, not wanting to give her name.

"So, Miss Doctor, can I maybe have a glass of water? Just a sip." His face twisted in anxiety. "I am very thirsty."

"Uh, no, Mr. Ciss. I can't allow that. If they have to operate on you . . ." She knew chances are they would, if the X rays indicated he could tolerate surgery.

He sighed. "Yes, yes, I know. My wife, she was not allowed to drink before her operation. But just a little?" He lifted his eyes upward and back in the direction of Cole. With a cervical brace immobilizing his head, it was hard for him to do anything else. "I promise," he said conspiratorially, "I won't tell if you won't."

In spite of her own worries, Meredith had to smile. This old man was so much like . . . No, she quickly wiped the tears from her eyes. Meredith Fischer could not permit herself to think about it, not, she thought, if she valued the life she had now.

"I'm sorry. I can't." She hurried off to get Margaret, who was now helping Josh.

Meredith stayed away from Julius Ciss until one of the aides had taken him to X ray. Then she stared at the spot where he'd been.

And Dr. Meredith Fischer realized that she was afraid—and that she had some past history to deal with. But could she?

How would Sean O'Neill, her Irish psychologist, react when he learned the truth about her? No. She could not and would not tell him. And she could not let him learn it from anyone else.

CHAPTER 7

The air stilled as Margaret dropped the helicopter down for her third and final trip. She actually hadn't planned on returning to the Chandler estate again, but Sophie had made her promise that she'd check for Lisa. She'd agreed reluctantly thinking that if she had time . . . but then Cole had radioed her, asking the same thing. It was hard to refuse both of them. And so she'd circled back.

Margaret somewhat resented this enforced baby-sitting, especially since she felt she'd be more useful helping Josh at the hospital. She worried, too, that the medi-copters might take the more injured patients directly to Baylor if she wasn't there to oversee.

She'd landed in the fields next to the herb garden on the western side of the house. The hail had stopped, but it was still freezing as she ran for the shelter of the gardens and gazebo. *Está frío*, Margaret thought in Spanish as she saw one of their housekeepers cleaning off the patio.

The neighing of Sampson, Margaret's favorite bay, stopped her. Sampson had been her baby since she helped foal him. Some thought it strange that she could distinguish his voice from the other dozen horses, but at least Josh understood.

Sampson hardly ever cried out unless something was happening, something that worried him. Maybe she credited him with too much intelligence, but she knew he had it.

Like a mother protecting her child, Margaret ran toward the barns. Her first thought, being that Lisa was already on her mind, was that the girl had done something to the horses. Cole's daughter or not, if that girl had hurt her Sampson, she was going to be history.

Breathless both from the cold and the wind, Margaret found the strength to fling open the stable doors.

She ran to her horse. "Are you all right, baby?" Her cold hand stroked the horse's thick mane. "What's wrong? What scared you?" Margaret glanced around, certain that she would find Lisa here. And she was right.

Straw sticking to her clothes and hair, the sixteen-year-old had burrowed into the haystack and was fast asleep. Next to her lay the danger Sampson had sensed: a box of matches, a tiny fire still burning, a bent spoon, and a much-used syringe. The rubber hose still lay loosely around Lisa's arm.

Disgusted, Margaret stomped out the fire. She was glad that she had come back looking for the girl and glad that she'd been able to prevent damage to the horses. With horror she recalled the other fire only a few months ago in which the barns had burned to the ground.

If Sampson hadn't called to her, the matches, angled in their position near the flame, would no doubt have caught fire, and from there burned down the whole stable—just as it had happened once before.

She ground out the ashes with her heel and threw some of Sam's water on the remains. Then she gave her horse a hug, and quick rub. "You're a good boy, Sam. You continue your watch."

The teenager was still out. Margaret wasn't sure if she was sleeping or merely unconscious from the drugs. She had no idea what the girl had taken, but whatever it was, Margaret didn't like it around her horses.

"Okay, Lisa. Time to get up." She removed the rubber tubing and took the girl's arms, lifting her to a standing position. From the labored breathing she knew the girl was in bad shape.

"Lisa! I want you awake." Margaret forced the girl to walk the stable's length with her.

"I'm awake! I'm awake," the groggy teen said, pulling away from Margaret and rubbing her eyes. "What's the big—? I just came in here for . . . for a chance to be alone." Lisa wheezed slightly, apparently still having trouble breathing.

Margaret glanced at the paraphernalia still on the floor. "Yeah, I see."

"Oh, Margaret." Lisa shook her head. "You are such a prude." She glanced where the older woman was looking. "Hey! That stuff's not mine! Don't look at me like that." Lisa unsteadily bent down to examine the small propane setup, the syringe, needle, and rubber hose.

"It's here with you, Lisa. You were using it. I may not be a doctor like Joshua, but I can see you're having difficulty breathing."

"Like hell. I'm having difficulty breathing because I have a goddamn cold. I took some Actifed Mom gave me. And I guess I forgot I shouldn't drink with it." She gestured toward the drug setup again. "Margaret, I don't know who, but someone set me up." Her arms were on her hips.

Margaret shook her head. "And put the rubber hose around your forearm? And lit the fire . . ."

"Look, if I was out cold and had been using whatever it supposedly was, you'd better believe I wouldn't be so alert and able to talk to you right now. And if it was coke, then I would have been up and about, not down for the count." She looked directly into Margaret's eyes. "Shine a flashlight in my pupils if you don't believe me."

Margaret glanced at the materials on the floor, pressing her lips together. "I'm not judging you, Lisa. I'm only concerned about the animals."

"Well, so the fuck am I."

"No one who cares about horses lights a fire in a barn." Seeing the girl was now perfectly able to stand, Margaret turned her back on her. "I'm going into the hospital right now. They need all the help they can get. I suggest you come with me and let your folks know you're all right. They might actually be able to use your assistance, too."

"Margaret"—Lisa planted herself in front of the other woman—"I did not use anything tonight. Look." She thrust her arm in the woman's face. "No marks. Not new ones, anyway." She hurried outside, following the Chandler sister. "Are we going in the helicopter?"

Margaret nodded.

"Oh, man! Wait till I tell my friends. Will you let me fly it a bit? Please! Pretty please."

It was hard not to suppress a smile at Lisa's enthusiasm. Margaret truly wanted to believe that the girl hadn't been using anything and didn't realize the fire was there, but the evidence strongly denied this. Still, something nagged at her. Margaret vowed to watch more closely over the animals. If someone else had set this up, maybe Lisa wasn't the reason.

"I can't give you any lessons tonight. But if your folks say yes, I will after the New Year."

"Right on!" Lisa ran to the helicopter, forgetting just how cold it was. Boy, would Ray be impressed if she could fly a helicopter. Maybe he'd even let her help him with a few runs.

Margaret followed the girl reluctantly, glancing back at the barn every few steps. She should go into the house and let their security guard, James Lee, know what she had found and maybe fetch Lisa's coat, but she was anxious to help at the hospital. Besides, if the girl didn't care about the cold, neither did she. Margaret would call James from the air.

Maybe the girl was right. There was definitely something odd about the setup, and Margaret instinctively knew she would have to be more conscientious about possible danger. She only wondered who the source of it might be.

CHAPTER 8

Darkness surrounded her as Hillary Johnston stirred. For a few moments she couldn't think of where she was, but she slowly realized her legs and arms were bound.

Hillary cursed. "Goddamn him!" Twisting and turning, she tried freeing herself, but it would take time to work the leathers.

These bastards weren't as simple-minded as the CMC crew.

Hillary smirked. Back at Emma's, Joshua Allister, that smug New Yorker, had tied her down so loosely, it had been a cinch getting loose. Of course, she'd never tell him.

But the imbeciles at the hospital who had put these leathers on knew just what they were doing. What was the plan? To torture her until she told them she didn't believe Rosa and Ellis were seeing each other. How much was her darling husband paying these geeks?

She tasted the cotton in her mouth and tried wetting her lips. What had it been this time? Haldol or good old Thorazine? Damn it! She was not psychotic. All she wanted was her husband back—was that so wrong?

If your husband never came home before two a.m. and was *always* "too tired," never having time to look at you, pay you a compliment as he used to do, or be around to discuss problems with the kids . . . well, it was all too obvious.

A Carpenters' song, "Rainy Days and Mondays," played softly over the air. So softly you could almost swear you were hearing things and yet you were not. It was one of their ways of making you seem insane.

Hillary knew from the music and the "ambiance" of her "suite" that she was having a stay at the courtesy of Houston's "Inn"—the psychiatric facility where the best families of Texas all sent their near and dear ones. Its real name was Inez Nations Institution for Behavioral Health, but everyone knew it was really a lockup. A swimming pool, pool table, VCR, library, and cafeteria with a New York chef who had "food to die for"— and Hillary was sure many people had.

Of course, the patients never got the good grub or the good movies; it was only for the doctors and those bitch nurses.

As she listened to the words of the song, Hillary's face scrunched up into tears. She sniffled and wished she could yank her arm out of the restraints to wipe her nose on her sleeve. "Damn leathers!" The music reminded her of when she and Ellis had been on their honeymoon in Jamaica. Who would ever have thought it would end up like this?

Hillary knew Ellis was screwing the Mexican bitch. Had to be. They spent so much time together, and she certainly wasn't getting any. "Bitch! Bitch! Bitch!" Hillary screamed at the top of her lungs, her voice already hoarse.

"Knock it off, Hillary." An anonymous voice from the outside came through, followed by fingers rapping on the door.

"Who the hell is that?" she screamed back.

"Quiet down, Hillary, and we'll take you out. You know the routine."

"Yeah, right. I *know* the routine like I know my ass, Tommy Twosome! I hav' t'go to the fuckin' bathroom. You want me to pee in my pants?"

The door swung open. Thomas Thunderbird, the half-Iroquois/half-Irish was framed inside the door, his red hair flaming like a fiery halo in the hall light. Six feet five inches and a belly like Santa Claus. She knew him from prior admissions, especially the take-downs. A former alcoholic, he'd found sobriety in dealing with the "mentally challenged." *That was the term they used for retards and loonies,* Hillary thought. Considering what he faced here, it surprised her that he was still clean and dry.

"Must be nights still. Christmas?" She didn't think it had been a whole twenty-four hours, but she couldn't be sure.

The grim aide came over to her side and checked the restraints. "Yeah. Double pay. Not much but it's something."

"How many else on tonight?" She gave him one of her coy smiles. It was a mistake.

"Why are you asking that, Hillary?"

Damn these people. Too smart for their own pants. "No reason. Just curious. Wanted to renew old acquaintances."

He grunted as he bent down to loosen the center strap, which tied her in the middle.

"So I heard you went after your old man with a knife. Not too wise, Mrs. Johnston."

She shrugged the best she could considering the restraints. "He asked for it. Making eyes at a bimbo Mexican."

"Oh, yeah." Tommy became thoughtful a moment as he mentally scanned her record. "Dr. Rosa Sanchez. I don't know, Mrs. J. Sure seemed to me like he was awfully fond of you."

Hillary rolled her eyes up. "Give me a break, Thomas. Just loosen these cuffs please."

What's happening now, Hillary? With you out of the way again, they could be making plans to run away. Do you really believe that crap about the accident? There was no accident. It was a ploy so they could put you here, Hillary.

"What did you say, Tommy?"

"You hearing things, Mrs. J?"

"Is that what you think? Just because I asked you what you just said? Well, fine. Then don't tell me what you said, because it doesn't matter." She narrowed her eyes. "I don't have to hear things. I know what's going on." She struggled against the leathers.

Don't you know that all the Chandlers and CMC are in league with each other? What do you even want to do with them? Everyone in that town hates you. It's time to get back your own life.

"But I . . ."

Tommy paused, the key had not yet turned in the lock. "What's going on with you, Hillary? Maybe I oughta just get you a bed pan."

"No! No!" she shrieked and then calmed down. "I mean no, I'm fine. I was just thinking out loud." She took a deep breath.

Sure you were.

This had to be some trick being played on her. Jesus, how she hated that CMC group and everyone in Chandler Springs. Meredith Fischer must have been the one setting up this little play. Some shrink she was.

Hillary glanced at her arms. In the bright light flooding the room, it was possible to see the reddened areas where she'd struggled to escape. But she didn't need to see them. She felt them. Still, the pain was kind of good. Made her forget that emotional pain jabbing its sharp knife into her heart.

But I don't want to forget. It makes everything too easy, boss. We need to go back to Chandler's Mental ... Medical Facility. I'll show you how they're saving lives.

Hillary, determined to not hear whoever was talking to her, began humming to the Neil Diamond song which came on next. "Well, To-mas? Waiting for the second coming or something?"

Tommy shook his head. His hand with the key hovered over her arm—the proverbial carrot, just out of reach. "Do you agree to go to the washroom and return quietly?"

"Yeah. Yeah."

"Why don't I believe you?"

"Damn it, Thunderbolt, I have to pee! This is against my Constitutional rights—"

"No, it's not. Not if you're considered a danger to yourself or others, my dear. You should know better. One of your friends, I think it was a Dr. Allister, signed you in on a seventy-two-hour hold."

"Shit! Yeah, he's in league with the bitch."

Tommy shook his head. "Hillary, that language is not appropriate around here. Must I recite the rules for you?"

Hillary put on her "Miss Priss" look. "No, you do not. I know perfectly well how to act like a lady." She glared at him. "I am a member of the DAR! My mother was a member and my grandmother was a member—"

"And her grandmother before her," he continued and smiled. "Still doesn't mean you know how to act. I want your promise, Mrs. J."

With an exaggerated sigh Hillary said, "Okay, Tommy Tunes, I agree."

He stood back a moment, evaluating her. Then he bent down and undid her right wrist and right ankle, and started to do the left wrist, pausing. Only her left ankle remained captive. "Is this a trick, Hillary?"

Stay cool, girl. Don't let him know what we're planning.

Hillary shook her head. Her blond hair flew in her face. She opened her eyes wide, hoping that she looked innocent. Surprise was her element.

The psychiatric technician had no sooner undone her left ankle when she jumped up into an almost perfect *ecarte*, her arm and leg extended as she hit her "punching bag." Miss Zanadane, her ballet teacher, would have been proud of her.

What a way to go, Hillary!

Hillary ballooned toward the open door, gliding as she had when she performed *The Nutcracker*.

Great! Great!

Applause from the peanut gallery?

She glanced back toward the aide on the floor, clutching his stomach, and staring at her in shock.

No time to think about him. He doesn't understand. No one does, except me. I'm on your side, Hillary. Let's move it.

"Sorry, Tommy. Nice seeing you again, but I gotta run."

Still wearing her evening gown, but shoeless, Hillary sprinted from the room as if she were her daughter's age. Swimming those laps in their pool, with or without Ellis, had been worth it.

The trouble now was getting out of a locked unit. "Shit!" She hadn't thought about that. Glancing behind her, she could see their very own Nurse Rached, Susan Francis, rounding the corner, with Tommy huffing and puffing behind.

"Code green! Code green! Unit Four." Echoed through the halls. It was the Inn's way of telling staff that their coworkers needed assistance with a patient.

Hillary had watched often enough as the day room, or wherever the event was taking place, swarmed with doctors, nurses, security, housekeepers, and whoever could get their butts over fast enough.

"Jesus," she whispered, looking for a place to hide or a way to make them think that she had gone out.

There was only one possible escape. Her ears picked up at the telltale jingle of keys. Security! "Yes, please!" With a running leap Hillary made the doorway just as the latch released. Taking advantage of her element of surprise, she swung the door open, slammed the uniformed guard in the groin as she pirouetted, laughing gleefully, and headed out.

She was definitely going to have to take that aerobics class at the gym in town.

Hillary leaped over the Ethan Allen Queen Anne sofa in the lobby, landed on her back, pushed it down for their obstacle course, then scrambled up and away. Like the Pied Piper, they came from every doorway, following the music of her laughter. There were six after her now and one more had come up from the basement. Too bad he'd interrupted his dinner break. He should have stayed where he was because she wasn't going to let anyone catch her.

"Hi, Dr. Waldman!" If only she had a camera to see the administrator's surprised expression. It took him a moment to realize what was happening before he, too, joined the conga line.

Throwing the flowered Chippendale chair so it blocked the width of the hall, she burst out of the hospital, nearly tumbling down the steps, righting herself just as she neared the curb. Her heart raced as she glanced around. Dawn was breaking. Hillary didn't know if it was the medication they'd given her or if she was high solely on her escapade.

But there was no time to think about how gracefully she moved. She had to split.

A honking horn startled her as the driver of a red

Ferrari opened up the passenger side and leaned toward her.

"Hillary Johnston! What a nice surprise! Get in."

"What the f— are you doing here, Bill Martin?" She turned to see her private following emerge from the hospital's oak doors.

Get in, you ninny. Beggars can't be choosers. Besides, if I helped you get out, do you think I'd leave you stranded?

"Right." Hillary no longer cared who this voice was or why. She only knew she wanted out of here.

Bill's tires screeched away from the curb even before she'd slammed the car door.

CHAPTER 9

It felt as if they had been running for hours. Jennifer Stauton didn't recall the last time it had been so hectic. But for the moment, until the next slew of patients, came in they could rest. She glanced at the tiny figure of Angel, the Asian girl who had been rescued from the crash. What had she been doing there alone? There certainly didn't seem to be any parental person there with her, except maybe for the old man. Her grandfather? She supposed the girl could be adopted, but if she wasn't, if she had been traveling alone, Jennifer shivered. If that had been her daughter, she would never let her travel alone. Not ever.

Exhausted, the surgical nurse slumped into a chair for just a moment. Twinkling lights of the hospital's Christmas tree sparkled against the glass. As Jennifer took a gulp of hot coffee to wake her brain up, she realized what day this was . . . one of those that she usually tried to forget.

Briefly an image flashed before her of her husband and her daughter unwrapping their presents. Waldo, their blond overweight, cocker spaniel, snoozing by the fireplace.

Lin would have been nearly twenty-seven now. An adult. The ache speared Jennifer's heart. Where was she? What had happened to her? Did she ever wonder about her real mother? She had tried so hard to find her baby, but even with Jen's connections the girl had disappeared.

And Vinh, well, he would be here in the States with her, a successful business owner, just as he'd always talked about. Maybe they would have had more kids, Jennifer mused. A boy would have been nice, looking just like his father. She didn't know whether to cry or smile. She just knew she hurt. Oh, God. Why did the pain have to stay this long?

She didn't know how, but someone had leaked her story to the press. They seemed to hound her almost forever. That was why she'd left the big city and come to Chandler Springs.

Maybe if she'd been married now, maybe if she'd had children, she would have forgotten the baby girl she had borne, Lin, and Lin's father, Vinh Du. But she hadn't. Oh, how her heart ached. She could almost taste his sunburned skin and luxuriate in the feel of his kisses. He had been more of a man than many of the Americans she'd known.

It hadn't taken her long to fall in love with the quiet, shy young Vietnamese who'd shown her the ways of his country and brought her to his village. The other nurses had ridiculed Jennifer for having a native lover, but none of them knew just how sensitive and caring he had been.

Even now she still did not and would not believe that he might have been a double agent. If only they had been able to get away before ... before he'd been shot.

Instead she had lost herself in drinking and drugs for those first few years after his death, and after his mother and her village had taken the baby to raise. She would have kept Lin, herself, but as a single nurse in the military, Jennifer had been forced to keep her condition a secret and only a few of her close friends then knew her story.

Besides, at the time she didn't think she could deny Lin's grandmother a chance to get to know the baby. After all, Lin was supposed to return to the States with her.

She picked up the coffee again, absentmindedly drinking it, almost as though it was the Scotch with which she used to drown her thoughts in those early years.

God only knew how many patients she messed up, gave the wrong medication, the wrong IV, the wrong surgery while she was in her state.

Sent to a rehab hospital in England, Jennifer pushed through her grief. She knew she should have been dishonorably discharged, especially after that pilot nearly died, but she'd been hustled onto the nearest plane without having a chance to find her daughter. Having connections helped. Her mother was a distant cousin to Lyndon Baines Johnson and somehow the first three letters of the dishonorable discharge were dropped.

Jennifer returned to Houston *sans* military baggage and would have given anything to return *sans* memories. It was for that reason she'd jumped from 'Nam into the emergency crisis center at Ben Taub. The gorier the accident, the more alive Jennifer became. Seeing and helping relieve the pain and suffering of others somehow helped her feel alive and cope with her own loss. And with each emergency, Jennifer thought she was pushing the memories further and further away.

And now this . . . this plane crash had brought it all back. Having just worked a double and now in the middle of her third straight shift, a full twenty-four hours since she'd last closed her eyes, with another four hours yet to remain, Jennifer found herself teary-eyed and weepy. Damn! Why did this have to happen now—just as the memories were fading?

The cry of the Chinese five-year-old brought Jennifer running. "What is it, honey?" Jennifer reached out and lifted the tiny girl up, being careful not to tangle her IV or mess the bandages which covered her whole head.

Just as soon as Ellis and Rosa finished with the old man, Angel would be taken in for stitching. Thank goodness the X rays didn't reveal bone fragments lodged in the brain and the CAT scan showed no hematomas building up. An accident like that and a wound like hers could cause not only brain injury but a painful and perhaps slow death.

Even with the best of luck, the little girl could still lose memory and perhaps other areas of brain activity.

Lost in her own world, Jennifer began rocking back and forth with the baby, her daughter, her daughter, Lin. "Hush, honey pie. Hush, Mama's coming back for you."

A tap on Jennifer's shoulder startled her so that she almost dropped her fragile package.

"Hey, sister, you all right?" Avon Dupree stood ready to catch Angel should Jennifer let go.

"Uh, yeah. Thanks, Avon." Jennifer glanced at her co-worker but felt as if she really wasn't there anymore. She wanted to return to the world where she had held her Lin in her arms.

"You don't look so well, Jen. Why don't you go lay in the lounge? Take a break. I can cover for you."

"But I . . ." Jennifer reached out with a mother's yearning toward the Asian treasure, and then with a slight shake of her head, realized that her own treasure was lost and this one belonged to another family.

"Yeah . . . yeah . . . you're right. I do feel kind of strange."

Avon put her arm around her friend. "Come on, gal.

I'll take you in. You can have a little rest. And maybe if things aren't too bad, we won't even need you for the next round."

"But I . . ." Alarm flushed through Jennifer's face. Since losing Vinh and Lin her whole life had been lived only for how she could help others. If she wasn't helping, what good was she?

"You won't say anything about this, will you?" Jennifer asked, regaining some of her wits.

"Course not, sister. We all have our secrets. Tomorrow or the next day, you and I, we's gonna have a coffee chat."

Jennifer nodded and started toward the nurses' rest area.

Carrie Harper, L.V.N., felt good; she had actually felt useful. Running with the gurney, her mousy brown hair flying unprofessionally in her face, she'd held the IV up all the way from the medicopter to the emergency room. Just like in the movies.

She flushed as someone pushed a stand toward her. It was for her to hang the IV on, but she didn't want to let go of it. It made her feel . . . well, professional.

Gosh, damn! She sure would like to have a picture of this to send to Pa. He and his big mouth, tellin' her that she wasn't going to mount to much, tellin' her that she'd be a failure at whatever she did. Her anger tightened her muscles just as she thought of him. She sure would like to stuff that cow dung in his mouth now. Just like he used t'do to her when he thought she was tellin' a fib.

Helping like this made her feel important; it made her feel like someone else, not just Carrie Louise Harper, L.V.N.

Pa hadn't wanted her to go to the nurses' training. He said she'd never make it through the first sight of blood, let alone graduate. But she had. Proudly so. True, she had to do a few "errand" things for some of them professors to get her passing grades, but by skunk's water, she'd done it.

Neither her pa nor her six brothers had come to the graduation. She had hoped Pa would be proud of her after that, but he didn't let up. Still saying that she was no-good and worthless. Saying that she'd never be able to keep a job because she ain't good enough.

Carrie wasn't going to admit that Pa had been right about those first two jobs in the big cities, Dallas and Houston. But she felt confident that out here in Chandler Springs, without all that citified pressure on her, she could do better. Of course, she hadn't given her real references. If they knew what she'd been accused of . . . but that was just it. Carrie hadn't done those things, and she wasn't going to take the blame for the other nurse's mistake.

Clipboard in hand, Carrie tried to look professionally busy. She glanced up at the pilot as she passed his curtained bed. He'd be going into surgery within the hour, she noted.

Since he was her patient, Carrie took great pride in knowing all the facts, or what she thought were the facts, about Mr. Williams.

His IV was due in another twenty minutes. Maybe she ought to make up a fresh one, just to be ready. Yes, she decided, Ms. Drummond—she still had a hard time remembering it was Morgan now—would be pleased with that.

Then Carrie's eyes focused on the blood. The blood in Williams's IV line. Her heart pounded. Oh, my God. She'd let the IV run dry and now blood had backed up, and they'd have to start a new one and she'd be blamed and maybe fired again and maybe . . . Carrie pressed her lips together, unable to think, unable to concentrate. She looked around, frantic that anyone might notice her mistake. Oh, damn! What should she do? She didn't know if she should just hang a new one, call Dr. Cole (but he was awfully busy), or call one of the R.N.'s, or what.

Carrie's face flushed as she glanced toward the medication room. A new IV. She had to hang one. Maybe if she washed it through fast, the blood would rinse out and the others, especially Ms. Drummond, would never know what Carrie had done.

"Damn! Jesus! Mother Mary!" She ran, her keys and bandage scissors dangling at her side, knocking together like wind chimes. She scurried into the medication alcove, glancing around her to make sure none of those catty nurses had noticed. They would report her for sure.

Reaching into the IV supplies, she pulled out a dextrose in saltwater. Was this the one? She didn't know, but she thought so. For sure her notes said Dextrose, so it had to be the same, or certainly close enough. She hadn't looked to see if the pharmacy had made up a new one with his label on it, but if it was all the same, what did it matter?

Carrie started back across the hall and then recalled that Mr. Williams was supposed to have an additive put into his IV. *Jesus! Mother Mary! What the hell was it?* Carrie unfolded the smudged paper where she'd taken her report. It had been folded and unfolded so many times that the creases were already lined with dirt from her pocket.

Okay, here it was. Damn! Why can't I read my own writing? You would think if I wrote it, I can read. It looked like a "D."—maybe that was digitalis. Didn't they say he had a heart problem? Or it could be an "F"—maybe ferrous salts? He was probably anemic after all that blood loss. And it could be a "B." Maybe

Benzene Hexachloride? She'd forgotten what that was used for and it looked too difficult to mix up.

She hurried back to the medication station.

Gosh, damn! She almost felt like she was on that *Jeopardy!*™ show. You know with the time ticking away. Funny how she always got the answers when she watched at home, but when she tried playing the game that one time, it was like Jesus had wiped a clean eraser over her mind.

She tried reading her notes again and quickly glanced toward the pilot's bed area to make sure none of the other nurses had gone over to him. *Jesus! Mother Mary!* Carrie closed her eyes and let her hand sway over the three. Whichever she stopped near was what she would use. It would be that simple. She knew that Jesus would guide her. He had to.

Taking a deep breath, Carrie grabbed the ferrous salts off the counter and drew up about twenty cc's in one of them big old syringes. She wasn't exactly sure how much he'd been ordered. She'd forgotten to write that down, but hell, it was only iron. Couldn't hurt him, could it?

Jabbing the additive into the side port for the IV, Carrie ran again toward his room. If only she was in time. If only the other IV hadn't stopped completely.

A winner of the Boston marathon couldn't have done better, except for the fact that Carrie's weight caused her to huff and puff as she ran, her arms moving frantically in a rowing motion at her chest level.

She saw Miss Stauton . . . too late.

Skidding to a stop, her new rubber shoes making track marks on the linoleum floor, Carrie collided with Jennifer, who hadn't yet left the unit.

Both women fell to the floor. The fresh IV solution in its plastic casing bounced a moment and then rolled to a stop next to Jennifer.

"I'm sorry, Carrie. I wasn't looking," Jennifer said, shaking her head to rid herself of the noises surrounding her. "Are you all right?" She wiped her hands on her pants and stood, offering Carrie a hand.

The dazed L.V.N. just sat there looking at the older nurse. "Uh. Yes, ma'am, I do believe I am." Not trusting herself to take Miss Stauton's hand, Carrie pulled herself up by a gurney positioned off to the side. Thank goodness it was locked into place. She hadn't thought of that until afterward.

Walking over to where Jennifer stood, Carrie picked up the fresh IV, mumbling something about having to hang it.

"Let me help you," Jennifer said. Actually, she would rather be kept busy than be with her thoughts at this moment. Avon meant well, but no one could possibly know the torment she had or was going through. She leaned down and scooped up the solution. "Who's this for?" She handed it back to the L.V.N.

"Uh . . . uh . . . Mr. Williams . . . over there." Carrie pointed. "Bed C."

"Are you sure, Carrie? This is dextrose in salt water. I don't recall his orders reading that." Jennifer shook her head. "I know that he's been pretty badly burned but . . ."

"Well, I . . . um . . ." Carrie knew her face had turned an ugly persimmon orange. She couldn't even blush right, her pa would say.

"Carrie, this doesn't even have his label on it. The pharmacy may be rushed, but I don't think they would have sent up something without a label on it. Besides, isn't he supposed to be getting a supplemental antibiotic added? There should be a side label, if that's the case. Carrie?"

"Uh . . . yes . . . ma'am. Antibiotic, did you say?"

Carrie rolled her eyes skyward. *Shit!* "Not iron . . . I mean ferrous—"

"Where did you get the idea of ferrous salts? No, Carrie, Dr. Morgan did not order anything like that for this patient. Besides the amount of ferrous salts you'd need to put in here to turn the solution this color brown would probably push him into acidosis." Jennifer glanced at the L.V.N., trying to assess if the girl knew what she was doing. "Carrie, he's bordering on the edge of alkalosis now. Don't forget he's a burn patient as well as being a chest wound. They can flip from acidosis to alkalosis in a matter of minutes, and either of those conditions can be fatal for him."

Carrie glanced around, looking for someone else to blame. She shrugged. "I just asked Miss Dupree over there to hand me his next IV. And this is what she gave me."

"Avon gave you this?" Jennifer cocked her head, glancing toward the black R.N. now charting at the desk. "Come on. Let's go into Mr. Williams's cubicle. We'll check his chart though, before we hang it. I just want to see what he has dripping now."

Carrie's lips were becoming drier and drier. Her mouth, too. Her heart was beating faster than a speeding locomotive. She'd always liked that term. Always wished Superman would come save her. But he never did. No one *ever* saved Carrie Louise, not even Jesus.

She didn't know if she could even speak. But her hands, moist and slimy, as they always were when she got nervous, couldn't seem to grasp the bag. Like a comedy sideshow, the IV kept slipping from her hands, adding to her embarrassment. She knew everyone had to be looking at her, whispering about her. She wiped her palms on her dress as she followed Jennifer toward the pilot's cubicle.

Carrie had only taken a few steps more when Jennifer pulled back the curtain for better light.

"Carrie, he doesn't have dextrose and normal saline, he has plain sugar water."

"Well, I, uh . . ." Carrie wiped her hands again and glanced around, hoping that Miss Dupree wasn't around to stand up for herself. "It's what that there black nurse gave me."

"Carrie, you've worked here long enough to know that Avon does not just hand IV solutions out willy-nilly. Not without checking. Neither should you. And look here. His IV's run dry. Carrie—" Jennifer shook her head, frowning—"do you know what could have happened if you'd have infused this whole bottle of normal saline into him? He'd probably go into dehydration. And that would be the least of it."

Carrie's lips were dry. She wet them, feeling pretty dehydrated herself. A nice cool beer would hit the spot right now. Just like the ones Pappy used to drink. "No, Miss. I didn't think it would do no harm since normal saline, I mean it's mostly the same thing as blood."

Jennifer's eyes rolled upward. "No, Carrie. It is not. With this patient's current levels of sodium and his blood gases the way they're reading, you could have caused him to arrest."

"For what? He didn't do nothin' wrong."

Jennifer stared unbelieving at the overweight girl. "No, Carrie, I didn't say arrest as in jail. I said arrest as in cardiac arrest. Heart attack."

"Oh." Carrie's lips rounded in a pout. She looked down at her scuffed shoes and knew she was turning that horrid persimmon color again.

Jennifer sighed. "Go bring his chart, the proper IV for him, and the IV kit. I'll have to restart it. It's a good thing I ran into you before this was hung."

"Yes, ma'am. A good thing," Carrie mumbled as she hurried off.

Jennifer glanced at his dressings. He had second-degree burns on his face but third-degree on his arms and legs. And the chest wound still oozed. She wasn't quite sure where she would restart the IV. Maybe his left wrist?

In his bed, the pilot stirred. He'd been apparently listening to the voices ping-pong back and forth.

As soon as Carrie left to fetch the supplies, Ian spoke up. "You sound very familiar, Nurse." His eyes weren't focusing properly, but he could see the wisps of blond hair escaping from the neat bun at the back of her neck and in his memory he recalled the most beautiful nurse in 'Nam. When she was off duty, her blond hair had cascaded down her back. Jenny had been her name. Some sort of political connections. He'd been told not to mess with her. Shit! But he'd had the hots for her. What a body! He would have liked to have had her as a pinup on his locker rather than Marilyn. And what a voice. She'd been in the choir. He'd go two and three times to the church services. His buddies thought he'd turned religious, but he just loved hearing her sing.

If only he'd had the guts to talk to her. But then she'd fallen for some *gook,* who supposedly knocked her up. Then one day she'd just disappeared. He never knew where she'd gone.

He tried staring at her again. "Are you sure I don't know you? There is something . . . I . . ." he paused and tried to think. "M'name's Ian Williams. Does that mean anything to you?"

It was Jennifer's turn to redden and wish she could melt down into her shoes. *Ian Williams! It couldn't be.*

She picked up his chart again. It had to be. Even to the same blood type. He was the pilot that she'd thought she killed. Giving him the wrong medication had pushed her over the edge and out of the military.

Again, she recalled how her commanding officer had quickly ushered her out of the hospital and pushed her toward the plane. No time to pack, no time to say good-bye to anyone, not even her daughter.

She'd been so positive the pilot had died. But here he was—alive. Why hadn't anyone ever corrected her assumption?

She cleared her throat and put her hand on his wrapped brow. "Hi, Ian!" Her heart raced quicker than a bunch of stampeding ponies on a Texas plain. "Of course I remember you. I'm Jennifer Stauton."

CHAPTER 10

CMC had been one of the few hospitals in the area to use equestrian therapy. Margaret had insisted and now she was glad she had. Their rehab department had become one of the best known in the state. Even other hospitals in the area were recommending CMC, at least for this. If only they had a qualified rehabilitation specialist but most of those stayed in the bigger cities. Emma would have to offer more than the big bucks she'd given Rosa to come from UCLA to attract a doctor of note.

Since Margaret had started the process, she'd read numerous articles confirming what she had learned. Riding a horse helped patients balancing their bodies and those with back injuries, unfused cervical breaks, motor problems, and head injuries were able to retrain their gait so that often the patient ended up walking again.

Margaret had also noted that some of the mentally challenged children who'd been given the lessons had progressed beyond their farthest potentials. Most likely Margaret thought the improvement was due to the children's relationship with the horses. Whatever it was, it worked.

Now that there was a lull, Margaret felt the need of some air. She stepped outside into the cold crisp morning. The moon was up and the sun would be peeking through momentarily. Hard to believe that they'd been up nearly the whole night.

Two of the victims had passed through surgery and were in intensive care. Cole was suturing the pilot as best he could. Ian would then get assembly-lined to Rose and Ellis for the surgeries Cole didn't or couldn't do. The pianist was still unconscious, which was probably just as well. Her fingers had been splinted as best they could. As soon as Patrick and Sara finished with the Asian baby, they would set Nancy's wrist and shoulder. Then it was up to whatever powers that were as to how she healed.

From the way she was dressed and the jewelry she'd worn, Nancy Hoffner appeared to Margaret as a clone of her sister, Allison: slender, pretty, spoiled, and used to getting everything her own way. Well, for this, Margaret hoped the girl would regain her playing power. She only hoped that she wouldn't be a nuisance while doing so.

Inhaling deeply, she smelled the woody odor of burning logs. If it hadn't been for the crash, this would have been a wonderful evening. Well, almost.

Remembering the incident at the Chandler stables earlier that night and knowing how freaked out the horses became with the noise from the helicopters, Margaret decided she'd better wander over to see how they were doing.

Could it have been someone out to harm the Chandlers? Or was it someone getting revenge on Lisa? Or had the girl lied and simply did not want to admit being caught using. Margaret didn't know the answer and that concerned her.

For a brief moment, Margaret wondered which nook or cranny had swallowed Lisa. That girl had a strange habit of disappearing and Margaret could understand, considering Lisa's history, why Cole and Sophie were so distraught. She was sure that Sophie's pregnancy didn't help her cope with Lisa'a new strides toward independence any more than it helped Lisa dealing with her mother's nesting instinct.

Hearing raised voices from the barns, Margaret hurried along, her feet cracking the few ice patches which had formed on the walkway.

John McNamara, Dr. Sarah's Down's syndrome son, was supposed to be there mucking out the stalls. But she didn't think anyone else was there.

"No, John, we have to do it this way." The strident tones of an impatient teen rose over the momentarily stilled wind.

"Well, at least we know where Lisa is," Margaret murmured to herself.

The huge wooden door pushed open on its rollers as Margaret touched the buttons. Security here was tight. But maybe it could be tighter. She would have to speak with Nana about that.

"What's going on here?"

Like naughty children, their faces both flushed as they turned to Margaret.

"No . . . nothing. I just came out here to help. I hope you don't mind."

Margaret shook her head. "I don't. But have you told your mother where you'd be?"

"Uh . . ." Lisa paused as if thinking. "Cole was busy in the triage room and—"

"Nevermind." Margaret reached over to the phone on the wall and dialed the ER. Luckily Sophie was at the desk and didn't have to be paged or taken away from anything life threatening. And she was relieved when Margaret told her about Lisa.

Hanging up the phone, Margaret walked over to where John was staring at a mare, lying down on its side heaving. He seemed fascinated and puzzled at the same time.

"Is something the matter, John? She's having a baby."

"That's exactly what I told him. Didn't I?" Lisa smirked.

"Yes, but . . . she . . . isn't breathing . . . well." John continued watching, his eyes transfixed on the mare.

Margaret adjusted the portable heater so that it was close enough to be effective but far enough that it would not burn the expectant mother.

Margaret smiled at Sara's son. "She's anxious about her baby and she's probably having a bit of pain, so she's breathing fast. How long has she been like that?"

"An hour or so," the girl responded. "But she only started heaving just now."

Margaret sat down, her feet folded one inside of the other, yoga style, and she reached over to pat the horse's swollen belly. The animal neighed in response.

Then slowly, gently, Margaret placed a gloved hand within the gaping opening. "I think the head might be starting to descend, but it could still take some time. After the head emerges and we can get the baby to breathe a bit, we're in good shape, but often it takes an hour or more for the rest of the body to slide down. If she goes on like this for more than four or five hours without a complete birthing then we'll have to call in the vet. Lisa, fetch me a quilt. Let's cover her so that she doesn't get cold."

Eagerly the teen hurried toward a stack of horse blankets.

Margaret was stroking the mare's forehead and showing John how she wanted him to do it when Lisa returned.

"I've never seen a foaling, Margaret." Lisa was just

as fascinated as John and not even as reserved. "Is it all right if I stay until it happens?"

"Me, too." John would not be outdone. "Me, too, Margaret."

Margaret shrugged and studied Lisa a moment. At times the girl seemed so overly worldly-wise, too dangerously ripe and rebellious for her own safety, and at other times she seemed just like an ordinary teenaged girl, low on self-esteem, hungry for love, for approval, and for something with which she could bond. A girl like Margaret had been. "Yeah. I'll ask your mothers, but I'm sure there's no problem. Although Lisa, John might have never helped with a birth, he does have more experience with the horses than you do . . ."

"All right. So?" Lisa shrugged. The rebellious child was back.

The mare tried standing, but could not. She was straining, and it looked like she was having some pain. Margaret preferred letting nature take its course, but sometimes, it seemed, nature needed a little help.

"I'd better call the vet and let him know we might need him." Margaret lifted the phone just as the scream from the hospital pierced through the air.

CHAPTER 11

"This is perfect." Dr. Bill Martin grinned, hitting his steering wheel with glee, as he turned onto the freeway. "I couldn't have asked for better luck. You just flew right into my lap."

"Excuse me?" Hillary's eyes narrowed. She shivered from the open windows. The evening gown she'd worn looked as if it was an antique, a very shabby antique.

"I only found out a few hours ago what Ellis did to you."

"A bitch, huh."

Use him. Learn what he has.

"Shut up."

"And now he's off with Rosa. . . . You don't want to know, Hillary? I would have sworn you'd be eager for this information."

It was all Hillary could do to stay in her seat. At her side, her hand clenched into a fist. "Yeah. I am. Tell me where they are." She grabbed his arm, yanking it off the steering wheel. Her eyes were coals of anger and hate, as if she were possessed.

"Will you be careful? This is a cashmere jacket made by my tailor on Saville Row." He pulled his arm back and rubbed his sleeve, nearly hitting a truck which had slowed in front of them. Bill swerved again, just missing a Chevy van in the next lane as he sped along. Straightening his suit, Bill Martin glanced in the mirror. Hillary was only vaguely aware of *eau de* liquor surrounding him. But who cared? All she wanted was information, like the voice said.

"Don't be a prick, Martin. Where are they? I want to know. I want a gun. I want . . ." Her brain was still foggy from the medication—

Medication, that's a laugh. Medication is supposed to make you feel better. They drugged you, Hillary. And they didn't even Reese you. That's one hell of a lawsuit. No one can medicate you, not even if you're crazy, unless they have a court hearing first or unless you're an immediate danger and we both know you were only joking with the knife.

"Yeah," she responded, not even caring how Bill might perceive her answer.

The doctor, concerned with his own vengeance, hadn't even been aware of her speaking. "Hillary"—Bill yawned, not even covering his mouth—"I've had rather a rough day and night." He shook his head. "Don't make me feel sorry that I came to see you. Your timing by the way was *per-fect.*"

"Hillary, stop making a mess of my car! If that's how you're going to be, you can find your own way back to Chandler Springs." He slowed the car and began to pull off, as if to stop.

Use him. Use him. He can be helpful to you. Just say the right words. Abracadabra. Please and thank you.

Hillary took a deep sigh, closed her eyes, and drew her claws into their sheathes momentarily. "Bill, I want you . . . to know . . . just how much I appreciate this ride . . . especially since . . . I was . . . not discharged." She waited barely a moment before getting back to the focus of her anger. "Now, tell me, where is that Mexican bitch and where is Ellis?"

Bill grinned, his perfect white teeth showing fully. "Ah, the plot thickens. So that's why the good professionals were hurrying out of the building. And I thought they were looking for the morning coffee cart." He pulled the car into traffic again, glancing behind him to make sure they were not being followed.

"Why are you doing this for me? You were never friends with Ellis."

"Oh, Hillary, my dearest lady, you have totally misunderstood me, as has Ellis. I think the world of your husband. I think he's one of CMC's finest." Bill hit the accelerator, the needle tipping over eighty. "And I want to repay him for all the help he's given me.

"It's my pleasure to escort you to see your husband, my dear. I'm sure you've never watched the famous Dr. Johnston in action."

Actually, he was right. She hadn't. Ellis had never asked her to view one of his surgeries. Not that it would particularly interest her but . . . "Thank you." Hillary tried muting her emotions. She didn't want *him* reading her mind or knowing what she had planned for Ellis and the bitch.

Hillary clenched her fist, taking care not to grab the leather dash, and feeling her nails digging into her palm. "Take me home first. I need to change clothes."

"That's the first place they'll be looking for you, my dear. Why don't I take you to my place. I'm sure some of Karen's pre-pregnancy outfits will fit you. Or we can even stop and see Coral May McQuade. Her new place is somewhere along here. One of those new developments, you know."

She just nodded. "Whatever."

Danger alert!

"Where?" she asked.

"I don't know what the township is called . . ."

Hillary tuned him out. Stupid Bill Martin. As the voice instructed, she glanced out of the car. Nothing. Then in the rearview mirror she saw them. He gave a fake French accent to the last word. His forefinger and thumb pinched together.

Hillary didn't even think the louse had ever been to Paris, much less London. Saville Row, her ass.

"Had I known you were being discharged, I wouldn't have made the torturous journey. But I had felt the need to pass on the information that *they* were both still at the hospital.

"And seeing as I was not called in to assist in this crisis, I can only assume that CMC does not need the income *my department* generates.

"I can tell you, it was quite a shock to come into the hospital this morning and find everyone still at it. Bloodshot eyes. Coffee cups staining the counters. And two patients still waiting for surgery." He shook his head. "I doubt Allister was able to diagnose anything with his immature technique. So they're probably going in blind—"

"Will you shut the fuck up? I don't give a damn about your bruised ego. After the way you treated Karin tonight, you deserve it. What do you mean they're at the hospital? In one of the rooms? What?" Hillary dug her nails into the dashboard, the leather pitting where her hands kneaded it. Two helicopters hovering in the distance above them. She glanced up. "Get off the free-way. We're taking side streets."

CHAPTER 12

Someone might have called it "The scream heard around the world," but that had been another event. Others later wondered why Nancy hadn't been an opera singer as well as a pianist.

Just about everyone felt sympathy for the girl who had worked and practiced her whole life to achieve her dream of musical stardom, only to have her hand crushed at the pinnacle of her career, maybe never to play music again. But they felt she should feel lucky to be alive, considering how few of the other passengers lived.

At this moment especially, Cole Morgan was in no mood to be sympathetic. He wanted to finish setting the girl's broken bones and go on to some of the more superficial of her wounds. Damn! Why did she have to wake up now? That sounded almost like he wanted her to remain unconscious, which of course he didn't. Nevertheless, he didn't want to deal with a prima donna right now.

With Leroy, their anesthesiologist, occupied in the surgical suites and hopping between the two surgeries, Cole had been forced to try it alone. What an unfortunate time for Denise Perkins, the backup nurse anesthesiologist they'd just hired, to fly back to Chicago and see her family.

Well, everyone had their strong points, but the mixing of anesthesia gases was not Cole's. He gave it the old college try. Unfortunately, he must have given her too little because here she was, wide-awake, sitting upright in the makeshift surgical suite, like some corpse come to life in the morgue. He'd never respected anesthesiologists as much as he did now. The tricky mixture of oxygen with the numbing gases, not to mention the constant monitoring of the blood pressure which, not having a doppleganger, he hadn't had a chance to do, was what kept the patient under sedation and quiet enough for the surgeon to work on.

So groggy with sleep deprivation, as he knew all the other staff were, too, his stomach irritated by the constant caffeine, and his knee and shoulder joints aching from the prior wounds, the now damp air and the overwork, he didn't even know if he could think properly, and yet he had to keep going. There were lives still depending on him, people still to be patched and repaired.

Granted these were the lesser injured, but Cole did not want to slight them. Nor did he want to deal with this.

"Will someone come help me?"

Both Fred, their physician's assistant, and Vicki, the other former OR nurse, ran in to give Cole assistance.

"Nancy!" Vicki's voice echoed like a conductor. "Desist! Quiet!" The girl stopped her screaming almost immediately. "Nancy, relax." Vicki touched Nancy's uninjured shoulder. "I want you to pretend that we're leading an orchestra. Listen to me. Okay?"

The frightened girl nodded, still not speaking.

"Good. You are going to be meditative, reflective, and serene. I want you to watch me and I will tell you when it is your turn to join in."

Nancy nodded again, mutely staring at Vicki as if the nurse had a private hold over her.

"Good. Good. Okay, now, I'm going to give you a shot of Valium mixed with some Ativan, hon. And then . . ." The pianist's eyes widened as she watched wordlessly while Vicki expertly injected the medication intravenously. "I want you to count backwards now . . . and when you wake up . . ."

Nancy heard no more. She closed her eyes and became quiet. Her breathing deepened. The medication given through the vein worked faster and reached the brain quicker than did an ordinary injection. Even if she had put it into the IV tubing, it would have had to circle around and been diluted with the IV solution, taking slightly longer to act.

Vicki motioned for Cole to continue his work while she wrapped the blood pressure cuff around the girl's good arm and began monitoring her vital signs.

She'd be fine for right now and possibly even through the surgery with Patrick repairing her wrist and clavicle, especially when they added additional muscle relaxant to the IV solution.

Maybe after, when she'd woken, Vicki would stop in and have a chat. Knowing what it must have been like to be a child prodigy, Vicki prayed that this girl would return to music, while Vicki had not.

Patrick studied the exposed surface of the brain where the skull had opened. He didn't like the small petechia which had started forming. That meant underlying injury and worse yet, perhaps a hematoma. Obviously, he would have to order neuro checks on the girl every fifteen minutes. If only he could see the hematoma, he could aspirate it quickly and prevent it from killing the tissue around it, but if one was building up, it hadn't yet shown on the CAT scan.

If any signs of hematoma began showing, they would have to bring her back to surgery immediately, or risk losing her. That meant she'd have to stay NPO, without anything to eat, until they were sure. As of now, her pupils were still equal and reacting to light.

Patrick felt sick just looking at this little girl and wondering what kind of damage had been done to her and how this would affect the rest of her life. He'd found out from the airlines that she'd been on her way to Corpus Christi to be adopted by a wealthy family there. Why the hell hadn't they flown someone out to meet her? Was there the possibility that they might reject her, now that she was no longer perfect?

In the very next room, the music floated over the air in the background. Ellis hated working without music. It calmed him. Some doctors used classical; others used jazz or even soft rock; and he knew one who used opera. He didn't care usually, as long as it kept him stable, kept him from thinking about the power he held in his hand. Once you started thinking about power, you started thinking you were God, and it was the beginning of the end.

"Looking good, Rosa," Ellis said, peering over the punctured lung of the wounded pilot. The chest wall had been penetrated by some of the flying glass as he'd gone through the window. "I think we can fix it," Ellis said with more confidence than he thought. Sometimes when he bluffed his way through. . . .

They swabbed the skin with Betadine and Ellis's hand, delicately holding the knife, prepared for his incision.

He'd just completed the cut and applied the retractors when the beeping of the alarms told him that Ian Williams's blood pressure was falling abnormally fast.

"Ellis, we're losing him," Rosa said. The patient's complexion had become ashen in a matter of seconds.

"Shit!" Just as he feared. Either he had a leaker here

or a ventricular rupture. He couldn't see it. "Bicarb, stat!"

"Ellis, he wasn't hyperventilating. *He's not in acidosis* and we don't have current blood gases on him," Rosa argued. "The last ones were an hour ago, showing that he was going into alkalosis. You can't give him bicarb. It will throw him over the edge."

"Just give me the damn drug. It's my call." He turned back toward the patient. "2.5 dopamine."

Excess fluid was seeping into the pericardial space. As a cardiologist, Rosa knew that when the heart compressed, it decreased the output and stroke volume. The only cure for cardiac tamponade was to remove the excess fluid immediately, before the patient arrested.

Okay, it was Ellis's call. She motioned Jennifer to prepare backup medications in case they had to swing him the other way. Then Rosa injected medication.

The pressure stabilized for a moment. Rosa pulled back the clamps as Ellis desperately searched through the open cavity for the seeping artery. She glanced at her colleague, worried that the stresses of tonight, not just the emergency but Hillary's actions, had made him unable to think clearly.

Still he was one of the best damn cardiac surgeons she knew.

"O_2. Five liters. Stat." Maybe if they could enhance the tissue perfusion . . . Ellis reached out for a pulmonary artery catheter.

Rosa mistakenly picked up a scalpel. She hadn't meant to, it was just there.

His look was enough to make her cringe as he grabbed for the needle himself. Of course, she knew better. They were all tired and under strain.

Peggy, the lab tech, ran in to take a stat blood gas level. But there was no time to wait.

If they wanted to save this man, Ellis would have to

begin aspirating the fluid. "Hang a Lactated Ringer's," Ellis now ordered. The fluid would replace some of the lost blood. "We might need to do . . ."

He didn't have to finish. Rosa nodded and undid the sterile wrapping on the thoracotomy set. She wasn't even going to question him. Next to her were the internal defibrillator paddles.

Jennifer stepped to the head of the patient, monitoring his blood pressure and hemodynamic indicators. She wanted to be in the other room assisting Patrick with Angel, but she knew that if she went in there, she'd become a useless blubbering tear duct. This activity kept her focused.

The ECG hookup on Ian Williams showed PVCs. With preventricular contractions, the pilot still wouldn't get enough blood to the brain.

"Time!" Ellis shouted.

Rosa glanced up at the huge double-sided clock, its second hand sweeping away the life-giving moments. "Forty-two seconds," she responded.

Only forty-two seconds. It seemed like forty-two years and yet a patient without oxygen for even thirty seconds could be damaged. After four minutes, you almost didn't need to bother trying to bring them around. And by ten minutes, they'd kicked over.

"Lidocaine." He glanced at the monitor. "And then defib!"

Rosa injected the painkilling medication, which also enhanced the reception of the current.

Ellis reached for the paddles. They were both awash in blood.

"One, two . . . now!"

The ECG line jumped.

Peggy ran in with the lab results. Rosa had forgotten just how quick the computers could work when they were set right.

Rosa was relieved that Ellis had been correct. The pH of the blood had somehow reversed itself. There was no time to question how.

As soon as Ellis had removed twenty-five milliliters of fluid, the pilot's pressure rose to within reasonably normal limits, fluctuated a moment, and then stabilized. Color momentarily returned to the pilot's face.

"Okay, gang, I think we're out of the water, for the moment." Ellis wiped his brow on his sleeve.

Ellis held out his hand expecting a number four needle and cat gut to sew some of the internal organs. The cat gut would melt and disappear into the body as the injury healed. Later, the remaining pieces would be eliminated with the rest of his bodily waste. It was certainly better than having to open him up again to take the stitches out.

Realizing his need wasn't being automatically taken care of, as it usually was when one of the nurses worked with him, he glanced up. For a moment, irritation made him squint.

Then he saw Jennifer hurry from the other room, where she'd been drawn for a moment. Ellis nodded in her direction.

Immediately assessing the situation, Jennifer placed the proper needle and sutures in Rosa's hand. It wasn't the cardiologist's fault. She didn't know the setup here.

Rosa didn't know how Jennifer, Vicki, and the other nurses were able to read Ellis's mind so easily, but it certainly made for smooth work. Now that Sophie was back from her honeymoon and director of nursing again, instead of Pam, Rosa would see if they couldn't move these nurses back to OR.

"He's going to be okay?" Jennifer's voice was strained as she held back her worry. Ian Williams was not going to die twice on her.

"I think so," Rosa whispered as she handed a new needle to Ellis.

In response, Ellis Johnston made the mistake of looking up. It was his undoing.

All he could see were Rosa's wide brown eyes, just as red rimmed from overwork as his were, but they were beautiful brown eyes nevertheless.

A second. Only a second. That was all it took for them to be forever linked in time and memory. Maybe Hillary had known something he didn't.

Ellis swallowed hard and turned back to the patient.

"Counting sponges," he said, as he began to lift one blood-soaked gauze out after another. He forced himself to pay attention. It seemed so simple and yet one of these left in could cause an infection, not unlike the one which took Jacob McQuade's life. God only knew, Ellis did not need another lawsuit, even though that other one was Bill Martin's doing and not his.

And God only knew that Ellis did not need what was happening to him right now. He would have to push it away and forget it . . . at least until this thing with Hillary was resolved.

"Dr. Johnston," Vicki spoke over the loudspeaker into the surgical arena.

He didn't look up. He didn't even acknowledge.

"You have a telephone call, Ellis. They say it's urgent."

"Nothing's more urgent than the life of my patient." Ellis heaved a sigh of relief. It had been touch and go for a few moments, but he'd managed to seal up the lung. With luck, the repair would heal. He began stitching up the other cuts.

"Ellis, it's Houston Psychiatric services. Dr. Waldman's calling. Hillary's escaped."

Ellis Johnston closed his eyes for a brief second and sighed. That was all he needed. "Okay, Vicki. Get on the horn, please. Call Frank at the police station. If he finds her, he can evaluate her. If she seems reasonably safe, tell him to take her home and I'll deal with the hospital later." His voice faded with the effort this cost him.

Now, in addition to everything else, he had to worry about Hillary's safety and that of the kids.

Up above the surgical suites, in fact surrounding both of them so that students (should CMC ever open its doors to interns and residents, which Emma would love to do) could watch and comment about two procedures at once, a lone figure dressed in black and hidden by the darkness, stared down, watching intently. Yes, she was a student . . . a student of life. So she had every right to be up here.

And she had just received the answers to the test she'd wanted.

Hillary Johnston silently crept to the exit door. There wasn't going to be any more cheating on exams. Not from this school.

CHAPTER 13

When Nancy Hoffner woke the second time nearly fourteen hours later, there were tears in her eyes. She'd been dreaming about her career being a huge aircraft and it had fallen out of the sky, crashing just like her hopes did. Her whole right side felt numb. She tried reaching out to touch something, but she couldn't feel anything.

Once again, she sat up in bed screaming. "Someone tell me what's happening?" But it didn't sound like that. Her words were garbled, similar to someone with a recent stroke. Though Nancy Hoffner had not had a stroke, she had suffered a severe concussion.

The pianist's reaction had been expected as a possible side effect of Haldrone, a medication given to reduce the swelling. Pam thought this girl was a textbook case of the drug's ability to increase instability. This was one place where Meredith Fischer was definitely needed. Pam tried calming the hysterical young woman.

"It's all right, Miss Hoffner," Pam said in her most professional manner. "I know you're scared. I want you to take this Ativan. It will help your anxiety, and then when you wake up, you should be able to talk a little better."

Frustrated that she could not be understood, Nancy sadly nodded and took the pill the young nurse offered.

Without her hands, her whole life was over. She might as well just end it now.

Until the swelling in Nancy's brain went down, it would be impossible to tell what, if any, her further injuries were. The first seventy-two hours after an accident were always the most critical. It was then one looked for the real damage, separating what had merely been due to the shock and what other injuries there were.

Her fingers, crushed by the metal of the plane, were now in individual metal splints. Maybe she would be able to use them again, and maybe not.

Her blood pressure during the procedure had been higher than Cole or Patrick would have liked it. They hadn't been sure if it was from the edema to the brain or if it was possibly a kidney problem, since Nancy had contusions on her back as well, though the scans had all proved negative as far as renal damage. For that reason Patrick hadn't left any orders for narcotics even though he knew she'd probably have a great deal of pain. In cases like this, there was always the fear that by giving Demerol, Morphine or the like, they might mask other symptoms. Another point which he had to consider was that most of pain medications caused urinary retention as a side effect. He wasn't going to risk that if this girl might have renal problems.

After finishing up his notes, he asked Rosa to evaluate the girl for hypertension. The best an exhausted Rosa could do was write orders that should take care of the patient until later that evening when she'd have had some rest and could diagnose more clearly.

While he was at it, Patrick put in a request for Meredith's services. The new Chief would be useful here. Patrick didn't know how he, a surgeon, would handle the loss of his hands, and he wasn't sure how this girl was going to handle it either.

Everyone was surprised that Pam Roberts volunteered to stay over after working the ER to assist in the ICU where Nancy, Mr. Ciss, and the little girl had been placed. Ian had gone to CCU because they wanted to keep an even closer watch on him. A tube running out of his chest drained the excess secretions from his lung and kept the pressure in his heart from building up again.

Margaret wondered if her "cousin" was just doing this to curry favor.

"I have a detective friend in Houston who could probably use some side work," Allison said. Even though she was still on crutches, she had been useful during the emergency, in filling out paper work and doing the admits.

The fact was, this time Pam's desire to help had been above board. It simply had not struck Pam yet that as a Chandler, she didn't have to work these crazy nursing hours. Of course, having grown up as she did, Pam did not and probably would never feel like a Chandler.

The one bedroom apartment approximately a mile from the hospital was what Vicki Kantera called home.

After nearly thirty-six hours at work, it was all she could do to feed her cat, Mozart, a white, very spoiled Persian, throw off her clothes, jump into a hot shower, and crawl into bed, hoping not to be awakened at least until the end of the century.

It was an impossibility, she knew. Given the shortage of nurses at CMC, the odds of her being called back within twenty-four hours were three-to-one. With luck,

Vicki thought as she flossed her teeth, she'd get a little sleep.

"Come on, fish breath." Vicki hoisted the fat cat up onto the bed with her, stroking him for a bit while he purred contentedly and then fell asleep cuddled in her arms. Vicki closed her eyes, too. But somehow sleep eluded her. Tired as she was, scenes of the night kept flashing in front of her.

All she could think of was Nancy Hoffner and her screams at finding her fingers in splints and her wrist immobilized.

How would Vicki have felt? She didn't even want to remember.

She shut her eyes tight and began breathing deeply, hoping that would inspire lethargy to overcome her. She'd been so sleepy while forcing herself to work—and now? Now, she felt wide awake. Wasn't it always this way?

Having counted to one hundred, Vicki started again, feeling herself on the edge about to cross over into never-never land when *Bam! Bam! Bam!* woke her.

Vicki groaned and put the pillow over her head. "Why don't they teach the boy to play right, Mozart?" she asked the cat. "And why does he have to practice now, at this very moment?" She opened her eyes. Mozart stared at her with his one blue and one brown eye. Only that questionable defect kept him from being a show cat, but Vicki didn't care. In fact, she loved him all the more for his imperfections. If only her folks had felt the same about her.

"Do you think they'll ever tune their piano?" She picked up the phone to dial her neighbors and found the line busy.

Slipping on a robe, she rose and stood by the window, watching a blustery Christmas Day come in off the plains. It would probably be cold again like it had been last night, but for the moment the air was heating up.

Mozart purred, rubbing against her feet, trying to draw her back to the bed. Vicki absentmindedly picked him up and rubbed her cheek against his soft fur. Damn! "Mozart! How come your fur is wet?"

Vicki didn't have to hear Mozart's answer. She sniffled and wiped her eyes on a nearby tissue. Even after all this time, she still wondered if she'd done the right thing. "They" said she had promise, but how did "they" really know?

Vicki had always tried harder and harder and felt more mediocre and more mediocre. No matter what she did, she'd never been able to come up to her parents' standards. All the more reason to put her past behind her.

Besides after years of being out of the music circle, it would be almost impossible to jump back in. It just wasn't done. Still, it didn't stop the wondering if she, Vicki Kantera would have been as well respected, as well received as Nancy Hoffner. And would she want to trade places with the young pianist now?

She kissed her cat and rubbed his stomach. Mozart was probably the closest she'd come to being in music again. He'd been a present from her folks after she had graduated from Northwest Music Academy as a classical pianist and a first violinist. She stared out into the flat Texas fields beyond her apartment building.

Vicki began to feel the familiar itch in her fingers, almost like the phantom-limb phenomena. Soldiers or others who'd had legs or other body parts amputated would swear they felt their legs moving, but they'd look down only to remember their legs weren't there.

She recalled the practice chords she had to memorize, and Mrs. Snitzer with her little beagle yapping up a storm everytime Vicki hit the wrong note. How could anyone say she had been destined for greatness? Not even those at the school could predict.

She let her fingers glide over the imaginary keyboard, feeling the smooth ivory of the keys and black obsidian of the flats and sharps. Then she played the strings, hearing the music in her mind as she pressed one and plucked another, holding the Stradivarius just at the right angle to her chin. Oh, yes, only the best for her, even if it meant Mother and Father had to sacrifice.

To achieve success in two very different types of instruments was considered difficult if not impossible. And yet, Vicki had persisted—because her parents wanted her to and she wanted to please her parents.

Her whole life had been music: no after-school events, just practice; no outings with Girl Scouts or the church group, just practice; and no dates until she was eighteen (and then only with other boys from musically minded families)—just practice. Even television had been unheard of in her house except for the few public broadcasting specials about music.

But there was no piano in her life now and no violin. She had sealed her fate when she turned her back on her scholarship. Unlike Nancy, Vicki would never have a chance to return.

Had Nancy been raised in such a single-minded atmosphere or did she truly enjoy her music?

Both Vicki's parents had been professionals: Father played the horns and Mother, the strings. Each had won their own set of awards and expected nothing less of their daughter. But each had been lost within their music and could relate only to that. They played wonderful duets, but the more she knew of her parents, the more she was surprised they had ever mingled long enough to have her.

As an only child, her life went on much the same, day in and day out, sort of a dry contentment, until she joined the Academy . . . and met Bart. His full name was Bartholomew James Kirkpatrick III. Unlike her own family, Bart's parents were not only rich but influential in the community. She didn't know if emotionally he was really better off than she was or not—his folks gave him money, hers gave her music. But what Bart wanted he usually managed to have.

She knew now that Bart had been attracted to her virginal innocence and wide-eyed adoration—her fascination with him and his world. At the time she believed everything he said, even when she lost her virginity, even when she realized that he did not really want her.

A hunger for human companionship had pushed her forward and the need to be acknowledged in a way that her parents had never done for her made her follow the young playboy to Dallas, throwing away a complete scholarship to Juilliard.

There at the Dallas stadium, she sat and cried on the sidelines while Bart wooed not one but three Dallas cowgirls and acted as if she had never existed. They had adored him, too.

Vicki thought that probably those years were the worst in her life. Her parents begged her to come home; begged her to take up the scholarship before it was too late, but Vicki had been a sleeping beauty locked in a trance and once awakened, she never wanted to sleep again, even if those cushions supporting her head were the floating wings of Beethoven, Bach, and Mozart.

Vicki tried suicide twice that year and ballooned up from 109 to 145. Not that heavy, but when you're only 5'1", 145 was, as her Jewish friends would say, *zaftig*. She dyed her blond hair a harsh red, but didn't like it and let it grow out. Losing the weight again, she became an expert horsewoman, finding the animals better companions than the men she knew, and now she competed in the annual CMC rodeo events.

Finding herself was not an easy thing to do, and for a long time she didn't think it would happen.

It had taken several years of therapy to realize that Bart had never really meant anything to her except as a means out of her rut. And that once she had found him, she entered his groove, and changed the needle on her recording, she didn't want to play the same song again.

Refusing to acknowledge anything about her musical background, Vicki had enrolled in nursing school at the University of Dallas. She loved helping people, touching and hugging, comforting and holding her patients, especially the kids. Somehow it seemed to make up for the lack of emotion in her own family.

Other than a call at Christmas and her birthday, her parents were usually on the road performing; she hardly heard from them anymore.

But Vicki supposed that her nursing, as close to anything else, provided her the satisfaction and the chance to be in the real world. She'd always wondered if and when the real world would find her. Maybe Nancy Hoffner was the reason Vicki had been propelled into nursing. Maybe through Nancy, Vicki would again hear the joy of synchronized harmonies.

The kid upstairs continued to bang away. Vicki shook her head, sadly. A Mozart he'd never be, but maybe she'd offer to give him a few lessons—after she had some sleep.

CHAPTER 14

Sophie leaned over the toilet bowl. She remembered when she'd carried Lisa how sick she'd felt, but somehow she hadn't expected to be as ill this time. Not only was she nauseated, but she was running a slight temperature, which she knew affected her work. Every muscle in her body ached. She didn't remember that from last time, either. But Dr. Ken Stevens, CMC's head of OB, had assured her that there was nothing to worry about. Especially in older women, it wasn't unusual to have a slightly elevated temperature.

"Maybe you should rest a bit more, Sophie? These thirty-six-hour stints are okay for me, but not for you," Cole said. He'd been cheated out of experiencing the last pregnancy with Lisa and by God, he was going to fully participate in this one. "You're pushing too hard. When do you have to start Lamaze?"

"Chauvinist." Sophie shook her head and then reached up to kiss him on the nose. Cole was acting worse than her mother.

She sighed. "Lamaze classes don't start for another couple of months yet." She patted her stomach gently. The queasy feeling was still there.

Sophie'd first realized she was pregnant a week before their original wedding had been planned—Halloween. But then Cole had played hero when that hotshot cowboy had murdered Dennis Green and forced the crew to work on his already dead girlfriend.

So, she'd been three months pregnant when they sailed on their honeymoon. Of course, she'd told no one but Cole and Dr. Ken Stevens, her OB. But she was sure others at work had guessed and were already counting the months with their midget minds on their midget fingers.

Her mother never came right out and said anything, but Sophie knew that Mom was disappointed. First she had become pregnant, and told them Lisa was John Drummond's. Mother had been happy that she married the baby's "father." After she'd left him, her family never let her forget it. A divorce was a major disaster for the staunch Southern Baptist family she'd grown up in . . . and now Sophie was pregnant again before she'd gotten married.

At least her mother couldn't complain. This time the baby was legitimately with his father as Lisa, for many years, had not been.

"I should probably begin them in my sixth or seventh month. But even if I could start now, I don't have the time, or the energy. Until we hire more nurses—"

"That is not your problem. It's Emma's." Cole guided her to the bedroom. "*You* are going to be a mother."

"No, Cole." She sighed. "I'm already a mother. I am going to be a mother for the second time. But I am also the director of nursing. It *is* my problem. I have to speak with Marcus Laurence and see about budgeting for some new hirees. The agency nurses cost too much."

She slipped her hand into his. "I'm going to lie down a bit until Lisa returns from helping Margaret in the barns."

She moved awkwardly toward their bedroom. It looked to Cole as if she was in pain, but he didn't want to say anything. It was bad enough she thought he was like her mother. No, if Sophie needed his help, she would say so. In the meantime, he would try to stay out of her way.

Cole went to stand by the dormer window, where as a young boy he would often look out and wonder about his life. Hard to believe that this was the house he'd grown up in, and that now he was looking out of the same window, wondering about his daughter. Molly, his yellow Lab, slipped her head under his hand, indicating that she was his "woman" too and wanted her fair share of attention.

He turned and glanced at the tree filling the room, which he, Lisa, and Sophie had picked. Because of the emergency last night, the presents were still there, unopened. Well, they'd take care of that later when Lisa returned.

Meanwhile, Cole decided he'd lie down next to his wife.

Sophie woke from a nightmare, sweating profusely and out of breath, as if she had been running the rapids.

Even though it was only perspiration, Sophie felt as though she was swimming in her own blood. She turned, surprised to see Cole at her side. Of course, he needed rest as much as she did. She was sure he was having sympathy pains along with her. His big hand covered the area of her stomach, of their baby. She lightly placed her hand on top of his.

How she loved him! She just wanted to reach out and touch him, but lately, it seemed their communication had gone stale. Sophie had adored Cole Morgan, basketball hero, since their high school romance. Her stupidity had lost him once. She wasn't about to let him go now. Whatever it was, they would work it out.

Maybe, she thought, as she reached for the thermometer, she was coming down with the flu. It was the season for it and with the hours she'd been working lately . . .

She had the same low grade temperature she'd been running for weeks now. But somehow she felt worse. Two aspirin? No, Tylenol was better. Aspirin might make her bleed. Certainly near the last trimester it was especially *verboten*. Anyway, the studies that had been done showed Tylenol just as effective in most cases.

An imaginary knife appeared from nowhere, cutting through her kidneys as she tried turning. Damn! What was going on? It had to be just the flu, she reassured herself. The chills followed as if to affirm her thought. Yes, it was the flu, and if she rested a few days, she'd be just fine.

Thinking that she'd feel better after a hot shower, and being as quiet as she could, Sophie stepped into the bathroom.

Conscious of every movement she made, Sophie felt like she was the tin man, who'd stood out in the rain too long. She peered down. Her urine was slightly blood tinged.

Jesus! Was she aborting? She hoped not.

She touched her stomach and gently palpated the shape of the baby. No, she wasn't having the pains usually associated with a miscarriage. But maybe, just in case, she'd go in to see Ken tomorrow.

She frowned as she undressed and studied the scaly red patches on her skin. They were slightly swollen, almost like hives or bug bites. But so many of them? Maybe that's why she was feeling so lousy. Maybe the blood in her urine had something to do with that.

Had she eaten anything she was allergic to? She didn't think so and yet . . . Glancing at the medication shelf, she studied the pink and white pill a moment, before placing the Benadryl under her tongue. Normally, it was best not to take any drugs when you were pregnant, but Ken had told her that an occasional Sudafed or antihistamine would not hurt the fetus, as long as she was careful, which of course she was. Benadryl was an antihistamine, which would help the swelling and redness go down and maybe take care of some of that achy feeling. It would also make her sleepy, but at this moment, she didn't care.

She glanced up at her butterfly mask, flushing her cheeks and bridging her nose. It, too, had small raised blisters and white scaly skin. Why hadn't she noticed this before? She leaned closer into the mirror.

Sophie had never thought herself beautiful and this didn't help, even when Cole said she was the most perfectly beautiful woman in the world.

Yes, tomorrow, when the hospital staff returned to normal, she'd check things out with her OB, Ken Stevens. "Dear God," she prayed, "don't let anything happen to this baby."

CHAPTER 15

Monday morning's M and M (morbidity and mortality) meeting was slower than usual in getting started. Not only was everyone still exhausted from the Christmas emergency, but there were several announcements to be made.

In their own little corner, the maverick table consisting of Ellis Johnston, and his partner, Patrick Thompson; Josh Allister; Cole Morgan; Rosa Sanchez; Leroy Porter; and Sean O'Neill made their own private jokes and comments, and each and every one grabbed for the watery scrambled eggs, sweet rolls, hash browns, and coffee. A colony onto themselves, there were times when they'd very much like to rebel and declare themselves a separate state, but thus far there had only been rumblings of succession. And no one truly believed their words meant anything more than an outpouring of steam.

Even though he didn't like the rush and push, Tyler Van Fleet, the pathologist, liked the company and had joined them today, since where he usually sat at the head table there were several extras: including Pam Roberts, Meredith Fischer, and a stranger with slicked-back hair, which looked more like a bad toupee.

Tyler glanced over at Pam, seated next to the stranger. She was looking extremely uncomfortable, but then it could just be she wasn't used to being onstage. Though she certainly had upstaged a few people, Ty thought.

Dr. Richard Bell, the prior chief of staff, made the formal introductions bringing Dr. Meredith Fischer, their head of psychiatry, up to the podium. She would be succeeding him.

Having been chief of staff almost from the hospital's inception, it was Richard who had broken the news to Emma about her son, Tommy, dying, about the survival but injuries to Tommy's two daughters, Margaret and Allison, and about the death of her beloved husband, Caleb. Dr. Bell could have probably been convinced to continue another year, as he had in the past, if his Parkinson's disease hadn't become noticeably worse.

In his wavering voice, he praised Meredith's duty to the hospital and her participation in the various associations: American Psychiatric and American Psychoanalytical groups, as well as her handling of the plane crash.

As soon as Meredith greeted everyone, she nodded to Emma who stood momentarily at her seat and said that there were two announcements.

One surprised almost everyone. Marcus Laurence, their resident Yankee, and hospital administrator announced he was leaving the position due to personal reasons.

A few words were whispered back and forth but none so plain as to openly embarrass Marcus, who looked as if he wanted to fall through a trapdoor.

Everyone knew who that personal reason was: his wife, Joyce, who'd made it clear that if Marcus stayed, it would only be because of Pam Roberts and that meant she, Joyce Jenkins Laurence, would leave—family fortune and all. As it was, the couple was on the verge of divorce because of his dalliance, and Marcus wanted it to develop no further.

There were a few pointed stares in Pam's direction, but she effectively ignored them.

It felt odd having a nurse, just newly graduated, in a meeting reserved for doctors and other administrators, where not even Sophie, the head of nursing, came on a regular basis, but Pam was no longer just a nurse. As of Christmas Eve, she'd been acknowledged as the grand-niece to Emma Chandler and had been appointed to the hospital board by her great-aunt.

Everyone wished Marcus well in his move back to Cincinnati, and Meredith handed him a plaque for service well done.

The big-boned stranger with the black-as-night hair and the ruddy face of a habitual drinker was introduced as Nelson St. Clair, the new administrator. Nelson wasn't even a Yankee but a Canadian from Quebec. He spoke with a slight French accent and said that it was a long way to come, and he hoped the warm weather was worth it.

The audience clapped to welcome him and Meredith handed him the keys to his office and the key to the staff lounge. Since he was not a doctor, it was doubtful that Mr. St. Clair would be doing the doubles and triples during emergencies as she and the other staff did.

Marcus said he'd assist the new administrator, making him feel at home for the next few days, until he departed.

Meredith was actually surprised to see tears in Marcus's eyes. She had always thought him such a prim and proper man.

Joshua wondered why Emma wasn't standing up. His future grandmother-in-law had always been the feistiest and healthiest of all the staff here. He would ask Margaret later, or maybe even talk to her himself.

Emma hadn't always liked Josh. She hadn't seemed

to mind when he'd been dating Allison, her young, blond fashion-model granddaughter, but when he dropped her, after finding her in bed with Jinx, one of her handymen from the spa, and had finally broken through his own doubt and Margaret's reserve to see that they were the ones really right for each other, Emma Chandler had shunned him.

Somehow, he wasn't sure, but Emma had gotten the impression that he was after Margaret for her share of the Chandler fortune.

Still he and Margaret persisted, in spite of the anonymous letters sent to both of them when he'd gone to New York for a trip. Hers had said he wanted to be alone to see an old girlfriend; his had said that she didn't want anything more to do with him. No one knew who had sent those letters, but Josh was willing to bet it was the same one who started the rumor that he was after Margaret for her money.

He glanced at his fiancée now, seated at the head table as a member of the hospital board. Next to her was pretty Allison, her sister, still moving around on crutches from her accident.

Marcus sat down as quickly and as quietly as he could, eyes directed only to the floor.

Joshua glanced at Sean O'Neill, the red-haired psychologist, who'd also had a fling with Pam Roberts, now the newest member of the Chandler family. And Bill, too. Joshua momentarily looked in the direction of his former boss who had tried so hard to get him fired.

Dr. Bill Martin took pride in his greedy scheduling unnecessary tests and thus making money for the hospital, money that the patients shouldn't have had to spend, and of protecting himself from frivolous lawsuits by signing the names of other doctors to the charts and test orders. They wouldn't dare cancel any tests once he'd started and so the consequences of the results had to fall on the other doctors, just as it had on Ellis for "ordering" the test that caused McQuade to die. Bill smirked. They wouldn't dare do anything to him.

It had been the fight between Marcus and Sean, both showing up at Pam's apartment at the same time, which had caused the ruckus that nearly killed the huge red-haired Irishman. No one would have thought Marcus capable of fighting the way he had and in fact, if Joshua hadn't pulled him off, who knew what might have happened.

As soon as everyone had settled back down, Meredith made the second announcement. The Joint Commission of Hospitals would be coming for their tri-annual visit in two months.

The initials JHC were like a curse being spoken. At the best, they'd escape with some warnings and suggestions, maybe even a few small fines. But if they had more than the allocated points against them, CMC would be no more. At least not until it raised its standards to that of the commission's.

Very few hospitals escaped without the regulation committee looking inside crannies and under every bed for specks of dirt and when they found anything, watch out.

Two years ago they had been written up because of their failure to meet minimum OSHA safety standards. Cole feared what might happen if the committee investigated the matter of Jacob McQuade. Even though that was history, it was recent enough to interest the commission.

Without JCH's total approval and support, the hospital could be closed down. More than one hospital in this area had been forced to suspend services until the members of the joint commission thought they were up to snuff. A lot of people went without employment during that time, but JCH responded that the hospital had to be safe to be licensed. And of course they were right.

"Well, maybe they'll finally hire some new nurses to help Sophie out," Cole said, as he grabbed the last cherry danish.

The others at the table grunted.

He seemed to be the only one thinking some good would come out of the visit. From the looks on the faces of the rest of the staff, they were not pleased.

Cole knew that even with extra staff, Sophie would probably go nuts. It was the nursing department that always bore the brunt of these visits. They did the quality assurance, checked up on the documentation on the charts, rewrote all the policies, checked for safety hazards. They rode herd on the doctors to make sure all the orders were signed, did the histories and physicals, not to mention legitimate discharge notes, multidisciplinary team notes correlating to each other, and probably the most important, oversaw how the lines of communication between doctor and nurse were kept open.

No, as Cole tore apart the cherry center of his sweetroll, he wondered if maybe he couldn't take some hints from the process. Was there anything he could do to help Sophie? Sometimes he felt as if they were one of those voodoo photos, cut in half, so that neither side could speak to the other.

It worried him that they hadn't really sat down and talked lately and he knew it was mostly his doing. But he was nervous: If he upset her, the pregnancy might go bad.

And now he had this. How would the coming of JCH affect their pregnancy? Was there any way he could prevent her from becoming too stressed out?

*   *   *

Off to the side, where Bill Martin sat at a table by himself brooding and drumming his fingers, staring up at the dais, where *he* should have been conducting the meeting, he thought about the JCH.

It had been him who brought the NCR into town examining Joshua Allister's credentials. Maybe he could assist the JCH with their work.

If he had been made chief of staff, they would have passed inspection with a by-your-leave. Bill Martin knew almost everyone on the main committee, and a little grease in the right places did wonders.

Instead, the new head was that shrink who didn't know an arterial catheter from a Foley. Something was going on between Emma and that woman, and he was going to find out. Being head of the hospital was his rightful place and Meredith Fischer was not taking it away from him, even if he had to force the issue.

Yes, that was exactly what would happen. He knew some of the commission personally. He would see that they understood where his interests lay.

He also wanted to find out about Pam's role in this fiasco. With her conniving manipulations, he was positive she had played a part. He was also going to find out why the little cunt had suddenly turned against him.

Bill picked up his coffee cup and drained it, wishing there was something stronger at these meetings. But he knew that, with the exception of him, very few people could handle alcohol so early in the morning.

If he had his way, by spring either he'd be in charge of CMC or it would be closed.

CHAPTER 16

"Roberts! Roberts! Or whatever your fucking name is. Open up this door immediately!" Bill Martin, obviously having had not only his breakfast supply of ETOH (alcohol) but the afternoon's and evening's as well, first pounded and then kicked Pam's apartment door.

"I know you're in there. I see your car. Open up, goddamn you, or I'll break it down."

"Get away, Bill. I'm calling the police."

"Like hell you are." He gave the flimsy structure a hefty kick, cracking a panel. "Open it, Pam. You and I need to discuss some matters."

"Not the way you are now."

"You owe me an explanation, Roberts! And I'm staying here until I get it."

Pam peeked through her peephole. Bill's face was flushed with anger and drink. She rummaged through her closet and found what she was looking for.

"I don't owe you a goddamn thing, Bill Martin. Get out of here." She dropped a few shells in, cocked the hammer on the double-barreled shotgun she'd stolen from her old man the day she left home. It might not work. She hadn't oiled the damn thing in years, and she didn't even know if the shells were still good. But it sure did make one hell of a noise. Ah, yes.

"You hear that, *Dr.* Martin?"

"What?"

"Why, my daddy's double-barreled shotgun being loaded." Grinning, Pam peered out again.

Almost immediately Bill quieted. "What's that you got, honey bun? I don't think I heard you."

"You heard fine, *dar*-ling," Pam responded in kind. "Either you get the hell out of here or I'm going to blow a hole in you that an ambulance can drive through. Maybe *then* I'll call the police. You are drunken and disorderly, sir. I do not need you around anymore."

"Pamela," Bill whined, "darling, I need you. What about those plans we made? What about the clinic and the hospital? What about us getting married?"

Pam jammed a second shell in for effect. "You and me?" There was laughter in her voice. "Sorry, fella, you just lost by a long shot. You should of cashed in on your horse when you had the chance. I have everything I need now."

"But, baby. Pammy. You know I couldn't. Not until Karin . . . I mean Karin would have taken all—"

"Bill Martin, get away from my door now."

"You goddamn bitch." He kicked the door once more and this time broke through. The door hung on one hinge.

Why didn't one of those nosy neighbors call the cops? Pam cursed under her breath. Spied on her enough of the time.

He kicked it again and a surprised Bill faced an even more surprised Pamela.

The element of timing being on his side, the drunken radiologist took two steps toward her and yanked the shotgun out of her hands and threw it on the sofa.

"I think it's time I taught you a lesson, Pammy, on just who needs who here."

Smashing her against him so that she could feel his cock hard and ready for her, he devoured her with a sloppy kiss, holding her in such a way that she could barely move.

"You stink!" She tried fighting him off.

"Always was stronger than you." He laughed and pinned her arms behind her back, kicking closed the remainder of the door.

With his free hand, he pulled her blouse down and began sucking at her nipples until she squirmed.

"Bill—"

"Now we'll see who has the power and who needs who."

CHAPTER 17

The consultation request to see Mr. Julius Ciss came through regular channels. Meredith would have probably put the forms in the in box to have her secretary fill out, and then perhaps assign it to one of the students who sometimes rotated through, but even as her hand dropped the carbonless paper into her "to do" box, Meredith stopped.

She'd been following the old man's case since the night of the plane crash nearly a week ago, she hadn't yet gone in to see him—and she hadn't slept much in the last few days either.

"Something the matter, Merry, me love?" Sean kept asking her. Damn. Why was he so perceptive? Or maybe she was just too obvious. Whatever it was, she knew that she was irritable. She knew that she'd been avoiding him, and breaking their dates. *He probably thinks I have another lover*, she thought.

If only things were that simple.

She had thought that like her mother she could hide from the past but maybe her mother was stronger, or maybe her mother was just more repressed.

Meredith consulted her calendar and then opened her desk for her address book.

Wedged into the wood was the fabric bookmark she'd found a few days ago. A childish hand had written *Ahava*. The Hebrew name her grandfather had given her. *Ahava* meant "dearly loved." Meredith didn't recall anyone but him ever using it.

Her hand trembled as she picked up the phone.

Dialing her mother's number in New York, Meredith left a message on the answering machine. "I'm coming in for the weekend, Mother. We have to talk."

Carrie Harper paced the door in front of Sophie's office. The DON had called her in for her six-month evaluation and Carrie nervously wrung her damp hands.

She couldn't lose her job. She just couldn't. She had gone through so much to come here, to alter her name, using her papa's first name as her last instead of Dickers, which she hated anyway. She'd lied to the licensing board that she had upped and married so that they would give her a new L.V.N. license with a new name and no one would know where she had worked or been before. It was just a white lie. She didn't think it would hurt anyone.

But now, as she waited, she was sure that goddamn Miss Stauton had ratted on her. Would be just like her, wouldn't it? Jennifer Stauton reminded Carrie of her older sister, the one who had always been tormenting Carrie about being slow, the one with the shotgun hole right through her brain.

It'd been messy all right. Carrie even had to help clean it up.

No one ever knew how it happened, just that it did. Pa was told by the sheriff that it weren't a good thing to have a loaded gun around the house, but since Pa never listened to nobody, he wouldn't have listened to the sheriff no how.

For all Carrie knew, the same kind of accident might have happened again after she'd left home. But it hadn't. Just damned luck, she guessed.

Sweat was pouring from her arm pits. Carrie was sure she must stink. It was the first thing she'd learned when she started at nursing school. Not everyone smelled as pretty as her doll Rosie.

The hall clock read three. Ms. Drummond . . . that is Ms. Morgan had said to meet her at three. But where was she? Carrie was sure the nursing supervisor was preparing a last check or maybe talking to Ms. Stauton or one of the others and hearing all sorts of bad stories about Carrie.

Wasn't there something about a fair hearing? Hadn't she heard about that in the classes Pa had made her sit through?

She tried sitting in the vinyl chair outside the door. Got up. Sat down and got up again. It wasn't any good. She knew for sure there was bad stuff on the report.

Just as Carrie had worked herself nearly into tears, Sophie Morgan hurried up the steps.

"Sorry, Carrie. Were you waiting long?"

"No, ma'am."

Sophie smiled at the L.V.N. "The elevators have been acting up and I ordered a repairman. We don't want anything breaking down when the JCH is here, do we?"

"No, ma'am." She waited patiently behind Sophie as the director of nursing opened her office door.

"Have a seat. Can I get you anything? Coffee or a soft drink?"

"No." Carrie's voice squeaked dryly. She knew it had to be bad. "They" were never nice like that unless they had bad news they wanted to give you. Pa always gave her a lolly or a soda before he beat her. She didn't know why, but he did.

Her shoulders hunched together, waiting for the words that she was fired to smack her on her forehead. She wet her lips with her tongue as she waited, and her stomach felt like it was doing that Russian dance she'd seen on television one night.

Sophie poured herself some spring water and opened up the file.

There it was in big red letters neatly printed on the file. Carrie L. Harper, L.V.N.

Her chewed-off nails dug into her palms. Why in tarnation didn't Ms. Morgan get it over with? Carrie moved to the edge of the chair and was rocking ever so slightly until she became aware of the supervisor staring at her.

"Carrie, are you all right? Do you want to put this off for another day?"

"No, ma'am." No, she sure as shootin' didn't. Bad enough her whole day had been ruined.

"Okay, let's see here. You've oriented to ICU, peds, ob-gyn, and med-surg one. Is that right?"

Carrie just nodded. Her heart raced like a field mouse with a huge cat chasing it.

"And I believe you came in last weekend to help with the emergency. . . ."

The girl just stared at the wall behind the supervisor. Her eyes were wide. "I'm really sorry about the IV. I didn't mean to let it run dry. And it was just a mistake that I picked up the ferrous sulfate instead of the antibiotic, and—"

"Wait. Wait a minute, Carrie. What's this about an IV? Did you have a problem when you were working in Emergency?"

"Yes, ma'am." She nodded. "I mean no, ma'am." Tears welled up in the puppy dog eyes as the story, according to Carrie's abridged and annotated version, spilled out between sobs.

If she had doubts before, Sophie knew that this girl was not playing with a full deck. She probably would have fired her, but the joint commission frowned on nursing shortages. Sophie's records had to show that there was at least a constant ratio of one nurse for every four patients. Any less than that and they would face a penalty. More often than not, Sophie had to ask her nurses to work double time. But there was only so much of that JCH would allow either.

Sophie wondered: Did she have enough nursing staff to keep a watchful eye on this girl? It frightened Sophie that Carrie had almost killed a patient. *And* that the information had come out only by accident. She would have to speak with Jennifer and find out why the nurse had not reported this incident.

"All right, Carrie. Thank goodness no harm was done." Sophie glanced up at the master schedule she had on the wall. It covered all the units and all the shifts and gave her a headache each time she looked at it.

There was only one place she could send Carrie right now. "Tomorrow and for the next few weeks, you'll be assisting in the clinic. Does that suit you?"

Carrie's pudgy mouth dropped open wide enough for that mouse being chased to jump in. "You mean I'm not fired?" She leaped out of her chair and impulsively hugged the supervisor. "I'll be the best clinic worker, ever. I promise."

CHAPTER 18

It was past two A.M. on Saturday night when Dr. Rosa Sanchez left the hospital and she was bleary eyed with exhaustion. Was this going to be an omen for the rest of the year? She hoped not. This last week had been hell.

Try as she could, Rosa still hadn't caught up on her sleep from the events of the week before, or on her paperwork, but then who had really?

Rosa had heard the firecrackers start to go off just before midnight and by 12:10 A.M., barely into the New Year, she'd seen three accidental burns, two shootings from guns fired into the air and bullets having fallen where they weren't expected, and one drunken disorderly pair who, according to Frank Willis, had been having a grand old time of celebrating by scratching each other up.

Why weren't people more responsible? Just because it was a holiday was no time to let down their standards. But having worked New Year's before, Rosa had expected this and more.

Still she'd agreed to substitute for Cole Morgan, so that CMC's regular ER doctor could spend his first New Year's with his new family.

For a moment, Rosa was remorseful. Other than her two cats, Charlie Dickens and Jane Eyre, she really didn't have anyone to be with on New Year's. They were just as happy curling up on her blankets day or night. She could just as easily celebrate with them tomorrow.

Might as well work. Her family, what was left of it, still lived in Los Angeles and friends . . . well, if anything, she had them here at the hospital.

She had never been much for socializing or "pubbing" as her friends from England called it.

Rosa knew her family thought it odd that she spent so much time at CMC. They constantly nagged her to find someone else and settle down. But Rosa had had enough of married life for now. Her patients were her life.

Maybe if she was dating someone . . . she wet her lips. No. There was no one, at least no one she felt at ease talking about. And she wasn't even sure that her feelings were returned.

In *such a large town* as Chandler Springs, there were so many eligible men to choose from, *especially* for a New Year's date. No, Charlie, her Persian, was a much better date than any of the men she had to choose from.

The neighboring towns, Richmond with its bars, where Jacob McQuade had met and married Coral May, the waitress; or even Houston itself were not to her liking, certainly not the night life everyone else she knew seemed to crave.

Saturday night barhopping and one-night flings were for her ex-husband, still in Los Angeles at his private clinic where she'd left him. He and his young starlet wife could go to all the Hollywood receptions their hearts desired. That life wasn't for her.

To Rosa, the best part of New Year's was curling up with a hot cocoa, and her pile of *New England Journal of Medicines*; *Lancets*; and other journals that she hadn't been able to read in months, and the able assistance of her cats. She would go through the magazines one by one, sometimes skimming, sometimes reading in depth, but educating herself on the new treatments and technologies.

Meredith was the only one Rosa knew who'd taken some R & R and gone off to New York. She gathered from what the psychiatrist said as she rushed to the plane that it was some family matter.

From snippets of conversation overheard, Rosa felt many of the staff were still under stress from the Christmas plane crash and felt that they had not been adequately prepared for the emergency that night. Maybe they were right. It was true that they had not only been short staffed but short on supplies as well, and two of the injured had later been transported to Houston Medical.

Rosa would suggest an in-service and triage team practice to Meredith. Something like that would look good when the commission examined the records. They always wanted to know what and how you were training your employees. And what you were doing to keep them up on current trends.

Maybe she'd even do something from one of the journals about the experimental cardiac drugs coming on the market.

Thinking of Meredith made Rosa wonder why the psychiatrist had not yet been to see Mr. Ciss. She'd seemed so concerned about him in the emergency room, and Rosa knew that she'd put in the order for a consult nearly two days ago.

Meredith usually responded right away to consult requests. It wasn't like their new chief was overwhelmed with work here at CMC. Most of her patients were like Emma's friend, Carolyn Wright, Bubba's wife: Moneyed, bored, and probably a little depressed.

Mr. Ciss was a *real* patient. Someone with whom

Meredith, if she worked with him, maybe prescribing an antidepressant, could accomplish something. It worried Rosa that the old man would not eat. He drank a carton of milk and occasionally ate some yogurt, but that was all. She suspected post-traumatic stress complicated with the depression that often comes as one ages, but she wasn't sure. Mr. Ciss would not talk to her and constantly insisted that he was fine, "just fine."

At least he wasn't dehydrated. She placed the old man on intake and output. She checked to see that his I & O were charted. Rosa had also made sure the nurses were pushing fluids and monitoring his blood pressure.

Reading the nursing notes, Rosa was pleased to see the old man had no kidney damage. Nevertheless, his urine tests were spilling sugar. She hoped his diabetes would be controlled by diet—as with most elderly discovered diabetes. Just in case, she wrote a consultation for Dr. Catherine McCornack, their endocrinologist.

Rosa sucked in her lower lip, concerned. Just because he wasn't insulin dependent didn't mean he couldn't go into a diabetic coma.

Each time she heard a code blue being called, she feared it would be him.

As soon as Meredith returned from her trip, Rosa would hound her about seeing the old man, and Nancy Hoffner, as well

Rosa reached her blue Subaru Impreza wagon, one of the few in the parking lot this time of night, and inserted the key into the lock. Lost in her thoughts, Rosa heard nothing as the attacker stepped up behind her, grabbing her around the neck.

A startled Rosa stiffened. "What do you want? My money?" She moved her purse, which had fallen at her feet, behind her, toward the figure.

The attacker made no motion to bend down.

Rosa tried moving. The person—she wasn't sure if it was a man or woman—tightened his grip. "Okay, then what do you want? Prescriptions? I've a pad of triplicates in my purse, too. You can get all the uppers and downers you want."

This time a knife was pressed close to Rosa's throat.

"Look, I'm a doctor. I like helping people. It's my job. Maybe I can help you, if—"

The emergency room entrance to the hospital opened as white light flooded the ground around her.

"Rosa?" Ellis called out, seeing the car but not its owner. "Are you still there? I forgot that Amy took my car today. I need a ride." He hurried out onto the lot, looking for his colleague.

"Rosa? Rosa, what's going on?" He could see someone with her, but he wasn't sure who.

"Ellis!" Rosa screamed. With the suddenness of a master martial-arts practitioner, she twisted around and bit her attacker, even as she felt the edge of the knife slicing into her flesh. In spite of her pain, Rosa kneed this person in black. She hadn't survived East Los Angeles without some skills.

The assailant fell to the ground of the parking lot as Ellis rushed forward. Rosa tried absorbing everything she could about the movements, about the dress, all the while trying to catch her breath and stem her bleeding. She reached out, trying to grab the jacket, or nylon something . . . it all slipped out of her hand.

Rising quickly, the mystery person sprinted away, and within moments was lost to sight.

Ellis attempted to give chase, but he was too tired and not in the best of shape. Somehow, despite the openness of the fields around them, the assailant had managed to hide.

"Did you get a look?" He asked as he huffed and

hobbled back to where Rosa sat on the ground, in shock.

She shook her head. "No. But whoever he/she was, is certainly in good shape."

"Yeah," Ellis said as he stared out into the seemingly empty field. "Come back inside. Let's take a look at your cut. Then we'll call Frank and make a report."

Frank Willis, Chandler Springs' police chief, came almost at once. He'd just gotten off duty and had been almost asleep, but he didn't seem to care that he'd been roused.

Sipping hot coffee in the emergency room, he questioned Rosa, prodding her to remember anything she could.

"Just the fact that he managed to get away and hide so quickly had to mean this was planned, doesn't it?" Ellis asked.

Frank nodded thoughtfully.

"Dr. Sanchez, was there any reaction when you kneeded the person in the groin?"

Rosa shook her head. "If there was, I didn't hear anything. I was only trying to survive." She wasn't sure if she wanted to share her suspicions that the attacker might have been a woman, mainly because she had nothing but gut instinct to go on.

One of the deputies ran in with a black ski mask. "Found it near the motel, Chief." Frank looked inside. A man's size large. For him, that narrowed the suspects.

"Okay, Dr. Sanchez. You go home and get some rest. Don't worry none about this. We'll get your man. I don't think he chose you especially. Probably just loaded and wanted some cash for drugs."

"Are we sure it's a man?" Ellis asked, recalling Rosa's

comment. He looked at his friend, wondering why she hadn't voiced the same concern.

Rosa shrugged. Of course she trusted Ellis, but she wasn't quite sure she trusted herself.

Frank threw the ski mask at the cardiac surgeon. "Check it out for yourself."

Ellis picked up the knit mask, using tweezers so as not to get it contaminated. Holding it gingerly at one side, he turned it over, trying to dissect his feelings.

The ski mask looked exactly like his neighbor's. Tyler Van Fleet also wore a large size. And this cap had the same Swiss ski patch that Tyler's did. But why would he have attacked Rosa?

CHAPTER 19

After unsuccessfully calling the medical agencies in Houston and Richmond, Sophie reluctantly looked up the phone number for Betty Sue Green, her former secretary.

Between JCH's forthcoming visit and her pregnancy, Sophie really needed someone who knew the ropes and could fill in when she fell short.

Dennis Green, Betty Sue's late husband, was the nurse shot in the emergency room during the Halloween massacre, as CMC was now calling it, when he attempted to calm the young cowboy who would not believe that his lady love was dead.

Sophie knew that with the new baby having been born just before Dennis's murder, Betty Sue was probably having a hard time making ends meet.

Whatever insurance money Dennis had just hadn't been enough and yet, Sophie knew that returning to the place where her husband had lost his life would be a horrific task for Betty Sue. The former secretary was already seeing Meredith twice weekly, courtesy of CMC, and practically living on Ativan for her nerves. Could Betty Sue cope with the pressures of a JCH visit and all the last-minute preparations it entailed? Sophie's hand reached for the phone.

Lost in her own thoughts, Sophie hardly noticed anyone standing in her doorway.

Only the knocking made her glance up.

"May we have a word?" The new hospital administrator, Nelson St. Clair, stood there in his checkered Carney jacket, smoothly creased polyester pants, and slicked-back hair looking every bit the con man. Sophie scolded herself about judging him. The minister wouldn't be pleased with her thoughts.

Maybe that's just how they dressed in Montreal. Wasn't that where Nelson St. Clair said he came from?

His exaggerated mannerisms made Sophie's hackles go up, but she nodded. She wondered where Emma had found him.

The large man strode in.

Three times the size of Marcus Laurence, Nelson St. Clair practically filled the office with his presence, and what he didn't physically fill, his overpowering cologne did.

She coughed as the scent irritated her nasal passages.

But even with the proportional difference, their attitude was much the same. They were the "gatekeepers" of the hospital, making sure that costs stayed within reason, and patients whose insurance had quit paying departed almost as quickly.

Taking over as if he owned the office, he grabbed a pen and pad of paper from her side table, sinking into the chair directly across from her. She wanted him to get out of here so that she could finish working on her scheduling.

"What can I do for you, Mr. St. Clair?"

"Nelson, please." His tobacco-stained teeth overlapped his mouth ever so slightly as he smiled. He was about as appealing as a dirty ashtray. "Sophie, I want to see all your files on Pamela Roberts."

CHAPTER 20

A real wooden sign from an English pub, reading JOHNSTON'S GALLEY, swung in front of the bookstore on the main street. Hillary had gone through quite an effort to find that sign or something like it on her last trip to England, which of course she'd been forced to endure alone.

She thought it made a nice addition to her little store, which was a showcase of first edition and classical works—that never moved. Well, seldom ever. Some of the doctors from the hospital, who weren't native to Chandler Springs and some of Emma's political friends visiting from Houston or Washington, would occasionally drop by the shop and see what acquisitions Hillary had made.

But since the Christmas Eve spectacle she'd made of herself not many people came to browse.

Frank Willis had discovered her walking toward the red Ferrari. Bill was waiting to give her a ride back up the road. They'd been planning on having some breakfast because she knew that her husband wouldn't be home for some time yet. Not if what she saw was any indication.

She told Bill that if Ellis and Rosa were planning on running off, she was going to take the children with her first. He for one had thought that an excellent idea.

Hillary wondered why she had never liked Bill Martin before.

Of course, when Frank had found her, she hadn't let on that Bill was nearby. Fool that he was, Frank Willis hadn't even suspected, but he hadn't been taken in when she said that everything was fine and that she'd just taken a long walk. Wasn't it amazing that she found herself here by the hospital?

It certainly sounded reasonable to Hillary. She didn't understand what was wrong with her story, but when he called the INN on his mobile phone, she'd been prepared to make another run for it.

Imagine her surprise when he turned to her and said the hospital wasn't asking for her to return.

Not asking for her return? Hillary didn't comprehend what had happened, but she was just as happy to go home. "Didn't I tell you?" She'd given the police chief her special smile. Maybe she wouldn't leave right away after all.

It would have been a shame to go away without some of her book collections. She, or rather, Ellis had spent a fortune on some of them.

So why didn't the people of Chandler Springs appreciate it? Not that Main Street had much walk-in traffic, either. But at least there used to be more customers than this.

"It's because they're all afraid to face me," Hillary told Esther Ortiz, the young Hispanic girl who assisted her. "They know it's true about Ellis and Rosa and they just don't want to look me in the face. Well, I've got news for them. I know, and I am making my plans."

If Ellis suspected her thoughts, he hadn't said a word. Of course that didn't mean anything. She knew he read her secret diary and all her letters. She knew that he had someone spying on her, like the man standing across the street right now. Hillary wondered how

Ellis had gotten the CIA involved. What lies had he told them about her?

"I think we're going to sponsor some autographings," Hillary said, walking to the window and back. Her path had long since been worried into the carpet. "Maybe *Deadly Doses,* that book about poisons. Or maybe one of those medical thrillers."

Esther merely shrugged. She had held this parttime job long enough to know when to stay out of Hillary's war path, and she'd heard Hillary going on about Rosa Sanchez many times before. But the fact that Esther was of the same "race" as Hillary's rival didn't seem to help matters.

"Maybe the people just don't have money, Mrs. J. You know, it being Christmastime and all."

Hillary shook her head at the girl's simplicity. The glazed look seemed to pierce through her assistant. "It is *past* New Year's now, Esther. Everyone has money again."

It did no good arguing with Hillary. "Maybe if you offered some paperbacks, and even some comics, too. Why I bet we could get some of the school kids in here."

Hillary's glare gave Esther her answer.

"Really, Mrs. J., how many of the folks here in Chandler Springs really know or care about first editions? If you want to make this store a success . . ." Esther paused. "You even said just now about a medical thriller. I think that's a grand idea. Why I—"

Without even letting Esther finish her sentence, Hillary walked over to the cash register. Ringing it open, she pulled out a fifty dollar bill and waved it toward the Hispanic girl. "I do not need unreliable help. I will not carry such trash in my store. Ellis has already said he's moving my shop to Houston where *it and I* will be appreciated or—"

"But Doctor Johnston can't move," Esther was clearly puzzled. She was positive that Hillary's husband hadn't said anything about any such move. But whenever her boss was upset, that's what she talked about. "What about all his patients and his practice . . . ? What about . . . ?" Esther asked.

Hillary merely smiled and pushed the money down the girl's blouse. Then with hands stronger than one would have expected for such a slight woman, Hillary turned the girl around to face the door.

CHAPTER 21

Meredith's discussion with her mother, Gayle (Gitel), had been totally unsatisfactory. In fact, Mother had forbidden Meredith to ask questions and search further into her past. She did not want her to remember about *Sabtah*, and Gayle/Gitel's brother, Daniel Yosef (Daniel Joseph in English) whom she'd grown up with or anything to do with the family. "After all, they sat *shiva* for me, mourning me as if I was dead. So I am. Leave it at that."

"Why?"

Ms. Fischer shrugged her shoulders and walked away in the very same fashion she'd ended every conversation Meredith had ever started about her history.

Meredith knew that Gayle/Gitel's marriage to Albert Dengler, her father, despite the initial passion it had begun with, had not been a happy one. Her mother had left him when Meredith was five years old.

Try as she might, she recalled very little about Albert Dengler or any of his family. She knew only that he'd remarried and moved to somewhere in Arizona.

Fischer had been Gayle/Gitel's maiden name and she'd quickly taken it back. For a short time, Gayle/Gitel even returned to the family home, giving Meredith the memories of her grandfather and uncle. Meredith recalled her *Sabtah* saying that Gayle/Gitel should have been named *Adara*, Hebrew for fire, because she flared easily and it didn't take much of a spark to set her off.

Within two years of her divorce from Dengler, Gayle/Gitel and her daughter, Meredith, had moved out of her family's home and away from their heritage, never to return. She changed her last name from Fischer to Faith. It had taken years of soul-searching for Meredith to take on her mother's original name.

When Gayle/Gitel and her friend returned from the theater that Friday night, they found Meredith in the attic, digging through some of the old boxes. At the feet of the psychiatrist were pictures of a once happy couple, a smiling baby, and some of Meredith's early class work. There were also a few things of Danny's, her young stepbrother, who now did police work here in New York.

"You have to persist. You have to bring heartache? Go back to your life in Houston. Let me live mine."

"Chandler Springs, Mother. And I don't know if I want a life without any past."

"Whatever." Gayle/Gitel gave an expressive Jewish shrug.

In her typical fashion, Gayle/Gitel walked out of the room. Meredith shook her head. Her mother might disagree with their heritage, but she still had the mannerisms.

She stared at one of the photos and wondered if her grandfather was still alive.

On the flight back to Houston, Meredith found herself wondering more and more about her past. She recalled a photo of herself with her hands on her hips: The rebellious child, who always did what she was told not to do.

But maybe, just maybe, it was best to let the past

lay silent. No one at the hospital knew her background and it didn't have to change. Still, she wondered how they would regard her if they knew she was Jewish. From the few comments she'd occasionally heard, she knew that her colleagues and other staff were fairly ignorant of who and what a Jew was. Would they be surprised? Shocked?

There. She had thought it. Had that been so bad? No lightning had come down to strike her.

Meredith then realized that she herself didn't know what made a Jew.

From her purse, Meredith removed the small *sedur*, prayer book, which she'd found in one of the boxes. It had once belonged to her mother. The inscription stated the book had been given to Gayle/Gitel when she had been called to the Torah and "became a woman," in Jewish terms, at the age of twelve.

Meredith realized that the only information she really had was what she'd gleaned from movies, television, and the like.

She stared out at the dark sky. The suburbs appeared, then a few city lights growing progressively brighter.

They were descending into Houston and Meredith didn't know who she was coming back as.

Two days into the New Year, Avon Dupree stood impatiently outside the post office, which also served as the bus station in Chandler Springs.

Thankfully she had these next few days off. Not only because she needed the rest, but because her younger brother, George Lucas Dupree, had come to town to spend a few days of vacation with her.

She waited until he'd gotten his luggage from the bus station before going up to him and kissing him.

"How long has it been, Sis?" George towered over

her by a good five inches, but was nearly three years younger. Avon had always been the shrimp in the family.

Avon smiled up at him. "Too long, bro." How handsome her baby brother was; what a womanizer he would be.

She kissed him again and then held him back at arm's length. He'd changed, but she wasn't sure exactly how. Maybe it was just that, as he said, they hadn't seen each other for nearly three years. That was a long time, especially considering he'd only been fifteen when she'd left for school.

Her arm reached up and around him. "My God, I can barely reach your neck now." She shook her head. "You sure do know how to make a sister feel old."

They both laughed.

"So what great things in Chandler Springs do you want to see?" Avon had always loved Georgie the best. Maybe because she'd been the one most responsible for raising him.

"Besides you, what is there?" He pulled out a well-thumbed tour book of Houston. "But I sure wouldn't mind seeing the NASA Space Center or the Port of Houston Turning Basin."

Avon shook her head and laughed. "Boats and rockets. Might have known. Might have known." She led him to her green, two-door Toyota, the one she'd driven down here from Chicago.

George kicked the side playfully. "Still getting dents, I see." He swung his duffel bag into the hatchback.

Avon blushed, and then felt her hackles rise.

In front of them stood the Chandler Springs's chief of police, Frank Willis along with two of his deputies.

"Can I help you, Frank?" She rubbed her forearms to get rid of an uneasy feeling.

"Well," Frank paused. "I do believe you can."

He nodded politely to Avon, tipping his hat. "You know this man with you?"

" 'Course I know him." Avon laced her arm through George's. "He's my baby brother."

"I see." Frank smacked his lips. "Well, if you don't mind, I'd like to have your baby brother down at the station house. Got a few questions to ask him. We've been investigating this area for new people coming and going."

"Why?" Avon's hands were on her hips. She'd forgotten that in the south here, especially in these small towns, things were still much as they'd been *before* civil rights.

"Yeah, why?" George asked. "You're not being very cool, man. I just came down here to spend a few days with my sis. Got a problem with that?"

"No, sir, I don't." Frank spat out some tobacco still in his mouth. "Don't get me wrong, son. I'm not arresting you or anything like that—"

One of the officers put a hand on George's shoulder. The tall black boy shrugged him off.

"But there's been some mighty strange things happening here the past few days. I just want to check up on everyone's whereabouts, especially strangers."

"Frank, he *just* came into town. I *just* picked him up. Right now. You can check the bus schedule. It only pulled in ten minutes ago."

"Maybe so." The police chief eyed first Avon and then George. "Maybe so. But someone thought he'd seen a man matching your brother's description right after Dr. Sanchez's attack."

Sophie tried shrugging off the headache that had persisted most of the day. She swallowed two Tylenol with some decaffeinated Diet Coke. "Why do you want

Pam Roberts's file?" she asked the new administrator. Hadn't she already asked him that?

Nelson shrugged. "I believe I know some of her family and I just wanted to check my facts."

Sophie was puzzled. "Then why not ask her?"

Whatever he said next was lost to Sophie as she stared into the distance, struck by the halo of light which seemed to surround Nelson.

"I . . ." Suddenly no words would come out of her mouth. She could hear herself speaking and yet she couldn't.

A floating sensation raised her spirit above her body as she saw her jaw slacken and her eyes glaze over.

Why didn't Nelson do something? Why didn't he say anything?

She felt immobilized and yet at the same time, she was moving, shaking. Was it an earthquake? In Texas?

Then she saw people running toward her in slow motion. She saw Wendy and Jennifer, Fred and Ellis.

She wanted to speed up the player, but it was stuck on thirty-three and a third. Even the voices were drawn out. They were making fun of her Texas drawl. They were . . .

Sophie tried grasping her desk, and then her chair as she fell to the floor, convulsing. The world was ending. She was Chicken Little calling out that the world was ending and no one could hear her.

Everything went black then as she suffered her own personal earthquake.

CHAPTER 22

Nancy Hoffner lay in her bed, not moving, staring at the dripping IV as if it were the most fascinating picture in the world. As a matter of fact, it was her whole world. She still couldn't move her injured hand or wrist, and her arm and left shoulder were in a cast. She needed help to move, help to eat, help just to pee. How humiliating.

And if everything else wasn't bad enough, she hadn't even heard from her family. She knew they'd been notified, but there was something about her father's new enterprise that needed attention, and they would come to Texas as soon as they could.

Not even her agent had shown. He was busy canceling and rearranging her schedule, or so he said.

At least that was how the message filtered down to her. They didn't let her have a phone in ICU. And besides, she still couldn't speak properly.

Tears seemed to be the only way Nancy had to express herself these days.

Why had she even survived? Why hadn't she just died? She was useless now. Her hands were useless. She would never get the acclaim she sought.

Tears flowed freely now. She was only twenty-two. What the hell was she going to do with the rest of her life? If only she could end it.

*   *   *

Peds was quiet today for a change, and Avon was glad of that since she still didn't know what to do about her brother George languishing in what Chandler Springs called a jail. There hadn't even been a hearing date set.

Frank had had no call to arrest him. George hadn't been in town when Rosa had been attacked; Rosa knew he wasn't her assailant; and even if he had been here, he didn't have any motive. But the police seemed to believe George had been hired by someone and they wanted to know who.

She was glad that Dr. Rosa had been able to phone her lawyer friend, Francis Basta, who knew about civil rights. He had arrived this afternoon. Avon was meeting him at the coffee shop just opposite the police department. Then they would march in and demand bail be set.

All this was probably going to cost more than her annual salary, but George didn't have much and neither did her family. At least she had the credit union.

Before Sophie's attack yesterday, the supervisor would certainly have called Frank for Avon and asked that charges be dropped, or that at least George could be under "house arrest" at his sister's. But with Sophie's seizure, Avon could hardly expect help from that direction now.

She felt bad about Mrs. Morgan, but worse about her brother. And she was beginning to have second thoughts about staying in this small Texas town. In fact, she was beginning to have second thoughts about staying in the South at all.

Most of the southerners she knew mouthed the words of civil rights, and publicly acted as if they agreed, but in private it was all a different story. She wondered how many of her "friends" here at the hospital thought George guilty.

"Hey, gal, what're you doing here? Did Soph call you in extra?" Avon Dupree asked as she looked up from the nursing desk. She was trying to chart, but of course nothing would come to her. So she was just as glad for her friend's company.

Jennifer wandered back behind the counter. "No. I wasn't called in."

"So? You like it that much here?"

Jennifer shrugged. "Just curious about the . . . Asian girl."

"From the plane crash?"

The blond nurse nodded. "How's she doing?"

"Here's her chart." Avon motioned toward the green notebook on the desk.

"That's great. But I mean, how is she doing?"

"Oh. How is she doing?" Avon took out her report notes from this morning. "Well, the people who were supposed to adopt her are coming today. I guess they're going to decide if they want to bring her to a hospital closer to Dallas."

Avon watched her friend's eyes go blank. Then she glanced at the huge clock in the hall as dietary wheeled the lunch trays down the hall. "Hey, you know, it's time to feed the kids. You want to help me with Angel? Carrie's off in the clinic today and I only have Flora as an extra."

"I'd love to." Jennifer scooped up the tray with Angel's name on the label and hurried off to the girl's room.

Sophie woke and saw the dripping IV. She blinked hard, not understanding what had happened to her.

All she recalled was Nelson St. Clair in her office asking for information . . . on Pam . . . and then . . . nothing.

Her head ached, but as she moved, she was aware of someone else in the room.

"Cole? Is that you?" Her voice could hardly be heard.

"No, Sophie, it's Ken."

She rolled over, aching. "What happened to me? Is the baby all right?"

Dr. Ken Stevens was silent a moment and wet his lips. "Yes, Sophie, the baby is all right . . . for now." He paused, letting the words sink in. "But you're not."

Of its own accord, Sophie's hand started trembling. She swallowed hard. "What do you mean?"

Ken covered her shaking hand with his firmer one. "Sophie, the tests are not conclusive yet, but I would judge from what I've seen that you have lupus systemic."

"Lupus? But how? Why? No one in my family—"

The OB man shook his head. "It's not necessarily genetic. And it does favor young women, women who are under stress."

"Well, see, it can't be lupus because I'm not that young. And as to the stress . . . ?" She shrugged. "I can only do what I can do."

Ken shrugged. "I wish I could tell you how or why, but no one knows. I had hoped that perhaps it was only the cutaneous variety that stayed on the surface but with your seizure . . ."

"Is that what I had?" Sophie glanced up to see what was in her IV. Phenobarbital and diphenylhydantoin. Exactly what they used for epileptic patients.

She could feel her anger rising. She was fine. There was no epilepsy in her family and there was no lupus.

"Sophie," Ken called her name bringing her back into focus with him. "You have no brain lesions so the seizure was not a part of epilepsy."

"Yeah, right." She lay back and closed her eyes.

"Sophie, I want you to listen. You remember that

low-grade fever you've been complaining about? This is lupus erythematosus-systemic. What you have is affecting your internal organs, causing sections of them to die. And I have no idea just where in your body the tissue has become necrotic. It can mean renal disease or it can mean heart disease . . . or both . . . or none.

"You've been asymptomatic for renal disease, which is one of the hallmarks of LE, especially when it starts progressing, so I can only hope and assume—"

"No, I haven't." Sophie's voice was barely audible as she told him about the blood she'd seen in her urine. "I thought maybe I was miscarrying or something."

The obstetrician sighed. "If you had, it might have solved a lot of problems. I think this baby is aggravating your symptoms."

Her eyes went wide. "What are you saying, Ken? Are you asking me to abort my child? Is that what you're saying?"

Ken Stevens nodded.

"No. I can't."

"Not even if it means saving your own life, or extending your life a bit longer?"

Sophie looked away from her doctor and out the window, where she could see into the courtyard of the hospital. "Have you talked with Cole about this yet?"

"No, of course not. I wouldn't say anything like this to him until I had your permission. Do you want me to?"

Sophie's voice would no longer obey her. She merely shook her head.

"Well, then, I'll leave you to discuss this with your husband, but Sophie, this is something you cannot decide alone. There are other people involved in your life now . . . not only your husband, but your daughter as well."

"My two daughters," her voice croaked. She knew.

She'd peeked when Joshua had done the ultrasound scan of her uterus. "I have two little girls, Ken, and I want them both. If you tell Cole anything about this, I will . . . I will . . ." She shook her head, her voice gone again.

The ob-gyn man frowned. "Very well, Sophie. I will keep my own counsel for the moment. We will see how you progress. But I am going to continue the tests we need, to make sure your other organs are healthy. Rosa Sanchez will consult with me on the medical side."

She nodded.

"And if things start going badly and you don't tell Cole, then I will. I'll check with you in a little while, after Cole and Lisa have had a chance to visit."

Tears flooded Sophie's eyes. She didn't, couldn't say anything as he left. How could this be happening to her—after everything else she'd been through? How could she tell Cole that she was going to selfishly have to get rid of his baby?

Dr. Bill Martin looked around, put his suitcase down, and cautiously put his keys into the door. There was no one in the X-ray Department. Good. Exactly as he wanted.

Within moments, he had piled his suitcases high with not only his own files, notes, and patient lists, but with numerous supplies which he would need to open his new clinic across the street. Yes, he was finally doing it. Pam, or no Pam, he was breaking away from this crummy hospital. He'd signed the contract for the space today.

Cost him a pretty penny for first, last, and security, not to mention the decorating he wanted done—his offices were going to be a class act, not like the little crap space they tried sticking him in here. Seeing them squirm would make it worth the cost.

They might not miss him, but they sure as hell were going to miss the money *his* department brought in. Allister didn't have the style or the charm to encourage the type of spending that Bill's patients did. And if he had all the state of the art equipment, they would be forced to come to him. And Bill Martin wasn't about to give his former companions any discounts. Not after the way they had treated him.

The radiologist grinned. "Soon," he said, holding up one of the X rays that Dr. Allister had taken. Poor quality. Poor image. "Yeah. Soon, they're going to beg me to return, especially with JCH on its way. And I'm going to have that commission breathing down their necks."

Heaving the case up by its strap, Bill Martin hurried from the room, locking the door behind him. By the time they realized what he had done, he'd be set up next door.

CHAPTER 23

"Rosa, you're absolutely right," Meredith responded to her friend's complaint. "I was . . . just caught up in some family business. I intend to see both Mr. Ciss and Miss Hoffner today. I'll evaluate them for their psychologicals and see if perhaps we need to put one or both on some antidepressants."

"I rather like Prozac, despite what I've heard. I think it has the fewest side effects. "But," Meredith said, "I still have to talk to them. Maybe they might need one of the other new drugs like Zoloft or Paxil, or maybe even an old reliable one like lithium. Considering what I've read of Nancy's chart, I wouldn't be surprised. You yourself know that we have to do a blood panel and check her thyroid and liver levels before I can even think about which drug."

Meredith sighed. "Yes, Rosa, dear. I will be over to see them this afternoon. I promise." She paused. "Oh, and thanks for that suggestion about the class. I'll look into it. We need something like that to impress JCH."

She hung up the phone and shook her head. "Rosa on her high horse."

Sean stood in the doorway.

Meredith blushed. She hadn't expected to see him and he knew that she had clients all morning long. Besides, she really wasn't in the mood to talk with him now. But when would she be?

"Come on in." Meredith forced a smile. "Grab a *cuppa*." She pointed to the tea cozy he had given her. The cup of tea or cuppa was the British way of dealing with almost any problem.

"Ah, good old Irish Breakfast. Fabulous brew. And I must say, my dear," Sean said, pouring himself a cuppa, "that you are indeed turning into a regular little leprechaun. My mam would be proud of you as her daughter-in-law."

How could he talk like that again when just weeks ago, he'd been fighting over the charms of Pamela Roberts? It was true Meredith adored Sean. She had ever since they'd met, but that didn't mean this relationship was going anywhere.

Meredith looked down into her cup and refilled her tea.

Sean's arm went around her shoulders. "Are we on for Friday, m'love? It's been donkey's years since we've been together."

"I know." She nodded. "I am just swamped with work and I have to deal with this thing . . . about my mother." Meredith hastily completed her sentence. "So, I'm not sure. Can we . . . maybe . . . get together on Saturday . . . Saturday night?"

"Why surely." Sean kissed her brow. "Anything for my lovely princess."

She parted her lips in a half smile. "Maybe they ought to have a kids' show in Ireland, not the *Barney Show*, but the *Blarney Show*."

Luckily her next client had come in, flashing the light in the waiting area.

She kissed Sean on the lips and let him out the back entrance. "Cafeteria at one?"

He nodded.

CHAPTER 24

Karin Martin just knew that this year was the start of better things for her and Bill. Hadn't he asked her to pick him up from work today? She couldn't recall the last time he'd done that. Not since the boys were little.

She bounced along, pleased. When Bill was happy, it was just so very nice. Yes, things were going to be great, she told herself. Just like in the past.

Karin pulled up to the back entrance of the hospital behind the emergency room, just as Bill had instructed. The only other car next to hers was a Honda. Karin thought she recognized it as belonging to one of the nurses at the hospital, but she wasn't sure. Anyway, what did it matter?

She thought it a bit strange that since in the past when she'd picked him up, it had always been out front. But he said something about carrying his files home. Maybe this was closer to his office.

She tried not to think about questions like that. Bill hated questions and besides, he usually knew best.

Getting out of the car, Karin ran into the hallway.

Just as he had said, there was a house phone on the wall. She dialed it and paged him.

"Martin, here."

Oh, how good it was to hear his voice. In spite of everything, she *did* love him, didn't she? "I'm here, darling." There was a lightness in her tone.

"Don't call me darling, Karin. You know I think that's sissy stuff."

"Oh, you're absolutely right, Bill. I'm so sorry. I didn't mean it. Only I was so glad . . ." Her lower lip quivered slightly. She hated when he reprimanded her, because then she'd cry in public.

At least the night of the Christmas party, she hadn't made a spectacle of herself. Bill hadn't complimented her or anything—he never did—but at least he hadn't complained. He just always expected the best from her. And she was glad he did. Really she was. It meant that he loved her.

She wiped her eyes with the back of her hand. Glad that no one was at this back station to see her blubbering now.

"Cut it, Karin," he said.

He was being brusque. But she had to try and understand. Poor dear, he had so much on his mind. *Not just my problems, but our problems, and the boys',* and *all of his patients, too.* Her Bill was such a caring doctor. No wonder all the women loved him.

"Are you in a bad mood, Bill?" Karin asked tentatively. Her fingers clutched the phone. When he was in a bad mood, she did not want to be around him, because usually he was angry at her for something. ·

"No. I am not."

"But you sound just like—"

"Must you always interrupt me? Do you think you can read my thoughts so easily, Karin? Huh?" The knife edge to his voice would have been enough to slice through anyone's flesh. "Look, I'm coming out in a moment. Just wait for me in the car. I won't be more than five minutes."

"Yeah, okay." Karin sniffled. She was about to put the receiver back on the cradle when she heard him shout something.

"Bill? What is it?"

"I just asked you, Karin. How many times must I repeat it? Did you bring my blue suit for the meeting?"

"Suit? Bill, I don't remember—"

"Stupid woman. You never listen to what I say. Three times this morning I told you . . . Damn it. Now we'll have to go back home before going into Houston."

"I don't remember, Bill. I'm sorry. I don't recall you saying anything about Houston."

"Of course, I did, Karin. Do you think *I* would forget something like this?"

"Like what?" Karin could swear that he hadn't said anything about being in Houston this evening. They were supposed to go to the counselor that Emma Chandler had arranged, and then they were having dinner with his parents, she thought. Poor Bill, he was always so busy, he didn't even remember their appointments half the time. As soon as she got off the phone with him, she would call and reschedule again. It was the least she could do for him. He was always just so very busy.

"Sorry isn't enough, Karin. I distinctly remember telling you about this last night. This meeting could be crucial to my future here at CMC."

"Oh, Bill, I . . . I guess I forgot." Karin cringed. She had been properly trained as an abused wife to believe everything was her fault. She sighed. "Are you sure you don't want me parked in the front?"

"Don't sigh like that, Karin. It drives me nuts. You know that. Why must you always repeat the same mistakes? How long does it take you to learn to listen to me? I will say it again: No, I do not want you parked in the front. Must you always question me, Karin? Do I have to explain everything to you? Why are you being so dense? Don't you think I know what I'm doing? You know, that's the problem with these independent women like you. Don't know when to keep your big fat traps shut."

"Yes, Bill. I'm sorry, Bill. I'll be waiting." She hung up the hospital phone, her hand trembling.

Her heart raced like one of those old greyhounds after one lap. She wondered how long it would be before she learned to handle him and to remember what he wanted. He was right. After twenty years of marriage, she shouldn't have to ask what her husband needed. It was her duty to know.

Karin's lower lip quivered again. She recalled how at the party Meredith had asked if she'd been abused. No, of course she hadn't. Bill loved her. They just didn't know him or understand him like she did. He would never abuse her. He just didn't know how to express his love.

Karin had to admit it had never seemed so difficult before. Or if it had, she'd forgotten. But then he was under so much more stress now. Much more than he'd ever had been.

All she wanted to do was please him and keep things quiet.

Karin remembered how sweet he'd been on their honeymoon: so concerned about her; locking the room so that she could nap without the maid coming in; so worried when she went out late; and answering the phone and telling her friends that Karin needed her sleep and that they were not allowed to call after ten P.M. Then after the boys were born, he always made sure they obeyed her. He checked over the church activities she attended for which ones were the best use of her time, and made sure people treated her right. She always obeyed him. He knew best. Yes, her Bill had always been so considerate and caring.

Now, of course, Karin didn't have many friends who called. Not like she had before. Bill had weeded out the ones who weren't good for her, and carefully monitored the time she spent with the others. After all, he reminded her, he didn't want them to get sick of being with her as he often was. If she outstayed her welcome with any of her friends, they might drop her.

Karin hadn't wanted that. And so she'd listened. The few friends from before were too intimidated by Bill's rages anyway and too embarrassed to be present when he went off into one of his firecracker angers. But that wasn't his fault. If they couldn't handle her husband, well . . . then they couldn't handle her. And that was just that.

The only problem was Karin never knew what caused his tempers, never knew how to predict them. She knew only that they were, and that if she wanted to remain his wife, which she did, she just had to live with them.

Besides, having left college to help support him through medical school, she didn't have any real training. What could she do? Where could she go? Her folks were always telling her what a wonderful husband Bill was, especially the few times he would buy her things like a mink or a dishwasher. They were so pleased that she had married a doctor. How could she have managed otherwise?

Of course, the mink was only a stole and not a coat. But with all her friends—former friends—having full-length coats and bragging about how great their husbands were, Karin was glad just to have this small gesture.

And then there were times when he gave her the ten dollars for a new dress. Sure they cost a little more. So Bill was out of touch with the prices of women's clothes. Karin would save up what he gave her and then buy something nice.

Did it really matter that she had to lie to him, telling

him that she'd paid twenty dollars instead of fifty dollars? He was always so pleased when he thought she had gotten a bargain. Karin loved it when Bill praised her. It was worth lying for that.

And he really did care about her, she thought. Just because he occasionally went with another woman didn't mean he didn't love her. It just gave her a chance to rest. After all, his drive, as most men's, was greater than hers. Why shouldn't he have his pleasure?

She caught herself sighing and reminded herself that Bill did not like that.

Resolutely, Karin Martin returned to her Tempo.

Even as she got into the car, she wondered what had happened to his Mercedes, and why he hadn't told her that he was repairing it.

Shrugging, she told herself he probably had and she hadn't remembered. Maybe she would have to talk with Meredith about her memory problem.

It was less than three minutes before she saw Bill coming down. He was carrying a box, but she didn't know what was in it.

Karin waited until the glass door had closed behind him and he was out on the steps. Then she started the car. The engine seemed to grind for a moment and then finally it caught and she smiled.

The explosion was the last thing she ever heard.

Of course, Bill Martin was the first one the police questioned when they began investigating the car bomb and death of Karin Martin. He denied it, and other than a possible motive of wanting to marry another woman, the police could find nothing to link him to the car bomb.

Whatever had happened, Bill Martin had an alibi, since he was in the hospital talking with her when the explosive was most likely placed. But he could have hired someone. And didn't it look odd that his former lover, Pam Roberts, was suddenly taking huge chunks of money out of her savings?

Good thing the bank teller, Darla, had noticed it and brought it to Frank's attention. Yes, they were watching her. Either she was paying off blackmail or maybe paying for someone to hit the Martins' car. At least that's what the police theorized.

Pam had had nothing to do with the blowing up of Karin Martin's car, but yes, that had been her Honda sitting out in the back. It had suffered some damage with the explosion, but it was still drivable.

But the police were right about Pam paying off blackmail. The trouble was, she didn't know whom she was paying. She only knew why.

CHAPTER 25

Meredith picked at her lunch. Sean had left her a message that he had problems with a client and was going to be late. Just as well, she thought, because she really didn't know what she wanted to say to him yet.

She knew nothing about her heritage and didn't even know if she cared. So why did her life have to change and why was she finding problems where there were none?

The cottage cheese tasted stale. Meredith pushed it off her salad.

Within another moment, she had pushed her whole salad plate away, grabbed her briefcase, and was headed toward the elevators. She would see Mr. Ciss today and deal with him. Give him whatever antidepressants she had in her artillery, and then it would all be over. It was silly of her to let those memories haunt her. Mother was right. Meredith had an established life here. She wasn't going to confuse issues of the past.

The lunch trays were just being removed from the floor as Meredith exited the elevator. She stopped a worker for a moment and checked the cart for Mr. Ciss's tray.

Looked great to her. Meatballs and spaghetti, vegetables, salad, soup, and coffee, and cherry pie for dessert (her favorite). But apparently not a favorite of this patient's because he'd only drunk the carton of milk and eaten some of the salad without the dressing.

Meredith understood now why Rosa was concerned.

Buzzing herself in, she walked over to the nursing station and picked up his chart. He should have been moved to a regular medical surgical unit already, but Meredith noted he still ran a fever of one hundred and five. The IV dripping into him had minerals and vitamins as well as antibiotics. He was on an ice mattress, and still his fever remained high. Rosa thought that maybe he couldn't eat because the fever had taken away his appetite.

Puzzled, she entered his private cubicle of the ICU. A monitor above the bed did a constant reading of his ECG as well as his pulse, blood pressure, respiration, and temperature. She glanced up a moment, noting what the green lights told her, and then smiled at him.

"May I sit down, Mr. Ciss?"

"Yeah, sure. Why not?" He shrugged, indicating the one chair he had for visitors. "How are you today, Miss Doctor?"

Meredith smiled in spite of her determination not to be swayed. "I'm fine, Mr. Ciss, but it's you I am here to talk about." He was wearing a knitted skullcap (*Keepa*) just like Sabtah used to wear.

"Me? For what? Besides this *farcachta* fever, which seemed to be making everyone crazy, not only me, I am fine. Couldn't be better." He sat up right in bed, using his remote to raise his head. "Good. Now I can see."

Meredith took a deep breath and went into her psychiatric mode. "You're feeling fine?" she said, repeating what the patient had just said as a way of letting him know you understood what he said but were asking for more information.

"Isn't that what I said?" He unfolded a pair of gold-rimmed spectacles from a rather worn case. "So, Miss Doctor, what else did you want to know?"

It was just like her *sabtah*. Suddenly Meredith felt as if she were five years old, sitting on his knee, and hearing him tell her a story about the old world.

"Earth to Miss Doctor. Earth to Miss Doctor." Mr. Ciss waved his hand in front of Meredith's glassy stare.

"Oh. Sorry." Meredith came back into focus. "I was just thinking of something . . ."

He nodded. "I could tell."

Meredith blinked and moved her body into a more upright position. "Mr. Ciss, your doctor, Rosa Sanchez—"

"Such a lovely young woman. Like you, not married. But both of you, very nice."

Meredith smiled again and shook her head. Just like *Sabtah*, always putting his two cents in. "Mr. Ciss . . ."

"What's this Mr. Ciss? Julius, please."

"Your doctor is concerned that you're not eating."

"Pshh! I'm eating just fine."

"Does that mean you're not hungry? The only food you've eaten"—she glanced at the consult notes—"is milk and yogurt. Is that enough to satisfy you?"

"For right now, yeah, you could say so. Listen, Miss Doctor, Julius Ciss does not want to be a bother. My grandson, he will come and bring me good food."

Meredith paused as she tried to assimilate what he had said. "Good food? Are you saying you don't like the taste of the food the hospital has given you? Or is there something else going on?"

Julius Ciss shrugged. "Don't bother yourself, Miss Doctor. It's fine."

"No, Mr.—Julius, it is not fine. Dr. Sanchez is afraid that you might become dehydrated, especially considering your fever. And I gather from the chart that you are also slightly diabetic. If you don't eat properly, you'll go into a diabetic reaction. Whatever calories you are taking in are being devoured by the fever."

He wet his lips.

From the nightstand by the patient's bedside, Meredith removed a lemon and glycerin swab used to moisten the lips of people who were either unconscious, or NPO, that is forbidden to drink or eat anything before upcoming tests or surgery, or had high fevers and were therefore on calculated in and outflow.

Julius Ciss shook his head. "No. I don't need. Water is fine." He reached over and took a long gulp.

Meredith glanced at the package. Why didn't he want this perfectly fine mouth swab? She felt there was something right in front of her that she was not getting.

From behind her there were steps. "Papi, how are you?"

Meredith turned to see a tall, intense young man with a slight beard and a black hat. He smiled at Meredith and turned his full attention on the man in the bed. Judging by his posture and his stance, he was probably only in his early thirties.

The young man stepped up to the side of the bed, and bent to give the older gentleman a kiss. "I brought you some of Mom's chicken soup. That should help your fever."

"And what else?" The old man's eyes lit up like a little boy in an ice cream store.

"Fresh gefilte fish, horse radish, some bread, a corned beef sandwich with pickles—but you have to eat only a little because I talked with your doctor. Your salt is up."

The old man nodded, eagerly taking the Care package. Slowly he unwrapped several items. "Mandel-broit, wonderful."

"Just a few, Papi. We have to keep you on your diet."

"Yeah. Yeah. Sure."

Meredith cleared her throat. "Excuse me, Julius, but—"

"No. No. The fault is mine." The young man turned to Meredith. "I'm Mr. Ciss's grandson, Ari Micha Mendelson. Are you one of his doctors?"

Meredith nodded. "His psychiatrist."

"A psychiatrist for Papi? You're kidding surely. He's never had a depressed day in his life. Every morning he recites *Modei Ani,* the morning prayers thanking the Lord for bringing us back to this world, and the *Shema*—"

"Except now, Ari. Hard for me to put on *tefflin* with only one good hand." He showed her the little black boxes which supposedly contained the 613 commandments of the Jews—and the leather bindings, which attached them to the arm while at prayer.

The young man patted his grandfather's hand. "Is there something you're not telling me, Papi? You feel depressed?"

Mr. Ciss shrugged. "Not anymore I'm not. Praise God, you came with the cavalry." He smiled at his grandson.

Puzzled, Meredith shook her head. "So you are eating, but you aren't eating the food our kitchen makes because—"

Ari sighed and wagged a finger at the old man. "Why didn't you tell them that you keep kosher?"

Now it all made sense to Meredith. She vaguely recalled some of the laws of *Kashrut* from living with her grandparents. But since *Sabtah,* she hadn't encountered it again. It was her turn to flush. "I'm sorry, Mr. Ciss. When I saw your *tzizits* at the crash site, I should have guessed why you weren't eating, but that didn't even occur to me. I haven't encountered that for so long—"

"You know about kosher? About not mixing the mother's milk in her baby's meat?" Julius Ciss asked. "So why didn't you say so?"

"Why didn't you say so?" Meredith shook her head, making a note on the consult form. She had a memory of her *Sabtah* refusing to even have coffee at the non-kosher restaurant her mother and her ate at. He probably would have been the same as Mr. Ciss, stubbornly eating only what he felt he was allowed, despite major health problems.

"You know, Julius, it would have saved your doctor a lot of problems if you had told her everything from the beginning. Now that we know what you can and cannot eat, I'll make sure dietary comes up and talks to you. It might only be airline food . . ."

Julius was not listening to her. His mind was already working in other ways. "So you're Jewish, and you're not married . . . Ari . . ."

"Papi! Shah!" Ari Micha glared at his grandfather. "Airline food would be just fine, Dr. . . . ?"

"Fischer. Meredith Fischer."

"And I can bring him food from the city from time to time. And yes, of course, when he's well enough to be moved, we'll transfer him—"

This time Julius Ciss would not be silenced. "Dr. Fischer, my Ari Micha is a doctor, too. Internist. My own private doctor."

Grandson glared at grandfather and then glanced toward Meredith and shrugged.

Meredith returned to her office in the towers across from the hospital.

She was irritated with herself for not realizing the reason why Mr. Ciss wasn't eating, although she thought she recalled something about health coming first before the laws of kosher. Looking at the carton of yogurt, she saw that it had a *U* with an *O* around it—Union of Orthodox Congregations, one of the many bodies who regulated the kosher food industry. She wouldn't have known all this if Gayle/Gitel hadn't pointed it out to her as she purposely picked up the food variety that had no insignia noting that the rabbis had agreed the items in the food were kosher.

Calling Rosa, she reported what she had discovered about Mr. Ciss, leaving out that he had a handsome grandson whom she thought she might be attracted to, and the fact that Meredith felt she should have known the grandfather's problem.

"Stop trying to be a perfectionist, m'love," Sean said, taking a seat on the sofa while she talked.

She ignored her Irish friend until after she'd contacted dietary and was instructed that it would be a while before they could get Mr. Ciss any special food since they had only recently made an order from their suppliers and procedure stated they must use what they had in the current pantry first. He would just have to make do with what was there.

She started to explain to them, and then realized that despite the fact that some of these dietitians had college-level educations and were supposed to know a variety of special diets, they probably had never known anyone who'd kept kosher.

"Now how would you be knowin' so much about this kosher business, m'love?"

Meredith shrugged. She hadn't asked him to come in while she was working on this problem, and she had no intention of answering him, at least not right now.

Taking out the Houston phone book, Meredith looked in the southwestern section where Jewish stores and synagogues predominated. She didn't know who or which one of the places listed here would be able to help bring food into the hospital for the old man, but she didn't want to ask him or the grandson. She feared it would seem as if she was ignorant of everything. Certainly, there was a lot she didn't know, but Meredith hated letting it "hang out." No, she was going to get her own answers.

Sabtah had sometimes taken her to a small synagogue called Young Israel. She remembered how angry Gayle/Gitel had been each time she would wake up on Saturday morning to find her daughter and father gone. It was shortly after that that Gayle/Gitel and Meredith had moved to their own apartment.

But Meredith recalled holding her Sabtah's hand and walking side by side with him to the *shul*.

She ran her finger down the list of places. One name, Young Israel of Braisewood, Rabbi Aaron Simkin stood out. Meredith was sure this temple had to be related to the one her grandfather had attended in New Jersey.

Sean came to look over her shoulder and rub her neck as he often did when she had a problem. God, yes, she loved him, probably a lot more than he loved her. Could, without knowing it, her secret be in their way?

She smiled up at him. "Just a moment more." Then she dialed the phone number. "Rabbi Aaron Simkin, please."

As she waited for the synagogue's rabbi to come on the line, she squeezed Sean's hand and realized that she had already started across the bridge. It only remained now to be seen if she would get to the other side or turn back.

CHAPTER 26

"How are you, darlin'?" Cole leaned down to kiss his wife.

"Fine. Ken's going to release me tomorrow," Sophie said, as her husband sat down next to her on the bed.

"And the baby . . ."

"Perfect. Ken's very pleased." Sophie brought her husband's wrist to her lips and kissed it. *Why had she added that? What the hell was she going to tell him? Nothing. This was her problem and hers alone. Just like the pregnancy with Lisa had been.*

"But you'll have to rest a lot, won't you, Mom?" Lisa asked, plopping down on the opposite side with all the courtesy and grace of an elephant.

Sophie winced as razor-sharp pain stabbed her kidney as her daughter moved the IV slightly.

"Sophie"—Cole rubbed her hand—"Are you all right?"

She nodded, not trusting herself to speak. If only this pain was the start of a miscarriage, then all conflict would be solved. Tears momentarily came to Sophie's eyes. She had to talk to Cole. She had to tell him. This was a decision they needed to make together and yet . . .

"I don't like how you're looking. I'm going to talk with Ken."

Her eyes went wide. "No. You don't have to. I'm doing fine, honey. Really. I'll be home tomorrow and yes, Lisa, I am going to have to rest a few days."

"What are you going to do about JCH, Mom?"

Sophie closed her eyes. Just thinking of the commission's visit was enough to cause pain even when there wasn't any. Emma Chandler counted on Sophie, as director of nursing, to pull this visit off. Somehow she had to do it.

"Lisa, don't talk to your mom about work right now." Cole took his wife's hand again. "Betty Sue said she'd be coming in tomorrow and she'll stay as long as you need her."

Eyes still shut tight, Sophie nodded.

"Lisa, honey, would you please go to the station and ask them for a fresh pitcher of water?" Sophie asked.

The teen glanced from her mother to her father and back again. Obviously they had some big things to discuss because Mom wanted to be alone. "Yeah, sure." Lisa stood and grabbed the pitcher, which still had water in it, from her mother's nightstand. "Be back in a flash."

Sophie nodded. Her heart raced more than it had when she'd told Cole about Lisa. But Lisa was a live, if somewhat rebellious child. If Ken had his way, this one would not be. Would Cole still want her if he realized she was going to be a drain on him? What was the use of their even staying married?

"Cole, honey, I . . ." Sophie's voice thickened.

"Code blue. ICU. Code blue. ICU." The announcement came over the loudspeaker.

"Damn. I'd better see what's going on, Soph. I'll be right back." He leaned down, giving her a kiss on the brow, and then sprinted off to the ICU unit to see where he could help.

"What the hell are you doing here, Ray Webber?" Lisa hissed as she crushed her can of soda and threw it into the garbage in one shot.

Her doped-up ex-boyfriend had a thriving business in town, one that Lisa had often partaken of in the past.

"Missed you."

"Yeah, I'll bet." She lit a cigarette and crushed the match under her heel. "How's your other friend, Melody? She leave you high and dry, Ray?"

He grinned. "Of course not. Besides, Lisa, doll, we were just business associates, her and I."

"Right." Lisa took two more puffs of her cigarette and ground it out, too. "This conversation is getting nowhere fast."

Ray grabbed her arm. "Oh, but it will. I've got a real sweet deal for you, darling."

Lisa stared at him. "I'm clean, Ray, and I'm going to stay that way." She tried releasing herself, but the sinewy arm held her tight.

"I heard a rumor that your rich friend, Chandler, was teaching you some maneuvers with the helicopter."

Lisa shrugged. She'd stop struggling because it was useless. Ray almost always got what he wanted. "So?"

"So, I'd like to propose a little business deal with you, baby. Like maybe we'd take a ride down the coast a bit."

"No. I won't do it."

It was Ray's turn to shrug. "We'll see, Lisa. Got a lot of shit on you, girl. All I have to do is release it and you are history."

CHAPTER 27

Jennifer had been visiting with Angel again, helping Wendy, who worked peds todays, give the Asian girl a bath. She knew that it was a bad idea to bond with the little girl, especially since the about-to-be-adoptive parents had already been in to see her and started the process for transferring the girl closer to their home in Corpus Christi. But a glutton for punishment, Jennifer continued on her fatalistic course.

Sometimes when she was with the Asian child, she would pretend it was twenty years before, and that this was her Lin. She would rock the girl and cuddle her as if the child was indeed her own. But most of the time, Jennifer was only too aware that Angel could be taken from her at any minute.

When they called the code blue for ICU, she tucked Angel into her crib and hurried to see how she could help. The fact that she had been on her break and should have been downstairs in ICU nagged at her only slightly. She was, after all, allowed a few minutes to herself.

The department was frantic with activity by the time she arrived. Every nursing unit had sent at least one person down and most were being turned away because there was just no room to work.

Jennifer raised on her tiptoes, trying to find out who the code had been called on and if the person was still pushing it. Apparently, everything was under control because next to the old man's room she saw Leroy, their main anesthesiologist, arguing with Ellis.

"What the hell did you use halothane for if you weren't going to take a history?"

"Give me a break, Leroy. How many times have you encountered malignant hyperthermia? How was I to know this old man—"

"You get a history, Johnston. You find out if there has been anyone in his family who died mysteriously in surgery. You ask him if he's susceptible to high fevers. You . . . you don't use halothane if you think they might develop this."

Leroy and Ellis became the focus of attention now as Julius Ciss slowly returned to the living.

Ellis just shook his head. "Malignant hyperthermia, where the fever rises fast and high, and the body goes stiff, if it's going to happen, it only does so in surgery while the gas is active. I, for one, have never encountered it in all my years as a surgeon."

The large black man turned his back on his friend. "Then you have not been very aware as a surgeon, Johnston. I see it all the time. Several times when I've assisted Patrick and yes, even you."

Ellis shook his head, denying it.

"And you should know that sometimes the malignant hyperthermia comes after the surgery while the patient is in recovery."

"So he's been in ICU for over a week."

"And he's been spiking high fevers since that time. In a man like old Mr. Ciss here, it could cause all sorts of complications. Why do you think his heart rate's so fast? Where are his blood gases?" Leroy asked, as he picked up the chart. "Look. His CO_2 is sky high. No wonder he went into acidosis." Leroy shook his head. "I'm surprised at you, Ellis, not being more watchful and Rosa, too. At least we pushed some dantrolene in time to reverse some of the contractures."

After Leroy ordered more of the dantrolene into the old man's IV, which counteracted some of the hyperthermia's worst effects, the pair walked off. "All I can say is it's a good thing the grandson wasn't around. Those Jews would be at our throats so fast . . ."

Almost everyone but the regular staff had dispersed since the immediate crisis had been dealt with, but a few extras hung around the station because the hospital gossip line loved to indirectly participate in the doctors' quarrels and because they wanted to learn what was really going down.

Meredith glanced up from her chart only as the pair was leaving. She felt a tumor growing in her heart, pushing out so furiously fast that all she felt was pain.

CHAPTER 28

The funeral service for Karin Martin was simple. Even Pam Roberts, sitting in the front row with the other Chandlers, was surprised at how few non-hospital people there were there. Didn't the woman have any friends?

She glanced back and saw Frank Willis in the rear row, along with several of his men. The officer nodded to her. Pam quickly turned her attention back to the minister, and to Bill Martin sobbing on stage.

Was that an act? Or did Billy boy really miss his wife? If so, why had he been playing with Pam and Coral May? Yeah, Pam knew about Coral May. It didn't bother her. She knew that if she wanted Dr. Bill Martin, all she had to do was snap her fingers.

The question about Karin was: Did he kill her? Pam had to admit that she thought him guilty, too. And, alibi or not, it only takes a minute or two to attach one of those devices. There had to be something he was worried about, especially after the way he forced her to remove half her savings. He said it was to help him get his new clinic started—but it could have been paying someone off.

Pam wouldn't have given him the money, if he hadn't found out about her bit with manipulating the hospital records and giving Coral May the file on her late husband, Jacob. Pam didn't know how he found out, but he was using it against her.

Since she wasn't quite ready to leave Chandler Springs yet, she had had no choice but to go along and be pleasant to him.

Avon and her brother George were two rows down. The tall good-looking black man was apparently still under suspicion both for Rosa's attack and now for the car bomb, but for the life of her, Pam couldn't think why . . . unless of course Bill had hired him.

But Pam had more problems to worry about. Now someone else was phoning her at odd hours and leaving hideous messages on her machine, and at her door. She shivered and glanced around. Granny Dottie would have said someone "had walked on her grave." Pam didn't believe that foolishness, but she did believe someone was spying on her and she did not like it. She knew it couldn't be the cops. After years of evading them with her other profession, she knew how they worked. No. This person was different.

As the final resting prayers were said for Karin Martin, Pam vowed that she would find out who was watching her, and why. When she learned their identity, she would damn well make them pay.

Emma Chandler wiped the tears from her eyes. Having witnessed the interaction between the Martins at the Christmas party, the matriarch felt especially responsible for Karin's death. After all, she had promised to investigate and what had she done? Yes, she'd asked Bill and Karin to seek counseling, but she hadn't pushed hard enough.

Emma had wanted Bill and Karin to see Meredith, but, of course, with her having upstaged him by taking the new position, it was obvious that Bill wouldn't go to the psychiatrist, even if he could be convinced he was in the wrong and needed help which, of course, he had denied. Emma knew that if he hadn't counted on her "making his loss up to him," he wouldn't even have agreed to go into Houston.

As it stood, they'd had only talked once with her friend, Dr. Waldman at his Northwest Clinic. Karin had canceled every session after that. Neither Waldman nor Emma believed Karin had made the calls of her own volition.

As Dr. Waldman sat behind Emma at the service, Emma whispered, "Do you think Karin was an abused woman?"

He cleared his throat just as the minister glanced in their direction.

Emma didn't need to wait for her friend's answer. She knew the signs. Why hadn't she talked with Karin on her own and found out what was really happening there?

CHAPTER 29

The day finally came for Allison's trial for reckless driving and driving under the influence she was probably more of a wreck now than on the day it had happened.

When the police had helped Allison out of the lake where she'd landed her Jeep, her blood level showed three times the drunken limit for her size and weight. Jinx had been thrown from the car before Allison even entered the water and so suffered more severe injuries as he crashlanded on the rocks off shore.

Horrified that she had caused it all, Allison had not taken any alcohol since the day of the accident, not even on Christmas or New Year's. She realized that among other things, her drinking had gotten out of control. In fact, that was one of the first steps in Alcoholics Anonymous, admitting that you are out of control. The only way out, Allison decided, was to "work the program." She knew that the judge would take into consideration her having started AA, but she was doing the program for herself more than for anyone. It was time to face up to the pain she'd felt for so many years.

As she and Emma drove to the courthouse in Richmond, Allison knew that Jinx, her former handyman, spa organizer, and lover didn't really want to sue. But she also knew that since he was paraplegic now, as a result of her driving, the insurance company was giving him no choice.

She glanced at her grandmother. Emma had quickly recovered from her tumble at the M and M meeting a few days before. But she had the whole family concerned about her. Still, none of the tests Rosa had worked up on Emma, showed why she had blanked out and fallen.

Maybe, thought Allison, everything was just getting too much to handle for her dear Nana.

The death of her darling son, Tommy, had been a terrible blow for Emma. She had done her best raising the two sisters, but Allison didn't think the best was enough when it came to herself. She had been willful and headstrong, causing Nana and Grandpa Caleb numerous hours of worry and grief. Margaret had been the good, stay-at-home girl who never got into trouble.

Allison didn't blame Joshua for leaving her and falling in love with Margaret. Even though she had mercilessly teased her older sister while they were growing up, she knew inside that her shy, self-conscious sister was the more competent and more mature one. But Margaret had a few rough edges that could still be sanded down.

Still on her own crutches for another few weeks, Allison hobbled into the courtroom followed by her anxious Nana.

Margaret Chandler and her fiancé, Dr. Joshua Allister, were due to arrive momentarily in Joshua's car, but he had to finish up some early morning patients at the hospital first.

Allison had both been surprised when Joshua offered to be there for her, and uncomfortable. How did Margaret, with her low self-esteem, see his gesture? Allison knew that Joshua no longer loved her and probably never did, but she feared her big sister still felt uneasy about the love the man from New York had given her.

Maybe after the trial, Allison and Margaret could

have a heart-to-heart talk. Even go away a few days by themselves and perhaps start shopping for Margaret's gown, which Allison knew had to be exquisite.

The court was called to session.

Allison glanced around at the double doors and the clock above them. It wasn't like her sister or Joshua to be late, especially for something as important as this.

She hoped they would hurry, because she didn't think Nana could handle the strain of the trial and Allison worried that she might have to deal with Nana on her own.

The classic red Mercury '76 convertible, complete with wing tips, which Joshua had restored practically with his own hands, moved along the 10 freeway, darting in and out of traffic.

"Can't you go any faster, Josh? Allison's going to be so upset if we aren't there for her."

"I know. But I thought you'd filled the tank with gas last night. It's not my fault we had to make a detour first thing out."

"Josh, I swear I did." Margaret sat with her arms folded, angrily watching the road as they passed.

Maybe it was prewedding blues, but they seemed to be fighting more and more, and enjoying each other's company less. "You know Allison suggested that she and I go off for a bit next week after this trial is finished. How would that sit with you?"

"Fine. Perfect. I think you need a break, Marg. You're under a lot of stress right now."

"Oh, thanks a lot. And you aren't? Am I so fragile that I have to be the only one taking a vacation?"

Joshua just glanced over at his fiancée and shook his head. No matter what he said, it wouldn't be the right thing. Margaret seemed determined to pick fights over the littlest things. "No, of course not, darling—"

He hadn't even finished his sentence when he first noticed the odor. He'd just tuned the car up last week. There shouldn't be anything wrong with it and yet . . . the flames popped out from under the hood.

Joshua hit the brakes, throwing them both forward against the windshield. Before the car came to a complete stop, he grabbed Margaret and pulled her out of the car with him.

"What the . . . ?" Margaret started to ask and then saw for herself.

The couple scrambled and rolled into the dunes at the side of the freeway, running and holding each other tightly, stopping only when they saw the car engulfed in flames, igniting the two vehicles surrounding them.

"Oh, Joshua!" Margaret hugged his neck. "What happened?" Grease smudged her skin and his.

Joshua Allister shook his head. "I don't know, but I am going to find out." He glanced over at his lady love. "Can you walk to the nearest phone?"

She nodded. "We'd better call Allison and let her know what happened." And she thought she'd better let James, their security captain at Chandler Estates, know what happened also. It could be part of the same scheme with the fire and the horses, or it could be something totally different, or even totally innocent. But at this moment, Margaret wasn't prepared to hazard a guess.

CHAPTER 30

Friday night. The fourth week of the New Year. And Meredith had promised Sean that she would spend time with him, but at the last moment, she told him she had an errand to do in Houston and it couldn't wait.

She wasn't quite sure why she'd lied to him. He wouldn't have minded walking with her in this area as she peeked in stores and absorbed the atmosphere, but somehow this felt private. Meredith didn't want Sean knowing where she was going or why. She didn't even know the why herself, only that she was curious.

You're being a fool, she told herself. *What do you want to go and ruin your life for?* Meredith thought again of the comment Leroy had made to Ellis. She had always thought them both to be rational, liberal men, but it seemed that they weren't.

Of course, she reasoned with her reflection in the window of a store that sold wigs, *shetels.* She remembered that being a married woman, her grandmother had covered her hair sometimes with a hat, sometimes with a nice scarf and other times with a wig, when they went to synagogue. Some of the other women *Bubbee,* her grandmother, knew hadn't covered their hair.

Gail, Meredith's mother, thought the whole hair business not only stupid but hypocritical as she did most other customs. "Either you committed totally—" she would say to her daughter—"or you don't do anything at all. No halfway measures for me."

Meredith played with her own dark curls in front of the store's window. She had never really wanted or wondered about marriage until recently when she'd thought of Sean. Maybe because Mother had made it sound so distasteful, Meredith had kept the institution at arm's length.

She studied one of the wigs up close. Meredith had always been curious as to how she might look as a blond, but to keep her hair covered constantly? Maybe it was better she stay with the life she knew in Chandler Springs.

All around her, shops were closing as the Jewish proprietors started getting ready for the *Sabbath*, which started twenty minutes before sunset. The aroma of fresh *challah* baking filled the air.

While Houston Jews were not as varied as those in New York, Meredith wasn't surprised to find a few black hats from the various Chasid sects and even two fur *striemels*, huge round hats trimmed in beaver, rabbit, or even mink. Growing up in New York's Italian section, she'd seen people dressed like that all the time from the neighboring Jewish area.

It had taken her a while to find out why they wore those costumes. Being descendants of a rabbinical line from Poland, those worshippers had adopted the dress similar to the Polish nobility of the seventeenth century, during the time that country's Jewish population had flourished.

She wandered down the streets of Braisewood and Fonden, passing the modern-looking Jewish Community Center. From the modern glass and metal buildings, it seemed a large portion of these synagogues were reform. But obviously from the varied dress and the children wearing the *keepot*—skullcaps—as they ran home from their private schools, there were also conservative and orthodox and even super-orthodox—*frumies,* Mother had called them.

The area wasn't quite as crowded as *tumbledick* (one of her grandfather's terms) as parts of New York or New Jersey were, but for someone who'd lived the last ten years of her life in a small town surrounded by wide open spaces, it was cramped.

Meredith had thought that she would just walk around here for a bit, get her fill, and be fine with going back to her own life. Maybe she'd buy a few kosher items to bring back for Mr. Ciss to eat until the hospital got its act together. But she'd forgotten about the Sabbath, about the shops closing early.

But the more she walked, the more she felt like she was an outsider looking in, not unlike that movie *Stella Dallas* where the impoverished mother gazed from outside the window, while her daughter inside the warm and cozy room, married a rich man.

This was getting to be too much. After all, she only wanted to see a little. Time to get in her car and head back to Chandler Springs. Maybe it was early enough that she could still have dinner with Sean.

Turning down a side street, the one she knew positively she had parked on, Meredith glanced around. Either someone had towed her car or . . . she walked down yet another street and then another. They all looked the same.

Okay, don't panic, she told herself. She had had to squeeze her Camry into a tight space; one that she didn't know if *she* could easily get out of, let alone any thief.

Frustrated, Meredith returned to Braisewood, the main boulevard of the Houston southwest Jewish community.

Across the street, almost in front of her, stood the synagogue she'd called when she'd been trying to help Mr. Ciss. She could hear the men singing the *Maariv*—the evening service—and for that moment, she was a five-year-old again, clinging to *Sabtah*'s arm, singing along.

Well, she told herself, *maybe it wouldn't be such a bad thing if I introduced myself to the rabbi. After all, if we get any other Jewish patients at CMC, I might need his help again.*

Tucking her purse under her arm so that it wasn't quite as noticeable, Meredith flushed recalling now that *Sabtah* had not liked her to carry anything on Friday nights or Saturday; not even Tina, her favorite doll, could accompany them.

Taking a deep breath, she climbed the steps toward the open door and slipped inside. Automatically as she entered, her hand raised to touch the *mezuzah* fastened to the door. She didn't even realize she had done anything until her hand came back down to her side. She shrugged uncomfortably.

Being from a traditional congregation tending toward the orthodox view, Meredith remembered that the women sat separately from the men. Prayer books with both English and Hebrew covered a table just inside the door.

A warm glow filled Meredith Fischer. She turned, expecting to see a fireplace maybe. But there was only a pair of candles burning.

Someone here had already lit the Sabbath candles. The light flickered, just like it had at Bubbee's house. She watched the flames a moment and tried to remember the blessing over them, which Bubbee had taught her. *Nar . . .* something *. . .* she let it drop.

The nagging thought at the back of her mind was that if she started on this path, she'd have to give up

Sean. No, she wouldn't, she argued with herself. Nothing was going to change in her life just by entering this building on a Friday night. She wasn't starting on any path. She was just being curious about her history.

Meredith was positive about that. Magical thinking accomplished nothing. She often criticized her patients who believed in magical thinking. Therefore, she knew she couldn't do it herself.

She wasn't sure why she did it, but as Meredith picked up the holy book, she kissed it, the words *just like Sabtah used to do* echoed in her mind. Hand trembling, she found the page the men were on and began following along. Maybe somewhere in here she'd find the answer of what it meant to be Jewish—and live in the non-Jewish world of Chandler Springs.

CHAPTER 31

The whole month of January and first three weeks of February in the Johnston home had been like those in an armed camp. Ellis made a supreme effort to leave the hospital at a decent time and to call home or the bookstore almost every hour. The kids, Amy and Will, were ever so wary of what they said, not wanting to upset their mother. Ellis was especially proud of his teenage daughter who somehow had managed to contain her normal teenage bitchiness and stay calm, even when it appeared Hillary was losing control again.

The rain, keeping them indoors, tracking dirt on Hillary's perfectly washed kitchen floors and her new rugs, kept her tense. On a scale of ten being the worst, Ellis thought Hillary was probably an eight.

None of them really wanted to put her back in the hospital—the kids because they missed their mother and her taking care of them, and Ellis because he couldn't handle both his work and the children simultaneously. He didn't know how other fathers with ill wives did it.

Keeping a watchful eye on Hillary, he checked her medication bottle daily, making sure she took the proper dose, and trying to ascertain when she was hearing voices and when she wasn't. Of course he knew there were all sorts of ways to hide pills, to cheek them and to make it seem the medication was being swallowed when it wasn't. Ellis knew that the possibility that Hillary might be going back for far longer than seventy-two hours loomed in the air.

Once the first milestone was passed, there was the fourteen-day hold, then the thirty-day hold, and after that, more often than not, the court would appoint a temporary conservator who had control over the person taking medications, being in the hospital, and almost every move that they might have taken for granted before. If no family members were available, then someone from the public office would be appointed. He'd heard horror stories about that and hoped it wouldn't come to something of that nature. But he still could not trust Hillary, one hundred percent.

One time he'd come home earlier than expected and found her barefoot, dancing around the dining room table, laughing, talking, and acting as if there was at least one other onlooker. But no one else was home.

Of course, Hillary had denied anything was wrong when he confronted her. But it bothered Ellis. And he became more keenly aware when it seemed as if she might be responding to "internal stimuli."

Finally, near the end of the month, the rain slowed to a drizzle and then over the weekend stopped for a brief bit of sunshine. A childlike Hillary woke her husband Ellis demanding that they have a cookout with some of his friends.

"Are you sure you're really up to that?"

" 'Course, I am," Hillary chirped. "The new medication they've started me on is working wonders. I even want you to invite Rosa."

He stared at his wife. After the threats she'd been making, he wasn't so sure that it was such a good idea.

"Oh, don't be a spoilsport," Hillary said, throwing a pillow at him just as she used to do when they were first lovers. "Besides"—she wriggled her ass in front of him—"I know something you don't know."

Ellis frowned. "What?"

"It's about Will. But you have to guess."

Ellis rolled his eyes skyward. "I give up."

"No. You have to make a guess."

Sighing, Ellis said, "He got a raise on his paper route."

Hillary smiled tightly and shook her head.

He threw the pillow back at her, as he once might have, glad that whatever crisis she'd been going through seemed to be over. She was like a school girl again, so innocent and naive.

With her sly smile, Hillary said, "Okay, I'll tell you. Our boy Will's in love." Hillary hugged her pillow as if she was the girl in love.

"With who?" Ellis was horrified at the thought of his ten-year-old "in love." Totally ridiculous. He himself hadn't fallen in love . . . well, until he met Hillary at the college dance. He knew that kids today were progressing faster, but this was silly. "You're kidding me, aren't you?"

"Uh-uh." Hillary's fingers were in her mouth. She coyly sucked them. "Wanna know who?" She grinned.

"Damn it, Hillary, yes, I do."

"Oh, Elli, don't be such a spoilsport. Have fun." She paused, giving him a moment to assimilate the information. "It's Ophelia."

"Who?" Ellis was sure he didn't know any Ophelia.

"Patrick's daughter. Your partner, Patrick Thompson, remember." She nodded as Ellis became bug-eyed.

"Yes, I know who you mean. But she's only nine."

Hillary laughed and shrugged. "That's perfect then. He's ten and she's nine."

Ellis could see that his wife was having fun with this, even though he didn't consider it funny, but it made him glad to see her like her old self. Maybe she was in remission, or maybe the medication had cured her. One could only hope, Ellis thought to himself. Simultaneously, he felt the aching loss of what might have been if he had pursued Rosa, but if Hillary was well and treated him and the kids right, then out of good conscience, he could do nothing but be faithful.

The pillow fight lasted a good five minutes with both of them falling on the bed, laughing.

Hillary's fingers twisted among his graying curls. "Do you know how much I love you?"

Ellis wet his lips. "I think I do."

"Well? Don't you want to say something similar?"

"Hill, you know I adore you. You're the mother of my kids and the woman I married. You still have a great figure and I still lust after you."

She sat upright. Her eyes showed hurt feelings. "I had to make you say that. You don't really mean it." Her lips formed a pout. Hillary sighed. "Do you want this cookout?" Swiveling her head to face him, Hillary let her long hair flow over her shoulders. Ellis had always liked that before, and she was sure he liked it still.

He reached for his wife. She moved away. "Uh-uh. Too much to do if we're having people over." Hillary licked her lips. "Later."

Ellis cleared his throat. "Yeah. Later." He got up, and going to the bathroom, turned the shower on. "I'll take a quick one and then I can help you."

"Good." Still playful, Hillary threw her arms around his neck, rubbing her body against his, and then she gave him a playful slap, sending him into the steaming waters.

Once he had closed the shower door, Hillary went to the trousers she'd worn the day before. From her pocket, she pulled out a folded, very wrinkled paper that had obviously been torn and crushed and unfolded many times.

Rosa Sanchez and Ellis Johnston are lovers. I have proof if you need it.

There had been no signature, no return address, not even a postmark.

You know what you have to do, Hillary. The voice sounded like a concerned parent, maybe one on the verge of punishing a child for not obeying.

"Yes," she responded.

Good. Then do it.

Hillary wiped the tears from her eyes, crushed the paper and threw it. A basket in one. She hoped that was a good omen for her plan.

CHAPTER 32

The report from day shift said that Nancy Hoffner had been extremely depressed for several days. Meredith had been to see the pianist more than once, but Nancy was never in the mood to talk.

Both Meredith and Vicki, who was now floating on this floor, told Nancy of the physical therapy planned for her arm, wrist, and fingers and how they expected at least a ninety-percent recovery, possibly better.

Possibly wasn't good enough for Nancy Hoffner. It wasn't good enough for her parents.

From her first recollections, Nancy, like Vicki, knew only music as her companion. More devoted to Nancy's success than even Vicki's parents had been, the Hoffners had planned and groomed her for a career as a concert pianist with comparisons only to other child geniuses as Mozart. They had reasoned that with the DNA in their mutual families, there was no reason, given the proper training, that they could not have a musical genius for the world.

Not even the position Nancy had been offered with the Los Angeles Philharmonic was good enough for the Hoffners.

Nancy didn't believe that she had ever been happy before, and now there was no reason to believe she would ever have a chance to achieve that happiness now. Always she tried to do just a little better, to get bigger smiles from her family. Now all they could do was frown and it made Nancy's sorrow sink her into the quagmire.

The fact that her family had not yet come to see her probably dug deeper into her soul than she cared to admit. There was always this excuse and that excuse. By the time she'd been in the hospital three weeks, she knew not to expect them, or anything from them. Her value to them was gone.

Even if she recovered ninety percent, she would never be as good as she once was. Tears were a constant presence in Nancy's eyes as she relived moments when she had had standing ovations, when she had played before President Bush, and even when she had had a solo performance for the Queen of England, followed by a sold-out public performance at Victoria Hall near Knightsbridge. How many pianists got that type of recognition? How many, besides the early greats, had musicals and operas manufactured from their own compositions? She couldn't even read the notes now, much less play.

Nancy knew, even without her family saying so, that they would rather have the "fond" memories of her many successes than the present facts of her handicap. The most she could hope for now, she told herself, was to teach music to screaming brats who hated practice—probably the most humiliating of all careers.

The medications Meredith had prescribed: Prozac for the long term and the faster-acting Paxil, as well as a nighttime dose of Desyrel had done nothing to relieve Nancy of these many fears and worries.

On Sunday of the fourth week of January, Nancy waited patiently until after the day nurse had bathed her and helped make up her bed afresh. She even smiled pleasantly and talked with the aides that day and complimented dietary on the lunch, giving her autograph, for what it was worth, to one of the attendants who'd asked previously and been refused.

She had been in the hospital long enough to know the schedule: She knew that at 2:45 in the afternoon, the evening staff began arriving; that the day nurses were frantically running around, checking IV's, recording intake and output's, and charting their last-minute impressions on their assigned patients; that by 3:02 in the afternoon, they usually all crowded into their small lounge to hear report; and that being a weekend, they were probably understaffed as usual.

Sometimes a few of them came out at 3:20 to give early medications, or to cover the desk, but seldom were assignments made by the nurse in charge until 4:00 P.M.

It was during that time that Nancy took the extra bedsheet she had persuaded housekeeping to let her have, wrapped it around the light fixture, climbed up on her visitor's chair and pulled the sheet around her neck, and kicked the stool away.

Only pure luck, if you wanted to call it that, made Vicki decide to make rounds with the off-going day nurse. Usually the P.M. staff just accepted what days said about the patients, but today, of all days, Vicki Kantera had insisted on checking the status of each patient.

Nancy Hoffner had probably been hanging by her neck a good ten minutes by the time she was cut down. No one knew exactly how long she had been without oxygen, or how much brain damage she probably had, but the fact remained that she would live.

Vicki called a code blue as one of the housekeepers helped cut the girl down. Nancy's pulse, thready and weak, was amazingly still there. Her airway appeared to be blocked. Vicki then placed Nancy on the hard surface of the floor, swept the patient's mouth, trying to determine if this blockage could be loosened and began resuscitation technique, being careful not to compress the heart since she did have a pulse.

Within moments, Nancy's eyelids fluttered open. She was not at all happy to see the room filling with more people by the minute. She had hoped that this event would be a private show. But things were just not working out the way she hoped.

The fact that Nancy had attempted suicide in a public place where she would more than likely be found told Meredith that Nancy really did not want to die. She just wanted help. If the girl had really wanted death, she would have gone to an out-of-the-way place, where she would not be quickly found, and put a gun in her mouth. Death would come instantaneously.

Within a matter of hours, Meredith had assessed the situation and ordered Nancy transferred to the INN. Once she was mentally stable, Meredith would have her transferred to a rehab specialist. But the psychiatrist knew it would take a long time for Nancy's soul to heal.

CHAPTER 33

Dr. Ken Stevens frowned as he studied the blood lab reports on his patient and friend, Sophie Morgan. Hoping that the lab might be wrong, he pulled out the ultrasound that JoAnn, Joshua's assistant, had taken of the five-month fetus.

Just as he feared, the baby was pressing against Sophie's kidneys. In a normal pregnancy, it might cause some discomfort, and more frequent use of the washroom; but in Sophie, with her lupus pounding away at her body, and her white blood cells not gearing up to fight, this renal complication might even prove fatal.

He slipped the film back into its covering sheet. As an obstetrician whose main purpose was bringing life into the world and joy to parents, asking your patient to have an abortion, especially in the fifth month, was like asking them to jump into the eye of a Texas tornado. It was something most people just didn't do and if they did survive physically, they sure as hell were going to be some kind of emotional wreck.

After the past few days, he didn't think that Meredith needed any more clients to add to her list . . . and yet, something had to be done.

Patrick Thompson, Ellis Johnston's partner, exited the elevator.

"Making rounds?" Ken asked, as the younger man came to sit down next to him.

Patrick nodded. "Invited over to Ellis's. Something about Hillary wanting a cookout."

"Yeah." Ken shrugged. "I was invited, too, but I might just pass. Janice doesn't feel comfortable around Hillary anymore. Not since . . ."

"I know," Patrick finished. "But I'm his partner, so I'm kind of obligated. Anyway, thought I would check up on my patients and make sure all the orders were covered and cosigned before tomorrow's surgeries."

Ken stood. "Well, I'm just off to see a patient." He positioned Sophie's chart so that the name was not visible. Everyone knew that Ken took care of Sophie, but with the laws of confidentiality regarding patients, Ken felt awkward leaving her chart exposed for others on staff to read. What was going on was between her, him . . . and Cole.

"So, how are you feeling today?" Ken asked, stopping next to Sophie's bed.

She glanced up at the IV. "I thought you said I was getting discharged *yesterday*."

Ken shrugged. "Changed my mind." The obstetrician moved his jaw around, exercising it so that the words would come out easier. It didn't help. "Talked to Cole yet?"

Sophie gave him a slight smile. "Of course. I talk to my husband every day, several times a day."

His face assumed a serious look. "You know that's not what I mean. Damn it, Sophie, you are losing renal tissue and renal function. I don't know if we can get them to come back. You are endangering your liver, and you are endangering your life. For all I know, your LDH levels might be up, showing heart damage as well. If something isn't done soon, both you and the baby could possibly die."

CHAPTER 34

Jennifer watched as the Lockhursts whispered back and forth. They were the couple supposedly adopting Angel, but they didn't seem too happy about it.

Mrs. Lockhurst treasured her position in society and didn't know if she really wanted to devote the time to a child who was obviously handicapped, and perhaps even a little retarded.

Jennifer paced back and forth, cursing herself for not having the courage to speak up. But what could she say? At her age to adopt a baby, to be a single mother? No, Jennifer didn't think she could turn her life around like that. She'd gotten so used to living alone with her dog.

Besides, this was not Lin. It was Angel. Lin was Vietnamese; Angel was Chinese. They might look similar to the unobservant eye, but there were very distinct differences. Having been in love with the former, Jennifer knew.

And with Lin, she had planned on having her father around to help raise her, to give her part of the culture of where she was born. Jennifer knew nothing at all about China. It would be almost impossible to raise Angel properly.

Besides, didn't Dr. Fischer say that a child's personality developed before the age of three years? Angel was five. Whoever took her would have to deal with the trauma of her being abandoned by her mother, being institutionalized for so many years, and now this plane crash.

The idea seemed totally irresponsible to Jennifer and yet, she found herself watching the Lockhursts and how they interacted with their future daughter, not hugging her, not holding her, almost as if they were afraid of her.

"But Harrison," Mrs. Lockhurst said, making a face as if she had just touched dog poop, "she seems so foreign, so alien. How am I going to call this girl my daughter?"

"Please, Sharon, we agreed on adopting a Chinese baby girl because of their attitude toward females in China and because this one, especially, needed help. And yes, she is foreign, but she's not alien. Once she's home with us, you'll see, she'll be fine."

The look of disgust remained. "I only agreed because you said the Chinks were brilliant and I want a brilliant child that I can show off. But look at her now, will you. She doesn't look anything like the cute picture Father Norton took." Mrs. Lockhurst waved a narrow, beringed hand; her polished red nails glinting in the light. "That bandage on her head. Even that doctor, Thompson, said that it's impossible to know how much damage she has as a result of the accident, until we test her. And that may be several months from now." She shook her head. "Harrison, I don't want an idiot child."

Sharon turned and walked out of pediatrics.

Jennifer, who'd been standing in the doorway and overheard the whole conversation, just stared at Mr. Lockhurst.

He gave a sickly smile. "Don't worry. She doesn't mean it. She just . . . um, PMS today. Everything will be fine. We'll be back tomorrow."

Jennifer frowned and nodded as he walked past her without even noticing her reaction.

She pushed herself up and away from the wall where she'd been leaning and went over to pick up the little girl. So light, so tiny for five, and so malnourished in so many ways.

Angel smiled at her, putting her thumb into her mouth.

There had been a strange bonding then between them. Angel smiled and as Jennifer picked her up, the little girl began babbling in Chinese.

Unable to bear the moment as it was, Jennifer leaned over and kissed the girl's forehead. "Yes, Angel, you are special. And you are pretty." She smoothed the black hair with her hand. Tears formed in Jennifer's blue eyes. "And I would love to have you . . . but I can't."

CHAPTER 35

There were only two other women upstairs when Meredith took a seat in the back row. Since both wore hats, she knew they were married. Automatically her hand went to her hair, but she was not married and never had been, so there was no requirement that she cover her hair.

She opened a prayer book and, by glancing at one of the women's, found the right page. The *sidur* was in both English and Hebrew. Even though it had been nearly forty years before, the melodies came back to her as if she had sung them yesterday. Her hand trembled as she followed along with the prayers. One of the other women turned to look at Meredith, and she felt herself flushing. Maybe she was singing too loudly or off-key. Or maybe these women hadn't ever lost anything and felt the joy of suddenly finding it again.

In a fleeting moment, Meredith likened her sense of return to being reunited with a loved one and how that marvelous first kiss and hug felt. The more she heard, the more she felt like a child again at her grandfather's knee. She could close her eyes and picture everything as it had been in New Jersey. But the past was the past and she couldn't go back. Too much in her life had changed.

Meredith remained upstairs after the bowing of the knees at *Alenu* and the ending of the *Kabalat Shabat* service, which welcomed the beginning of the Sabbath. She felt the other women glancing her way as they greeted each other and hurried down the stairs to meet their mates. Uneasily, she sat where she was, watching the men, and studying the ornate ark. Since she had no one waiting for her, she decided to wait a moment and hoped she wouldn't be too obvious.

How would Sean feel coming to a place like this? He'd probably stand out like a Goliath next to David.

Mesmerized, she remained where she sat, continuing to think about the past and imagining what it might have been like if things had been different.

She recalled now, having been attracted to Ben Levy, the valedictorian of her high school graduating class. They had seemed to have so much in common, including wanting to be physicians. But her mother forbade her to date him—because he was a Jew. She hadn't understood then, nor did she comprehend why her mother disliked her having Jewish girlfriends. At the time her mother had already changed her name from Fischer to Faith.

As she entered college, Meredith found herself avoiding the Jewish men because her mother disliked them and the non-Jewish men because she hadn't felt she had much in common with them.

Only years later did she start recalling her memories of her grandfather and realize that *she was Jewish*. Defying her mother, Meredith entered medical school, and changed her name back to Fischer. Only that still didn't make her feel like a Jew.

She hadn't thought much about it, one way or the other, until she'd found Mr. Ciss in the plane.

Sean was the first man with which she'd had anything resembling a dating situation in years. And maybe unconsciously this was why she had never felt he totally accepted her. It wasn't just their age difference, but their histories as well.

Time was suspended until she felt a tapping on her shoulder. Lost in her thoughts, she hadn't noticed the dimming of the lights.

"Miss, is something the matter?"

Meredith blinked up into the bleary eyes of the old man, the *shamus*—guard—who made sure the synagogue had ten men—a *minyan*—for the prayers, that the proper people were phoned, especially when they were needed for shiva, that the building was locked up and other necessary deeds.

"Oh, no. I'm fine. I'm just going." She gave a sheepish smile and closed the prayer book as she stood, starting down the stairs.

The old man followed her as the lights in the building began to one by one automatically shut off. "You have a place for Shabbos?"

"Uh . . . I was just going to the coffee shop down—"

"A coffee shop? On Shabbos? What are you, meshuga?" He shook his head, staring at her. "No, I don't think you're crazy, but a nice young woman like you shouldn't be alone on the Sabbath. You'll come home to dinner with me."

"But I—shouldn't you call your wife?"

He glared at her. And then shook his head.

Meredith realized that he probably didn't use the phone on the Sabbath. And even if he did, his wife probably wouldn't pick up. That's right. *Sabtah* hadn't either. She recalled the horrible fight, the one time Gail had secreted herself in the bedroom to call a girlfriend.

"All right." She shrugged. She didn't want to be a bother and yet it had been a long time since she'd sat at a Shabbos table.

Tucking her purse under her arm so that it wasn't

as noticeable, Meredith followed the older gentleman down three blocks and up another. For the life of her, she still couldn't recall where she'd parked her car. None of this area was looking familiar at all.

"Good Shabbos, Mr. Ginsburg."

A couple strolling by nodded to her host. He nodded back and responded in kind.

They walked in silence for a moment. "So? You have a name?"

"Yes, of course. It's—Ahava."

"Ahava? Very nice. Anything goes with that?"

Meredith flushed and shrugged. She continued following him, climbing the steps to the second-story apartment, already smelling the wonderful odors of chicken soup. "Jewish penicillin," her grandfather used to say. "Chicken soup can cure you of anything." Meredith felt a melancholy ache in her heart.

She walked into the old man's house. Behind his wife, Meredith saw the pristine white table cloth, the Sabbath candles glowing, the egg *challah* covered with an embroidered cloth, not unlike the one she had tried making. Mother had probably thrown it away.

"Ilana, this is our Shabbos guest. Ahava."

"No last name?" Mrs. Ginsburg asked the same thing as she quietly placed Meredith's purse out of the way, but where she wouldn't forget it.

Meredith shook her head. She didn't even know what she was doing here or why she had even come into the city like this. She had known the shops would be closed early and yet she'd still driven in.

But as long as she was here, as long as she was making the pretense of being Jewish, she would go by the name her grandfather had bestowed upon her.

The apartment was smaller than her place in Chandler Springs, but it had the warmth of love inside it. Meredith walked around the book-lined room, picking up one book and putting it back. She tried assisting with last-minute preparations but Ilana Ginsburg wouldn't hear of it.

A couple of the books, in particular, drew her attention: *Regimen of Health (Regimen Sanitatis)*, advising the Sultan Al Malik al Afdal on proper hygiene, diet, and drugs, stressing that a "healthy mind made a healthy body." From the looks of the pages, the book was old. But as she glanced at the frontis-piece she realized it had been written in the original Arabic in 1198 by Maimonides.

Meredith shook her head amazed that Rambaum, as the scholarly physician was also known as, knew about psychosomatic medicine, even back then.

The other book she picked up was by the same author. *Treatise on Poisons and Their Antidotes* sounded almost like a modern-day text, even describing the method of caring for snake and insect bites in just the very same way Meredith had studied in medical school. Shivers ran up her spine.

"Ah, I thought you would like those. You know all this medical information, you know where he got it from?" Mr. Ginsburg asked.

"The Greeks? The Arabic physicians?"

Mr. Ginsburg shrugged. "Yeah, some. But none of them had the impact that the Rambaum had. He found all his answers in the Torah. Don't looked so shocked. There's a lot packed in those five volumes. Unfortunately, not many of Maimonides' works have been properly translated into English, but many are in Hebrew and German and of course in the original Arabic. You know that he lived most of his life in a Cairo suburb."

She shook her head. "I thought he was Spanish. Toledo or something."

"Cordoba, actually." The old man sank onto the sofa

and leafed through the book she'd just been studying. "But his family fled when the radical Muslims started harassing the Jews. That was 1148. Time never changes things, does it?" He gave her a sad smile and handed her back the slim volume.

This man who had lived in the early Middle Ages, who had had none of the advantages of modern technology, had interpreted and written all this based on one source: the Torah, which the whole Jewish existence centered around from the time of Mount Sinai onward.

It gave Meredith a thrill just to glance at these historical works. How could her mother have given this all up?

Before she could ask the old man any questions, Ilana was calling them to the table.

Meredith sat silently, absorbing the aura which surrounded this old couple, listening as Mr. Ginsburg recited the kiddish over the wine, and then washing his hands, he blessed the bread.

"You know why the bread has to be covered when we bless the wine?" There was a twinkle in his eyes.

Meredith thought a moment as she devoured the steaming chicken soup and fluffy matzo balls. Every bit as good as she recalled from her grandmother.

She could hear the words just as clearly as the day her grandfather had explained the theory to her. "Because the bread wants to be first, as it usually is during the week, and we don't want to hurt its feelings."

He laughed and slapped the table. "Now how did you know that?"

Meredith returned his smile and shrugged.

What a dinner she ate! Five, no six courses, not to mention dessert. "I don't think I'll be able to eat for a week."

"Sure you will," Ilana Ginsburg said, putting another piece of cake on Meredith's plate. "You're skinny. A little weight you could put on. During the week, you're busy being a doctor, yes?"

Meredith nodded. She was surprised. Had she told them she was a doctor? Maybe she had.

"And probably don't eat regular meals?"

The psychiatrist sighed. "No. Not usually."

"You see. You see. I am right. Therefore, you need a little sustenance. If it weren't Shabbos, I would give you some to take home. Maybe you'll return during the week. A few care packages I can fix you up. Just like my granddaughter."

And these people were just like her grandparents. It was all Meredith could do to hold back the tears. She bit her lower lip. "It's getting late. I'd better leave."

"You sure? We can make the bed up for you here." Ilana pointed to the sofa.

Meredith shook her head, unable to trust her speech. She was beginning to feel suffocated. She had to get out. She had to leave. Now.

CHAPTER 36

Hillary could hardly believe her plan was working. Not only had Ellis called several of his colleagues out to the house—some of whom she wanted to impress with how well she handled a last minute gathering—but Madam Bitch had also agreed. It was too bad Hillary's oleander flowers weren't in bloom.

But being Ellis was a doctor, there were plenty of samples around the house . . . enough to accomplish her purpose.

She hurried around, the perfect wife, preparing the perfect party for her perfect man.

"Will you cool it, Mom?" Amy, their teenage daughter, complained. "The way you're going at it, you'll have a cardiac before the night's over."

"Maybe then I'd see something of your father. He'd be forced to visit me if I was in the ICU, wouldn't he?"

"Mother! Will you come off it? Dad loves you. He just works very hard. You should have seen how he was when I had my tumor."

"Because you're his flesh and blood. He loves you. I'm just an appendage."

Amy stuck her fingers in her mouth pretending to gag. "Mother, you are full of it. Dad loves you and that's all there is to it." The teen stormed away to set the table as her mother had requested.

Hillary listened as her daughter slammed the back

door. She peeked through the curtains wanting to know what Amy was up to outside. Ah, just as she'd thought.

Careful not to let the curtains move, Hillary watched. She could see the girl talking with Ellis outside, where he was busy cleaning the pool. Stupid kid! Probably reporting their conversation word for word. Did they really think they could fool her? She wouldn't be surprised if Amy had a tape recorder on her, or even one of those gadgets advertised on the TV where you could hear someone talking from one hundred feet away—or was that miles?

Careful, Hillary. Don't let any of those thoughts enter your head. Remember, he can hear you. He has ways of monitoring you.

Hillary nodded silently. She took some deep breaths as she blanked out her mind just like the Maharishi had taught her. Hillary didn't really think he was an Indian spiritual leader. He certainly didn't look Indian, but it didn't matter. She knew that if she whitewashed her mind, Ellis would know nothing.

Still, she had to be careful. Even if her thoughts weren't there, Ellis was having her followed by the CIA, and who knew what tricks they had up their sleeves?

Stepping away from the window, Hillary opened the bottle of Haldol, her "medication." Crushing it to minute grains, she flushed the remains down the toilet, pulling the cord several times to make sure there were no telltale blue spots on the water. It was important to make Ellis think she had taken her dose. She never would have thought of crushing the tablet first, but her voices had told her how to do it. If she had thought of it, herself, she probably would have kept the pill whole—and been caught.

She glanced out the window once more to make sure that Ellis was still occupied.

He and Amy were discussing something while Amy

was swimming some laps. Her daughter. So beautiful. Hillary's heart swelled with pride for a moment before she heard: *Not your daughter. His daughter. He's turned her against you. Remember that. I am the only one on your side.*

The voice was right, of course. There was no one for her . . . not even her own kids.

Company started arriving around three, just as they had planned. Patrick Thompson came with his family and Ellis found himself observing his son as the boy watched Ophelia. The thoracic surgeon shook his head. How could a boy as young as Will think he was in love? It was not only absurd, it was ridiculous. And yet, in that at least, Hillary seemed to know what she was saying.

With a sigh, Ellis decided that after the party died down tonight, he would have a talk with his son and make sure the boy knew not only about the "birds and the bees" but the responsibilities that went with that, too. Even though he still adored Hillary, he wondered now if he would have still married her, pregnant as she was with Amy.

Will and Ophelia went off to talk near a corner of the pool, each seeming to have eyes only for the other. Ellis wondered if it would help for him to ban TV and some of those movies. Life was much simpler when he'd been young. . . .

He watched Hillary flitting in and out like the social butterfly she always was, offering drinks, canapés, cheese and crackers, hors d'oeuvres of various tastes and sizes, all the while laughing and talking. She seemed to be having a good time, which was important. But she also seemed somewhat nervous, always watching their back gate to see who was approaching and the back door, to see if someone might have entered through the house.

Where was the bitch? *She's coming.*

"Something wrong, Hill?" Ellis went over to take one of the small spinach things and put his arm around her. "You're doing fine. I'm proud of you."

Her thoughts must have been too loud. Damn it! She had to do better than that. She blinked away tears as she looked up into his eyes. "No, everything's perfect . . . I just . . . I'm happy."

Hillary began to take one of the wine coolers she'd prepared for their guests. Ellis reached over, taking the glass out of her hand. "Not with the medication you're on."

"Oh, Elli. Don't be such a spoilsport!"

Her fingers tried to pry his loose from the stem of the glass. She'd insisted upon using her Lenox crystal. "Ellis! You're going to break it."

"No, Hillary. On both counts. Forget it. I don't want to see you drinking anything but sodas, juices, or waters."

With a sigh, she finally let go. "You are such a spoil-sport!" Stomping her foot, she turned on her heel with the grace of an accomplished dancer. Her eyes widened with joy—no, just relief. Rosa had arrived. Hillary's plans could go forward.

Will and Ellis played chef while Hillary returned to the kitchen, balancing lightly on her toes. There was still the guacamole to make.

CHAPTER 37

The rains came down heavily for a Texas February. Dr. Sara McNamara thought several times they were going to be stranded at the hospital. Certainly many of the fields had closed due to flood warnings and muck so think it was impossible to walk.

Schools were closed due to flash flooding and so John was with her daily. Not that she minded. Sara adored her son. Still, it did sometimes complicate matters.

Ever eager to please, John ran, fetched and carried for those in the hospital, as well as doing his usual mail run. Sara didn't mind his working. She knew he liked being useful. But half the time, he was outside without his jacket.

"John, that hat of yours can't protect you, honey." Dr. McNamara pointed to the black Stetson, exactly like Cole Morgan's, which John proudly wore, even at bedtime. It was a wonder the hat remained in one piece with all the wear it received.

"Can, too, Mom. Can, too. 'Sides Margaret asked me to check the horses 'cuz she was feared of fires."

"In this weather?" Sara McNamara asked.

John shrugged, his eyes wide. "Don't know. She just said."

"Well"—Sara tucked his shirt into his pants—"just

wear your jacket when you go outside. And maybe take an umbrella."

"Not a baby, Mom."

"You're right, John." She gave him a hug. "You're a big boy and a very capable one."

He nodded.

"I just worry about you. It's what a mother does."

John sighed and glanced upward as if to ask help of the saints above.

Sara knew that she was overprotective of him, but being a late-in-life baby, John was the last of her brood, and she didn't relish letting him go so quickly.

Only two days after their conversation, John began sneezing up a storm.

Sara knew that antibiotics didn't really work on the common cold, so she only had him drinking a lot of water to loosen the phlegm from his cough, and gave him plenty of the soup he liked.

The sneezing progressed into a nasty hacking cough that made Sara want to climb the walls when it hit her son. His face would mottle so red and pink that she almost thought he would stop breathing. It certainly seemed to a mother's ears that he was having trouble breathing, but John didn't want to have his mother do anything to take care of him.

He even resisted by wriggling around when she tried listening to his chest with her stethoscope.

His fever started going up from 99 degrees to 103.

The rains still poured from the heavenly sponges. Enough already.

She finally made him sit still while she put the cold metal on his chest. The wheezing she heard worried her. Ever susceptible to germs and diseases, Down's syndrome babies seldom lived to old age. And while her son was a highly functioning Down's, he still had more than his share of illness. Sara's main concern was her son's heart, which had been slightly enlarged at birth. "John, get dressed. I'm taking you into the hospital."

"Ah, Mom, I don't wanna work." He shivered. She pulled a jacket around his shoulders.

"I know, dearest. You're not going to work, you're going to rest. I'm telling Dr. Joshua Allister to take an X ray of your chest. I think you have pneumonia."

CHAPTER 38

Now everyone was here. At least everyone whom Hillary had wanted to come. She really didn't care that Ken or Janice Stevens hadn't appeared and she could hardly expect Cole to attend with Sophie. After all she was just being released from the hospital that day. And Hillary certainly didn't want Lisa, that slut of a girl, around her kids.

Hillary hoped the director of nursing would be all right. She knew how she'd suffered during her pregnancy with Amy. Flat on her back for almost the full nine months. That hadn't seemed to bother Ellis too much. Thinking about those days now, Hillary wondered how she'd even had the energy to make the wedding. They were living together then and he had waited on her hand and foot. Anything she wanted or craved, she could have. If only it would be like that again.

Maybe once she removed the obstacle, the prevailing winds would set the course right.

She glanced out on the patio. Rosa sat next to Ellis. Naturally. She hadn't needed her voices to tell her that. On the other side of Miss Bitch was Leroy. Why the hell didn't Rosa bother him? His wife probably wouldn't mind a bit.

Carefully using what she'd taken from Ellis's bag upstairs, Hillary made up a special bowl of guacamole. She was lucky that he had brought his sample kit home with him on Friday. He usually didn't do that, but the drug retail man had accosted Ellis just as he'd been leaving the hospital that afternoon.

From the looks of things, Rosa would be too smashed to even notice anything different. And once she did, well . . . Hillary smiled to herself and shrugged.

Amy came into the kitchen. "Can I help you, Mom? You ought to be out there with the guests, having fun."

"So should you." Hillary spontaneously kissed her daughter.

"You all right?" Amy asked. Her mother was not normally given to bursts of affection, and even less lately.

"Fine, dearest. Just fine."

Amy grabbed the special bowl of guacamole mix. "I'll take this out for you."

"Uh . . . no, it's all right. I still have to finish—"

"Looks fine to me." Before Hillary could grab the dip from her daughter, Amy had dug her index finger into the bowl and scooped up a huge glob. "Tastes fine, too. You don't need to add anything more. I'll just—"

Hillary's eyes went wide as she saw the spasms start in her daughter.

"Oh, my God. Oh, my God. Oh, Amy. Damn it! Why did you have to be such a know-it-all? Oh, my God."

Hillary ran out into the yard. "Quick. Someone! It's Amy . . ."

All the medics ran into the house, Ellis leading the bunch. He leaned down to touch his daughter. "Baby, what is it? The same kind of pain as before?"

Amy was hyperventilating. She could barely shake her head. "I . . . just . . . ate . . ."

"Someone call 911," Ellis ordered.

"Already done," Patrick responded.

"Ellis, she said something about eating . . . you have syrup of ipecac?"

He nodded and ran to the downstairs bathroom where their medical supplies were kept. The bottle was old, maybe even outdated, but it was better than nothing. He'd try getting her to vomit with this and then feed her charbroiled toast with milk, the universal antidote, which wasn't as universal as everyone would like it to be.

Running back to the kitchen, he saw that Leroy had raised her head up so that she wouldn't vomit anything back. His daughter's face was ashen, worse than when she'd had the tumor. Patrick's fingers were on her pulse. "Thready."

They heard the sound of the ambulance coming up the road, but it would be a good five minutes before the truck could weave its way back through the complex to here.

"Hang on, baby. I want you to drink some of this stuff. It's nasty but . . ." Ellis wiped her brow. "What did you eat?"

"Mom . . . Mom . . ." was all she could repeat.

He looked up and glanced around. "Where's Hillary? Has anyone seen Hillary?"

There was a slight murmur from those in the room as everyone looked around, too, almost as if they thought she might be hiding under the table or inside one of the cabinets.

"Hillary!" Ellis called out.

The retort from the .45, which Ellis always kept by his bedside was his answer.

As the paramedics came through the door, two began a code on Amy, while the second group ran upstairs.

At Hillary's side was the packaging of the drug sample she'd used. But she herself had no use for the medical crew, not anymore.

Tears in his eyes, Ellis picked up the packaging. Maybe they could still save Amy.

CHAPTER 39

The next week's M and M meeting started out with a heated debate, Meredith leading the cause, of having an in-patient locked-unit psychiatric facility on the premises. She pointed out that if they took in some of the Medicare patients, they could make some decent money for the hospital, besides serving a need for the community.

She was shocked at how alarmed some of the other staff became. "What were their impressions of 'crazies?'" she asked.

Leroy and Ty seemed to lead the group of unenlightened personnel. What with Hillary having acted out, nearly killing Rosa the night of the Christmas party, and now this Hoffner girl attempting to hang herself, they were sure that the complete lockup would be nothing short of "Looney Tunes."

"Didn't you guys have psychiatric rotations in medical school?"

Both flushed and admitted they had, but also said they hadn't paid much attention to their professors, since they hadn't been planning on that field.

Meredith shook her head, unbelieving. "But you, Leroy, at least, deal with live people even though most of the time when you have them, they're asleep or knocked out. I can understand Ty and his necromania not understanding the human psyche, but don't you realize that the *will to live* can sometimes outfunction the organs?"

The men looked at her blankly until Ellis attempted to explain to the assembly that Hillary had been fine one day and had suddenly snapped. Her chemical interactions had somehow gone haywire and that by medicating her, they were moving her back into normalcy.

Meredith was surprised when Joshua spoke up saying that he personally felt uncomfortable dealing with the mentally ill, who could sometimes be violent.

The psychiatrist just shook her head. "Mostly they are violent only when they perceive a threat to themselves. The majority of injury is done to themselves—cutting wrists, pounding heads, banging fists into walls—because they want the physical pain to take away their emotional pain. The majority of the cases we take in," she repeated, "will probably be potential suicides and"—she held up her hand seeing Leroy about to comment—"we will be properly staffed to do one to ones, fifteen-minute head checks and prevent situations like Nancy. She was able to do what she did because we were caught unawares but the signs were there. We—I—just didn't read them. But I can't do it alone. You and your staffs need to be trained to recognize when someone who has acted depressed for a time suddenly perks up and starts getting back strength. That is the time, like with Nancy, that we should have been watching." Meredith glanced down the head table and into the group of those assembled.

With Sophie still ill, Pam had once again taken over the position of DON, mostly because with the JCH coming, no one else wanted the job.

From her chair, Emma stood briefly. "Pamela, why don't you appoint a committee and investigate the possibility of this? Get some of the social workers to help you."

Pam tried protesting that she had not only the work-load of Sophie, especially with the commission breathing down their necks, but that she had her own problems, as well. However, a look from Nelson St. Clair advised Pam to accept with dignity. One did not refuse Emma Chandler and stay in her good graces.

Yet, there was something about St. Clair that made Pam just want to take Papa's shotgun to his smug face, him and his carny dress and fake toupée. She sure as shootin' did not know what was up with that man, but she knew her hackles rose every time she neared him and she knew she did not like him. Not in the least.

Fist clenched tightly, Pam nodded her approval, glared at Nelson, and smiled at Emma, while appointing Meredith to assist her.

The page came over the loudspeaker. "Dr. Johnston, please report to surgery. Stat!"

Everyone turned to look at Ellis Johnston. The maverick table took turns being paged out early so that they didn't have to stay for the full meeting, boring as it usually was.

Ellis shrugged and stood as the page came again.

"Whoa, boy." Bill Martin stood and blocked his way. "I'm onto your tricks and those of the others here." He swept his hand toward the maverick table. "I've got something important to say and I am going to be heard by all." Bill shoved Ellis back toward his chair as he moved toward the podium.

No one, except Pam, knew what to expect. And even then, she did not think Bill's announcement would cause so much reaction.

Several of the staff thought that maybe Bill was going to take responsibility for Karin's death. They should have known better.

He waited until the room was totally silent and he had their full attention.

"I have noted of late that my work has gone unappreciated by a number of you." He glared at Ellis, Patrick, Rosa, Cole, and Joshua. "For that reason, I have gone where my services will be available to all on a first-come, first-serve basis. I have started a new radiology clinic across the street. We will have nothing but state of the art equipment—"

"And state of the art prices," Cole commented.

Bill ignored the jive. "Its name, as you will note, is Martin and Associates."

"Oh? Who's going to associate with you, Dr. Martin? I think your reputation has already preceded you to the medical schools across the country," Ellis said.

Once again, Bill chose to not hear. "I wanted to let you all know that this would be my last, *my very last*, Morbidity and Mortality meeting." He turned to look at Emma, the woman he'd worked with and for during the last six years. "*I* made *your* hospital a name and *I* will very quickly take away that name."

Emma stood again. "Why you arrogant—" Her words went unfinished as her eyes opened wide and she fell to the floor.

Margaret and Allison rushed to her side. "Nana! Nana!"

Joshua Allister pushed his way in with a stethoscope and sphygmometer to measure her blood pressure, while Cole ran to get the crash cart.

No one noticed as Bill Martin walked out the door.

CHAPTER 40

Sophie hated not doing anything. Having worked practically her whole life, lying on the sofa and watching TV seemed sinful. But Ken had ordered her to take it easy, and Cole had even hired an agency nurse from the city to make sure she didn't get up.

They could have better used this nurse at the hospital to fill in some of their shortages, Sophie thought. But Emma, or rather Nelson in her stead, was working hard at cutting costs, not increasing them. Sophie only worried how this was going to look when JCH came.

She knew she shouldn't take the commission's visit personally, but it helped her not to think about her other—real—problems.

Sophie knew that if she got up and paced, or in any way showed her anxiety, the nurse would report directly to Cole, as ordered. And she could not have him questioning her. She hadn't even told him about the lupus, yet; and she did not want to tell him about Ken's insistence on an abortion.

Maybe if she spoke with the minister, it might help. Was she being punished because they hadn't married in the church? Or maybe because she'd had carnal knowledge of her husband beforehand? All the various "what ifs" flooded her thoughts.

But even if the minister hadn't known that before, God certainly did.

Suddenly Sophie was sorry about all those Sundays she had overslept and not gone to services or weekly prayer meetings, because she knew only God could help her with her dilemma now.

She wiped the tears from her eyes just as the doorbell rang.

The agency nurse, whose feet were up on the lounge chair, watching the soaps in the other room, hurried to answer.

"Mornin', ma'am." Frank Willis respectfully took his hat off as he addressed the woman. "Is Sophie at home?"

"Well . . . I . . ." the woman looked behind her. She didn't know if her boss, Dr. Morgan, would be too pleased 'bout her lettin' this police officer into the house . . . even if Miss Sophie had dated him for a bit.

"Come on in, Frank," Sophie shouted over the sound of the television. "It will be good to talk to someone who knows more than the latest scandal on *Days of Our Lives*."

The agency nurse made a face. "You'll just excuse me." She pointed Frank toward the room where Sophie rested.

"Howdy, Sophie. You doin' all right?"

She shrugged. "As well as I can be, I suppose. But I'd rather be back working. What do I owe this visit to? Pleasure I hope. Got any new gossip?"

The agency nurse peeped in. "You want some coffee, Mr. Willis?"

"Uh, no. Not right now," Frank answered.

"I'll have some tea." Sophie nodded at the woman who then disappeared.

"Arrested Bill Martin for the firebombing of his wife's car."

Sophie's eyes widened. "You're kidding? He really did it?"

"Jury'll decide that. We just know that he'd taken out a million-dollar policy on his wife not three weeks ago."

"So he hasn't confessed?"

Frank shook his head. "Keeps saying he's being framed. Tried to make us think it was Pam Roberts who did it. We're keeping an eye on her, though we haven't officially questioned her yet."

"Maybe . . . maybe they were working together." This puzzle solving with Frank was always more fun than scheduling her staff, which in desperation for something to do, she'd just started.

Frank shrugged. "Could be, but I don't know. He's made bail but I've got someone watchin' him. Don't expect him to stay in one place."

"But you didn't come over just to tell me this, did you?" She didn't like the way Frank's eyes were looking downward and his hands pushing the brim of his hat. "So?"

"Sophie . . ."

She took a deep breath. "Is it Lisa?"

" 'Fraid it is."

A spasm of pain passed through Sophie's kidneys. Was that a reaction from the stress or would the pain have come despite this? She closed her eyes, trying to deny what was real. "Tell me, Frank. What is it?"

He measured his words, waiting until the nurse had placed the cup and saucer of Earl Grey on Sophie's over-bed table. "She's been helping Margaret Chandler with the horses up at Circle C."

"You know that. What's wrong with it?"

"Not a damn thing. Neither is her taking helicopter lessons from Ms. Chandler."

Sophie sucked in her breath. She hadn't known that Margaret was teaching Lisa to fly. The girl hadn't even passed her driver's permit yet. This must be something between Lisa and Cole. Damn it. Why didn't he share these things with her? Lisa was more her daughter than his.

And then she remembered that Lisa was very much both their daughter.

"Go on, Frank." Sophie could feel herself wheezing as she tried catching her breath.

"It seems young master Warner's been doing a mighty nice business between the borders and he's been using helicopters and horses for transport."

CHAPTER 41

The town of Richmond had several bars and even more lounges, but Bill Martin had always liked the Sundowner Lounge. It was right off the 10 interstate and only took a few minutes travel. Besides, he liked the girls who worked there—a number of them had visited his bed more than once.

He sat there with four empty glasses in front of him and nursing his fifth. Bourbon straight up. The best stuff, he'd asked for. Hell, when you've spent nearly $20,000 alone just on bailing yourself out from a hellhole of a prison, and you hadn't even done anything to deserve it, you had to treat yourself right.

As he drank down another shot, he remembered that Hillary Johnston had died yesterday, too. Another one down the drain. He wasn't sure that Ellis hadn't killed her, himself, but he'd at least drove her to it. But would they prosecute their "golden boy" as they were Bill? Of course not.

And now to top everything off, his new clinic was gonna go bust. All that equipment he mortgaged for his stupid bail, and then there was going to be legal fees and then . . . he felt as if he'd gone swimming but dived in the wrong end and couldn't come up.

Staring into the amber liquid, Bill wished right now—for the umpteenth time—that he'd never asked

Karin to pick him up, never told her to park in the back, and had never taken up with Pam Roberts.

Some inner sense told Bill that Pam had had something to do with his wife's death, but just what he couldn't be sure. He knew Pam was on duty in the ER when Karin pulled into that space. Then a few minutes later the car blows sky-high, just like his future. No. That didn't work. He downed another. Even if Pam knew how to rig cars, he had seen her almost the whole time Karin had been on the phone with him. Yeah, that was right. He'd been in the ER reading an X ray when Karin had paged him.

Pammy, Pammy, Pammy. God, but she was a good lay. Knew just how to please him, squeezing her buns so tightly around him that he felt he wanted to burst the moment he entered her. And that damn cute little ass of hers. In spite of his inebriation, he felt his cock getting hard, just thinking of her. His tongue licked the edge of the glass ever so gently, but with definite purpose as he imagined himself licking Pammy's erect clit. Just couldn't get enough of that girl.

But besides wanting to marry him, which she'd been attempting to do forever and a day, she really didn't have any decent motive for setting Karin up. No, sir, she did not. Besides, he hadn't told the nurse that Karin was picking him up that day, or where she was parking. Had he?

So who was responsible? And why were the police blaming him? He motioned for Scotty, the bartender, to bring over another double.

The Sundowner was also the place where Coral May had once waitressed. Lucky for her, the breast enhancement—which damn it, had made her orbs as hard as stone, but sure did do something for the men—had helped her meet Jacob McQuade. The darling old man had been hooked as soon as Coral May sank down on him.

Having been a widower for more'n ten years, the poor guy was awfully horny, and Coral May was just as happy to provide, long as he gave her something in return. And so Jacob McQuade had married her, making her a board member of CMC, and a part of the wealthy Chandler clan. But all the money in the world hadn't gotten rid of Coral's nasal West Texas twang. That, and her stiletto heels topped off with the miniest of miniskirts and sometimes no undies, had made the Chandlers sometimes downright nasty to her. But her Jacob had stood up for her.

For ten years, they made a right handsome couple. It wasn't until her poor Jacob been taken sick and became strange-like that Coral May had had to find other amusement.

She couldn't say she was too fond of his grandkids, but they'd actually been pretty decent, especially in the light of the fire which had destroyed her home.

Living way out there on the Rocking M with only the Mex maids and ranch hands to talk to had been pretty damn boring, especially with Jacob in the hospital and afterwards. She was still upset that she couldn't have gotten that ten million her friend Salty promised her for selling him the ranch. But after the fire, she'd gotten one of Salty's development homes on a right-nice lake—manmade, of course, but it was pretty none the less.

However, the neighbors, which she had wanted so desperately, were so stuck-up here. You'd think they were better even than the Chandlers themselves. Well, as it turned out, Coral didn't want to be friends with them, no how.

She much preferred coming back here to the Sundowner, sitting on the piano, her legs crossed and uncrossed, sometimes singing a song, sometimes even helping Barb with the waitressing when it got a bit heavy. Most times the piano player, a sweet young boy, would play songs 'specially dedicated to her. What more could Coral May ask for? Friends who really were there for her.

Almost as soon as she walked in that night, she saw Bill Martin. Poor Billy. She knew that he couldn't have murdered Karin. He'd always talked so lovingly of her, even while he'd be screwing Coral May. She wished she could have told Karin that, but somehow she didn't think the late Mrs. Martin would have appreciated being told that. Coral May knew that she would've wanted to hear such talk, but then again, she was different.

"How you doin'?"

Billy looked up at her, blinking as he tried to focus. It took a moment before he recognized Coral May.

"Go 'way." He waved her out toward the piano.

"Aw, Billy. You don't mean that."

"Sure I do. Jus' got out of jail. Everyone thinks I killed Karin . . ." His words were the most slurred she'd ever heard him. "Bet you do, too."

"Aw, Billy. I sure don't. I know how much you loved your wife."

" 'Sright. Only she . . . never understood. Loved her to bits."

Coral May reached under the table. When you'd had as much experience as she, it didn't take very long to undo a zipper.

She smiled, feeling the hardness of his cock and knowing that it was getting harder and harder as she stroked it. "I think you just need some consolation." Coral guided his big long fingers up to her naked crotch. Must have just been pure luck that today of all days she hadn't worn those confining underpants.

Dr. Bill Martin might have been drunk, but he was no fool. "I think I ought t'take you home before it gets too late."

Coral pressed her fingers to her lips and then to his rigid penis. "No. I think I oughta take you home. I'm just down the road here."

He grinned and stood unsteadily. "Good t'have friends like you, Coral May."

CHAPTER 42

Emma Chandler couldn't believe all this evil was happening to her family. It was all she could do to stand upright when the news came to her.

Immediately, she phoned the gas station where her granddaughter and her fiancé were waiting for one of the ranch hands to come pick them up.

She was sure now that Margaret had not told her everything, so she tried talking with Joshua, but the young upstart doctor from New York who planned to marry her granddaughter wasn't telling tales.

Returning to the trial, she tried smiling at Allison, but somehow her face muscles didn't want to move.

Topping off the terrible day was the fact that her friend, Judge Luis Mendoza, who had eaten at her table and drank her wines, not only took away Allison's driving license for a year, but fined her five hundred thousand a year for Jinx's constant care *and* he wanted a record of her attending those silly alcoholic meetings.

Of course, she knew Allison was contrite. The girl had done wrong and already ran to those crazy meetings at the drop of a hat. Did she or Luis think they would really work? Goddamn-old-fashioned willpower was what did it. You just made up your mind to do something, and it was done. Just those words alone had worked for Emma Chandler since the day she'd escaped from the Ozarks.

Maybe that's why she liked Pam so much. The gal had spunk, just like she had had at Pam's age. Much as she adored her grandbabies, they had had a pampered life from the time of conception. 'Course, they probably only remembered from the age of three or four onward.

Oh, she knew that her kinfolk thought the young Pam walked all over her. And maybe she did. And maybe Emma let her. There was a force surrounding Pam Roberts that Emma wanted to nourish and she would do so, no matter what anyone said.

She stood up, grasping the seat in front of her as dizziness overtook her. Everything was in a haze. Emma could hear voices but they spoke as if in a wind tunnel.

She glanced around for her granddaughter. Allison's face seemed frozen in time, staring at her Nana.

Emma tried telling Allison that she was fine. Just fine. But the words wouldn't come.

Rushing to the ER, Cole Morgan realized almost at once that the matriarch of Chandler Springs had suffered a stroke. Her blood pressure was 220 over 170 and her pulse sped along like a runaway locomotive.

"Get her to ICU," he ordered after he'd given her Catapres to bring down her blood pressure. "I want her hooked up to every possible monitor we have."

As the orderly pushed the gurney toward the intensive care, Allison broke down sobbing. She knew that it was her reckless behavior which had caused Nana's stroke . . . and suddenly she started feeling that her whole life to this point had been worthless.

Nothing Meredith nor Margaret could say helped Allison feel better. It was her fault that this had happened, Allison told them, and she planned to do something about it.

CHAPTER 43

It was time to meet him. The man who'd been making those calls and leaving those notes. Pam wasn't scared. Not much really. That is not until the fella said that he'd wired up the wrong car. The person scheduled to die that night had been Pam. It was Karin's unfortunate mistake to park in the back, next to Pam's car.

Everyone in town knew about the firebomb destroying Karin's car and her with it. But not everyone knew Pam had also been parked in the back, too. He made it sound as if it had been her car Bill tried to have firebombed, only the person he hired picked the wrong vehicle.

It made her antsy as hell. Could be anyone. Even one of the coppers, though she didn't think it was. They weren't that smart. Besides, they'd have no reason to be blackmailing her. And she was sure as positive that Billy hadn't tried killing her.

Pam clutched her daddy's shotgun, which she'd brought with her, just in case. Of course, it was hidden beneath her all-weather cape. She paced and glanced at her watch. They were supposed to have met five minutes ago. Where was this creep?

She suspected that it might be her brother Randy, though it shocked her when she first thought of that. After all she'd done for the boy, how could he be this ungrateful and frighten his older sister half to death?

Pam never would have turned her thoughts toward her siblings until Daddy called.

Wouldn't say a damn where he'd gotten her number or what had happened in the past. All he'd say was he wanted some of Emma's money and that it was coming to him, one way or the other. He instructed his daughter with his high-and-mighty attitude that he wanted a nice new vehicle, maybe one of those Ford double-cab pickups with the works: air conditioning, heat, radio, and all.

"Do you know how much those damn things cost?" Pam had asked him, aghast that her father would even ask for such a thing.

'Course he knew. That's why he was asking. He was sure that Emma could afford it even if she, his darling daughter, couldn't.

What right did he have to gain anything from Emma's money? It wasn't like he'd done much to help Pam. That's why she'd left home so early.

Her pa laughed when she said that. "Hell, Pammy girl, you wouldn't have known a damn thing 'bout pleasin' a man, leastwise I hadn't showed you." She could hear him spitting out the tobacco he'd just chewed and she wished he'd up and die of throat cancer already.

Granny used to say that the plum rots in the same orchard as the prune. Boy, was that the truth.

But so far, now nearly a half hour after the supposed meeting time, no one had come.

Pam shivered. She'd forgotten just how cold it got standing on these street corners, especially in the plains of Texas.

A jangling bell jarred her. Pam spun around to see that the phone in the booth on the corner was ringing.

Hesitantly, she approached it.

The ringing continued and seemed to vibrate in her ears.

She reached for the phone, but jumped back from it as she touched it. Like the hot coals of Satan, Granny Dottie would have said.

"Shit!" She wasn't afraid of no telephone.

Her hand reached out again. She just wanted to end that damn ringing. Most probably it was just a wrong number.

"Well, hello, Miss Roberts. I wondered just how long it would take for you to pick up." The voice was smooth. Too smooth to be her brother's. But it was vaguely familiar.

"Who is this?" Pam demanded.

The laughter annoyed her.

"Who the hell in tarnation is this?"

"Do you want to guess and go for the jackpot, little lady, or would you like another try at the kewpie doll?"

"Damn it! I demand to know who you are and what the f____ do you want from me?"

"Such language. Such language. Do you really think I would take a chance meeting you with your father's shotgun so handy under your cape."

Pam dropped the phone, stepped out of the phone booth, and swept her gaze around the area. Empty. How the f____ had he known she had Pa's gun . . . and under her coat at that!

Picking up the phone again, she was prepared to give him a bit of her mind, when he interrupted her before the words reached her mouth. "Now, you will listen to me, Miss Roberts, or whatever you want to call yourself, you will continue with your plans to ruin Emma Chandler and take over her fortune—"

"Bill Martin, is that you? Goddamn you, Bill Martin."

The smooth laugh was just like Satan, himself.

"Afraid to disappoint you, but this is not Dr. Martin, Pamela. He knows nothing of your plans: attempted murder of his wife Karin by injecting excess heparin into her IV, and that fall down the steps? I'm sure he wouldn't be very pleased, especially since he is now Mr. Willis's prime suspect."

"You can't prove anything!" Fear was making her talk fast.

"Are you a gambler, honey? 'Cuz if you are, call my bets."

Pam took a deep breath and tried steadying herself. "What the hell do you want with me?"

"Just what you've always wanted for yourself. Emma Chandler's fortune. And if my partner and I don't see some action soon, you'll be hearing from the police."

"Partner?" Pam shouted into the phone. "What's this about a partner? Who the hell is your partner?"

Her only answer was the clicking of the phone line.

CHAPTER 44

The wedding of Dr. Joshua Allister and Margaret Chandler loomed on the horizon. It should have been the season's society event and yet, Margaret couldn't even begin to think about the invitations, the catering, the band, or even her dress. Weddings were just a lot of fuss and bother, and if it weren't for Nana wanting a big party, Margaret would have been just as happy to run off somewhere, maybe even Las Vegas. She couldn't even decide what words to use on the invitation.

Joshua was no help. He said he didn't care. That whatever she wanted was fine with him. But Margaret knew it wasn't.

She knew that Nana, the Allisters, and all of Texas would be mortified if she worded it the wrong way. Somehow, it seemed as if putting the words to paper would somehow nullify them.

She wasn't quite sure, but it seemed to her that Joshua relished the hustle and bustle of the Chandler-created social gatherings. Guests Emma had invited listed almost like a Who's Who in Houston and even encompassing the whole state of Texas, not to mention a few Washingtonians and international trendsetters.

Joshua's family couldn't help but be awed by the plans Nana had already made.

Already made. Those were the words. Margaret told

herself that with Nana in the hospital, trying to recover from that stroke, there was absolutely no way she could even think of the wedding. And actually that was the best thing Margaret could say right now.

Emma had been lucky. Joshua's X ray had been able to pinpoint the aneurysm which had just burst and with lightning speed, and the matriarch had been propelled into surgery.

Within seventy-two hours of the surgery, the edema had begun subsiding and a minimal amount of speech had returned to Emma. She still had difficulty walking, and found it impossible to negotiate with a walker. Often in her frustration, Emma would begin to laugh instead of cry. But that was common with stroke victims.

Some of her handicap would remain, but with luck and work, Rosa felt confident that their Emma would return to at least ninety percent of function. There was no one who could fight harder than Emma Chandler when she wanted something, and everyone knew that returning to the life she'd known was something the Chandler matriarch very much desired.

Allison and Margaret visited Nana daily, and sometimes stayed to help her with her physical therapy. Often Allison took therapy for her leg at the same time as her grandmother so that she could look after the older woman.

Of course, Margaret had to drive when they went anywhere. She wondered if her sister felt bitter about that, but if she did, Allison didn't show it.

Her younger sister had never been sensitive to anyone's needs but her own and so it surprised Margaret even more when Allison cornered her and demanded they talk about Margaret's problem.

At first the horsewoman resisted, denying that anything was going wrong.

"Come off it, Ret, I know you just about as well as I know me."

Margaret wanted to laugh. Her sister hadn't known that she, Margaret, had been totally and helplessly in love with Allison's boyfriend. And Allison didn't know that Margaret had prayed and hoped for him to give her sister up, to notice her.

But now that he had and now that they were to be married, it felt altogether different.

"Well, you love him, don't you?" Allison asked.

"Did you?"

"That's not the question, Ret." Allison glanced down at her own painted toe nails. Allison herself feared that she could never really feel love. She just seemed to hop from one bed to another, seeking sexual pleasure and never really connecting . . . not with Joshua, who would have been a grand catch, nor with Jinx, her muscular he-man who'd been a fabulous lover. Always there was a part of Allison that stayed off to the side while she "watched" her other self indulging and playing.

"Come on. Answer me," Allison insisted. "What's going on with you, two? I hardly see him here anymore and there's definitely a strain. You guys have a fight?"

Margaret shook her head. The hot tears burned down past her repaired scar, washing away the makeup she'd learned to apply so carefully. "I don't know. I just . . . don't know." Her voice choked in her throat. Then she pulled forth the romantic letter from another woman she'd found in Joshua's apartment. Of course, he'd told her it was nothing, and that he did not even know the woman who wrote this, but how could she believe him? He'd tried talking his way out of New York, but this . . . no, it had to be true.

She was shocked as Allison took her sister into her arms, stroking her hair. There had been times growing up that she had absolutely hated Allison for being so beautiful; and other times for acting so callous. Even though they were devoted to each other, she had never thought her baby sister capable of really taking responsibility for her actions or of having compassion beyond her own problems.

"You know what I think it is?"

Margaret sniffled and tried quelling her tears. "What?"

"I think you need a bit of a vacation. As soon as Nana starts looking better, why don't you and I go visit your friend Katherine in Beverly Hills?"

CHAPTER 45

Emma gritted her teeth as she stumbled and tried the parallel bars again. This re-learning to walk was like riding a bicycle, she told herself. She had done it once and Emma was sure she could do it again. It would just take a little time and maybe a few falls, but that was all right. As long as she worked at it, Emma would be happy.

Actually Rosa had told her that considering the placement of the aneurysm and what her blood pressure had been reading, Emma had made remarkable progress in returning to a functioning life. It didn't seem to matter to Rosa that every moment seemed to stretch out for Emma and that she was impatient, no, frustrated, with her lack of progress.

Meredith had told her that this feeling was normal, but it wasn't something Emma liked. Since she'd married Caleb Chandler nearly fifty years ago, Emma had become used to asking for something and achieving or receiving it immediately, if not sooner. No one had dared to cross Emma Chandler . . . except herself, it seemed. She'd forgotten what it was like to struggle for a goal. Maybe the Lord was trying to teach her a lesson. She'd always been an obstinate learner. Could be, Emma thought, she should consider changing her ways.

Just to make sure that she wasn't caught unawares,

Emma had her nurse phone for her lawyer Ronald Roundtree. It was time she amended her will.

Sophie didn't want to confront Lisa, but she had to find out if Frank was correct. Bad enough her daughter had been using drugs and overdosed not once but twice, but if she actually aided the dealer . . . no, Sophie would not tolerate that. Even if it meant sending the girl out of town. Cole had a cousin in Chicago, she thought.

The police chief had talked of returning when Lisa came back because he also wanted to ask her questions. If only the girl came home before Frank came back.

Exhausted as she was, Sophie had dismissed the nurse and waited up for her daughter to return. She hoped that they could hash this thing out before Cole returned. She knew he could probably handle it better than she could, especially since, magically, Lisa seemed to listen to him—at least a larger percent of the time than she heard her mother. But she also did not want Cole thinking what a mess she had made of raising the girl.

As she heard Lisa's key turning in the lock, Sophie hurried back to the sofa. It wouldn't do to let Lisa think something was wrong.

According to what the investigators could reconstruct from the remains of the Mercury convertible, similar chemicals had been used in both Karin's fiery death and in Joshua's car fire.

"So, besides Bill Martin, who hates both of us?" Joshua asked Frank. The head of Chandler Springs police didn't know what to say.

"We're keeping the doctor under surveillance, but he did post bond on Mrs. Martin's death, and I don't want to go arresting him unnecessarily again, unless we have more than circumstantial evidence, that is. After all, he's a well-known man in these parts.

Margaret glared at the officer. "So, what you're saying is that because Bill Martin is rich, white, and a taxpayer here, and George Dupree is a poor black kid from Chicago's slums, with just his sister, a meagerly paid nurse, to help him, that you would rather accuse George."

"Whoa now!" Frank Willis pushed his hat far back on his head, catching it before it could fall off. "I think, Miss Chandler, if you're going to talk about meager pay, you ought to look in the mirror. Aren't you the one who pays Avon Dupree her *meager* salary?"

Joshua knew Margaret wanted to haul off at the policeman, so he put his hand on her leg, warning her to keep calm. She took a deep breath and gave a slight nod.

"Yes, Frank. I *am* part of the hospital board. But the nurses' pay is not my sole decision. However, I think you're missing the point."

He shrugged. "Maybe I am, and maybe I'm not. All I know is that things were pretty quiet when that black kid was in custody and jist as soon as that sister of his got together the money to bail him out . . . things started happening again."

"Bullshit! Now who's talking about circumstantial evidence?" Margaret stood abruptly. "If our car was tampered with, then I want you to find the culprit. The real culprit. Not some poor kid you hooked because you didn't like the color of his skin." Her eyes blazed. "Come on, Josh. We have work to do."

CHAPTER 46

"Where have you been lately, me love?" Sean O'Neill, Dr. Meredith Fischer's sometime lover and chemical dependency psychologist, who worked in her department, was sprawled out on her leather couch, waiting for her as she turned the key to her office.

Meredith stared blankly at him. "What do you mean, Sean? I've been here working, at my apartment—"

"No, you have not." The huge Irishman swung his long legs up off the sofa as he stood. His red hair had been tousled by his reclining position and now it stood up like little horns around his head, matching the Satanic temper he felt rising. "I have been watching yer place. I have called at all hours. I have kept tabs of your office hours here. . . . Loretta has told me when you've been in and . . ."

She stared at him, unable to believe this was the man she loved; the one she wanted so desperately, hoping one day that he would love her as she had always done him, and perhaps that one day, she would give her hand in marriage to him. He had asked *her* secretary to spy on her!

"Just what are you saying, Sean?" Meredith sank down into the Queen Anne chair opposite her desk. "Are you accusing me of seeing another man?"

"If the shoe fits—" he began the cliché.

"Well, it doesn't." She swiveled her body around to

face her paperwork and tried controlling her anger. She wasn't ready to talk to him about her memories and everything else she was discovering. Not just yet. "Now, if you'll excuse me, Mr. O'Neill, I have a report to write. And I believe you have a group starting in"—she glanced at her watch—"fifteen minutes."

"Screw the fuckin' group." Sean advanced toward her. "I want to know who you've been seein'. I'm a man. I have me rights you know."

Meredith shook her head. She couldn't believe she was hearing this. "Rights? What rights?" Meredith held out her left hand. "Oh, you're a man all right, but I don't see any rings on my finger proclaiming those rights over me." She waved the one that might one day hold an engagement ring. "And even if I did, even if we were married, those rights you mention would still be limited by the law."

"Damn it, woman. I've seen ya with that Jew boy, talking and laughing it up."

Meredith sucked in her breath so sharply that it hurt. It actually felt like a knife sticking in her ribs. She glared at her lover and somehow managed to keep her voice even. "Mr. Mendelson is a man and he happens to be a doctor. I have every right to discuss his grandfather's case with him, especially in the light of his new tests."

"Over lunch?"

Meredith tried recalling when she and Ari had eaten lunch together and then she remembered that they'd had coffee the other morning just after she'd made her rounds. Because he kept kosher like his grandfather, black coffee was all he would have. He told her that some of his friends wouldn't even have that in a public place that hadn't been certified by a rabbi.

Their conversation had mainly centered on old Julius, and his depression over the fact that he was going to need a new kidney, but then, their talk had gone off on a tangent. She had started asking Ari about Maimonides and he'd been impressed with the little knowledge she had. When Ari had questioned her, she had inhaled and then jumped into what she considered the deep end, telling him that she was Jewish, at least by birth, and had just begun rediscovering some things from her childhood.

Ari had told her about a rabbi, Shlomo Schwartz, whose specialty was bringing Jews back into the fold and teaching them about their heritage, culture, and history. As Ari had put it, Rabbi Schwartz was a one-man act functioning as a dozen or more.

When he'd come to see his grandfather the next time, Ari had brought her a list of the classes the rabbi taught at his Chai center.

And Meredith had gone to a couple of them and thought she wanted to attend more, as soon as her schedule lightened up. She realized that was probably where she'd been when Sean had been trying to find her.

What was so important that he had to know her whereabouts?

"Sean, there is nothing between Mr. Mendelson and myself except the professional courtesy of sharing knowledge about his grandfather. And if we laughed a bit . . ." She shrugged. "For your information, though, we did not eat lunch. I ate a sweet roll with my coffee. He had coffee only. Hardly a date in my book."

"Right. I get it now. Our food isn't good enough for the pair of them, for none of them. That's why we have t'go to the expense and trouble of importing delicacies just for the *chosen* one."

Meredith stood. "*You* are not personally paying the bill for Mr. Ciss's kosher food. If you have a problem with this patient being here, bring it up at the M and M.

"Now I suggest you get out of my office." She looked toward the glass pyramid clock on her table. "You have five minutes to your group."

"So I'll be late. I gotta know what's going on with you, Merry."

"Why?" Furious, the psychiatrist walked to her door and opened it. "Oh, you're allowed to run around and have affairs all over the place with women like Pam Roberts, who's probably slept with half the hospital, but I'm not even allowed to *talk* to any other man." She shook her head. "You have the wrong person here. Ever since Pam threw you over . . ." She stared at him. "It's not been the same. Maybe we're not meant for each other."

Tears were in Sean's eyes. "For Christ's sake, Merry. Have pity. It's just that . . . I mean, doncha know what'll happen if you get involved with them Christ killers? Why they suck your blood and let you scream for mercy while you're dying on their cross. And especially now when the Easter and risin' of our Lord is upon us. That's when they always need the blood. Vampires. One and all. Four cups of red blood they drink. They claim it's wine, but me mam knew better. She saw them in action once."

Meredith's eyes went wide. Her stomach turned, nauseated. "Sean, do you really believe that nonsense? You're an educated man. I mean, I might expect that from some of the farmers, or peasants like your mother, or maybe even the punks who hang around the malls, but you?"

Sean shook his head. "Ain't nonsense, Merry. Truly. I know."

Her hand trembled. She was glad she held on to the door for support. Her voice, barely recognizable as her own, whispered, "No, Sean, you do not know." She paused, trying to get her strength and touching the star of David that she'd started wearing under her blouse. "I am one of *those* . . . those people . . . What did you say we were, Christ killers?"

"Oh, my sweet Lord. Holy mother of Jesus!" Sean crossed himself as he grabbed her by the shoulders. "Merry, my Merry, tell me that it's not so." He began sobbing like a baby, resting his head on her shoulder, so she could feel his tears wetting the fabric of her silk blouse. "Merry, it just cannot be. You've been bewitched by them people. I know they can do it. I've seen it done."

Pain surrounded her head. Meredith thought she probably knew what it felt like to wear a crown of thorns. She shook Sean off and stepped back. Pulling the small star out of its hiding place, she flashed the plain symbol in front of him. "Believe it, Sean. It's true."

With what could only be called a look of disgust, Sean O'Neill turned from her and ran out of the door as if Satan himself chased the Irishman.

Behind him, Meredith shut the door slowly, and as she heard the latch clicking into place, she sank down onto her sofa and began crying. Who was she? What did she do now?

CHAPTER 47

Carrie Harper stood gaga, mouth gaping as she watched the Joint Commission inspection team pass through the unit she was working in.

They actually used the white-glove test for checking the dust. She watched as they went into the medication room, counting narcotics and checking that the pharmacy sheets for the past few months reflected an accurate number. *Thank you, Lord Jesus for not having me on meds today*, Carrie thought. She just knew that even if she hadn't made any mistakes, they would probably find some, even if they had to create them. Or maybe someone else would and blame it on her. Yeah, she wouldn't put it past them. Had to watch your back, your front and just about everywhere that someone could sneak a trick past you.

She watched, holding her breath, as the committee sat down at the charting desk and randomly picked up charts. *Please Jesus*, she prayed, *don't let them choose one of mine. 'Cuz I just know they'll find a mistake*.

Carrie hoped she was unobtrusive as she stood in the corner, watching "them," anxiously swaying from foot to foot, almost like a young child trying to hold her bladder, as her palms sweated. The JCH had checked charts on every floor and every unit looking for proper utilization reviews, correct diagnoses, doctors' notes, graphics, and medications properly charted and the nursing notes following an orderly progress, not to mention all the legal papers. This was their last stop.

Carrie knew she would just die if *they* didn't pass the hospital all 'cuz of her.

Oh, my God, oh, Jesus help me. She felt faint as they picked up one of the charts she had written on yesterday. *Please Jesus don't let them know it was me.*

She thought of all the mistakes she'd made in the past week alone. Good thing Mrs. Morgan hadn't been on duty to see her giving the wrong medication to the wrong patient. Carrie had waited, worried that somehow the patient would have side effects or problems from the narcotic, and she was relieved when the old man had only just slept a bit heavier than usual. But then she had to pretend that she'd lost one of those small little Demerols and convinced Wendy to cosign for the missing drug. It was such a big hassle, but she knew that if she didn't do it this way, Hicks, the patient who was supposed t'have gotten the med, would have surely complained, and then they'd see that she had charted it out to her and think she was using the stuff herself.

Carrie knew she wasn't as bright as everyone else but she wasn't *that* stupid.

She shifted feet again. So far so good. Carrie knew she should be out on the floor. She still had two dressings to change, an Intake and Output to record, and an IV to check, but this was like a magnet drawing her to stay.

Jesus, maybe she did have to pee. She didn't want to leave the spot where she was, but it would be so embarrassing to do it here.

Closing her eyes, Carrie begged the Lord for some guidance. Even before she'd finished her prayers, she heard them talking and caught her breath just like it was a Frisbee headed for her stomach.

"Will you look at this? Two tests ordered by the doctor and no mention of it in the nurses' notes or cardex." That was the tall one with the turban on her head.

Carrie wanted the floor to open its trapdoor and swallow her, but that didn't happen. Her anxiety increased as she listened on.

"No graphics charted in this one either."

Damn! Had she forgot those graphs? Sometimes when she was in a rush, 'specially at the end of a shift, Carrie just pushed by everything and jotted her notes. Once or twice she had actually written a note that she meant for one of her other patients, and then she had to take out the whole page and studiously copy over everything on that page from the other nurses, so that no one would know she'd made the mistake. 'Course, Carrie knew that was supposed t'be illegal, but she didn't see why it should be. As long as what she said was the same thing as what they said, why should the courts care?

Then again she was always forgetting what the charting initials SOAP (symptoms, observation, actions taken to relieve the symptoms, probable outcome or result) meant. Half the time she didn't even list them and when she did, they were squeezed in between two sentences and not on a separate line as Mrs. Morgan had shown her.

The short fat one with the dark curly hair picked up the chart of the patient she'd had three days ago. Oh, shit. It was Mr. Williams's. Now she was in for it.

The episode of the IV in the emergency room flashed through her mind with the horror of one of them chainsaw massacre movies she always watched. Jesus, she'd rather be living though that right now than this. She sure would.

Then the L.V.N. recalled that she hadn't even charted that IV boo-boo.

Relief flooded her like a hot shower washing off her shame. 'Course they would get the hospital on not having noted that IV, but Carrie didn't care as long as *she* was off the hook. She never even checked back about that charting. Maybe Jennifer had written it up. But Jennifer hadn't told Mrs. Morgan about her . . . so . . . it didn't matter.

She heard the fat one comment about a patient who had been scheduled for surgery having to stay on a day longer because someone had given him breakfast after he'd been ordered to be NPO (without anything to eat) before the operating room came for him.

Carrie knew she'd been the someone, but hoped that the patient hadn't ratted on her. She'd just thought it was damn cruel to keep breakfast from them, especially when the patient was so hungry. Besides, she was pretty sure the old man didn't mind an extra day of rest. So, what did it matter?

Carrie tried shaking her head to get the buzzing sensation out of her ears.

"Miss Harper?"

Carrie spun around, damn sure now that she'd been caught and would get fired for it. Isn't that what Pa said they did to eavesdroppers? Shit! She felt some of that pee get loose and squeezed her legs tighter together.

"Yes . . . ?" She wiped her hands on her uniform.

Jesus thank you. It was only Mrs. Hicks wanting another Demerol pill.

Carrie glanced at the committee, busy with the charts. She wasn't on meds today, but she knew where Wendy had put the keys while she was on break. She should, she knew, tell Mrs. Hicks to wait until Wendy came back, but what did it matter a few minutes more or less if she could help now? After all, she had become a nurse to help people, hadn't she?

"Sure. Course. I'll bring ya one right away."

Carrie frowned as she checked the narcotic sheet. Mrs. Hicks had just had the Demerol two hours ago. Even though the order read PRN (as needed) it also said only every four hours. The woman was supposed to wait four hours between her pills. But the patient was in pain. Now how could Carrie make her wait? It made her feel really bad when she had to say things like that to those patients.

Maybe ... Carrie flipped through the medication book and saw that Mrs. Elton also had Demerol ordered *and* she hadn't had it all day long.

Her lower lip stuck out as she considered what she was doing. Well, she was pretty sure Mrs. Elton wouldn't be asking for her pain meds, at least not until the next shift, and then they could deal with the problem.

Without more consideration, Carrie charted out the Demerol under Mrs. Elton's name. A pill was a pill. She didn't really think it mattered. Two hours or four.

Medication and a cup of water in hand, Carrie hurried toward her patient's room. She'd heard enough of the commission's comments to know that they didn't have much of a heart, so she was sure no one in their right mind would heed them.

Satisfied with what she had done, Carrie hurriedly emptied her bladder, and then went about her business.

At two forty-five P.M., she clocked out. It was fifteen minutes to the end of shift, actually forty-five if you wanted to be picky because you were supposed to wait and watch the nurses' station while the evening shift had report. But how many people did they need to watch one counter? Carrie was tired and she had worked hard today. It didn't hurt if she left a bit early.

Wendy had been busy with her own patients and hadn't needed to give any other medications, so Carrie forgot to tell her about the Demerol. Well, she'd see it when she counted out.

It was only when she reached home that she realized she'd forgotten to finish her charting and that she still had the medication keys in her pocket.

CHAPTER 48

Unlike Karin's wake, the funeral for Hillary Johnston was a small quiet affair with just the immediate family in attendance. Her folks had flown in from Dallas, but her brother hadn't even wanted to take off work.

Amy had recovered sufficiently from the poisoning to have a pass for a few hours. She had sat there numbly listening to the minister eulogize her mother, a woman Amy had long forgotten knowing.

Ellis, too, scarcely recognized the person whom the minister described and yet, somewhere in the past, Hillary had been that fun-loving, sensitive, sweet girl. Hillary's body had been cremated. He and the kids would scatter the ashes out at sea. Hillary had always liked the water.

Tears spilled over onto his cheeks. He blamed himself for not watching her more carefully, for having brought home those samples from the detail man on Friday and not at least keeping them locked up in the car. But if she had wanted to do something, and she obviously had, Hillary would have found another way. Still, he wondered if it hadn't been partially his fault. He had loved her. Why couldn't he have done anything to save her?

Rosa stood next to him. Merely a colleague. Nothing more. "You tried your best, Ellis."

"Did I? Really?" The searching note was impossible

to keep out of his voice. "What would happen if I had moved back to Houston as she wanted? Don't you think she would have been happier?"

Standing on Ellis's other side, Meredith touched his arm lightly. "Probably not. Don't fool yourself, Ellis. A personality like Hillary's would have found other things to be unhappy with there. She would most likely have accused you of other relationships at whatever new hospital you moved into."

"Thanks, Meredith." He gave her a slight smile. "Maybe I might take advantage of your services in a few days."

"Be my guest. Professional courtesy." Very few doctors ever charged other doctors or their families for services rendered. It was a quid pro quo.

Ellis looked at her a long moment and then nodded. He had heard the rumors—he wasn't sure where they had come from—but someone had told him that Meredith was Jewish. Ellis had found that fascinating, more especially because no one had known it in all the fifteen years she'd served at the CMC.

He didn't know how Emma Chandler thought about it, but while it didn't bother him, he knew that some of the other doctors and staff at CMC were distinctly uncomfortable around her now. Was that causing her difficulty with her patients? Or with being chief of staff?

The service concluded, Ellis walked forward and took the urn of ashes. The last fragments of his marriage.

CHAPTER 49

Ian Williams turned restlessly in his bed. The pain in his chest just about killed him and he wasn't too sure about his arm and shoulder either, both of which felt as if they had been wrenched from their sockets.

Was it time for more medication yet? Damn, he hated this dependence on drugs. He'd had enough of that shit in the war. Still didn't make sense to him how President Johnson could pull out the way he had done, not with so many lives at stake and so much already sacrificed. And look what it had gotten them. Nothing. *Nada*. The place had reverted back to its former self. What a stupid waste!

Ian realized that he hadn't thought of the war in donkey's years. His thoughts drifted as he tried focusing on something other than pain. Donkey's years. He'd gotten that expression from one of his English "mates." Hadn't thought of Brian Edwards in a long time either.

He pressed the call bell and his eyes widened as his angel, Stauton, came in to find out his need.

"Baby, oh, baby."

Jennifer sighed. "What do you want, Mr. Williams?"

"Ian, sweetheart. Please."

Her glare was enough to silence him. "I'll check about your pain medication," she told him and quickly disappeared. The man made her feel definitely uneasy.

So why had she agreed to have him included in her assignment list this afternoon?

Jennifer had just started the shift but it felt as if she'd been on most of the day already. She actually hadn't, but she had been in the hospital compound itself since ten this morning.

The Lockhursts had said they were arriving at eleven to transfer Angel to a hospital closer to their home.

With tears in her eyes, Jennifer had combed the little girl's straight black hair over her white bandages. Physically, the girl was healing nicely, but she was still listless and barely talking. Jennifer hoped the Lockhursts would make sure their new daughter received some psychological counseling.

Bathing Angel, Jennifer dressed her in an outfit that she had bought for the girl, herself. *It was just from Sears*, Jennifer rationalized, meaning that it really hadn't cost her that much. But the fact still remained she had driven thirty miles to the Sears complex in Richmond to purchase this. *And other things, too*, Jennifer told herself.

Her thoughts didn't help the awful ache she felt as she prepared Angel for her new parents.

By eleven-thirty A.M., neither husband nor wife had shown.

She held Angel, rocking her gently, and feeding her lunch, thankful that she hadn't canceled the midday meal.

Noontime. She put the girl down for a nap and went to the desk and put a call into their hotel.

"Checked out?" Jennifer echoed the words of the clerk. "But that's . . ." Then she realized, of course, they would have checked out. They were headed here to pick up their daughter, and then they were flying home.

Tears formed in her eyes. Damn, she wished she wasn't so attached to the little girl. She wished the kid didn't remind her so much of Lin, opening up that wound which had never really healed.

Busying herself with catchup work, a care plan she had to finish on one of her primary patients, and some research on hematomas of the brain and the sometimes ensuing hydrocephalic syndrome, she found her gaze wandering down the hall toward Angel's room. She listened with the attention of a concerned mother for the waking of her child.

Two forty-five. Time to go toward the east wing where she was scheduled to work today. Maybe she could get someone to switch with her so that she could stay in Peds.

Immediately after report, she'd run back to Angel's room. The baby still slept.

Jennifer stroked the girl's smooth skin. "I wish I could be your mother."

"Well, such things are always possible."

Jennifer quickly wiped the tears from her eyes as she saw Mr. Lockhurst standing there. "Oh. Hi! I wondered what happened to you."

He nodded. "I'm sure you did. And I'm sorry we didn't call you." He paused and sat on the single guest chair in the room. "My wife and I have had some very heavy discussions over the past few days."

"Oh. Sure." Damn, she felt like a teenager being caught making out. "I mean, it's a heavy thing adopting, especially from a country where you don't know about the culture. I could send you some books on China if you wanted. I—"

The businessman shook his head. "I won't need them. My wife is concerned . . . well, I think you overheard some of her thoughts." He frowned. "Anyway, after much consideration, we decided we weren't going to take Angel."

"You mean not take her back today. You mean wait for a few more weeks for her to heal more."

"No, Miss Stauton. I mean not take her at all. Have her returned to the agency that sponsored her in the hopes they could find someone else who might want her more."

"But . . . but you can't do that. I mean, you uprooted her from the only home she knew and now just when she was getting used to your presence, you abandon her. Don't you realize what that is going to do to her psyche?"

Lockhurst frowned. "I understand that. And believe me, it worried me. But I didn't think I could subject Angel to my wife's . . . whims."

Jennifer wet her lips like a child being offered her favorite candy and told she could have it only on certain conditions.

She touched the girl's soft warm cheek with such longing. But how could she? She'd have to hire a housekeeper to watch the baby when she was at work, and what about when she worked a double or even triple? Did she even make enough to take care of a child? It didn't matter about her dating life. She didn't have any. But there wasn't enough room in her current apartment; she'd have to ask the manager if there were any two bedrooms coming up. Her head swam with thoughts both positive and negative and for that moment time stood still.

"So, will you take her off our hands?"

Jennifer couldn't believe he'd put it that way. She only hoped that he didn't plan on adopting any other kids.

Afraid to make any commitment that she couldn't

meet, Jennifer said, "Let me make some phone calls. Are you leaving right now?"

He shook his head. "My wife has gone ahead, but I'll stay here in town until this thing is settled."

Thing? She knew then definitely that she had no choice but to adopt the Chinese girl.

"So. What do you think, Avon?"

Avon's eyes were wide. She was the one in charge of pediatrics this evening.

"Go for it, girlfriend! It's a gift from God dropping right into your lap."

"But can I do it? Can I be a good mother? And we don't even know if Angel is going to be handicapped."

Avon took a deep breath. "You know I'm not too crazy about this place. But I do have to say that Emma Chandler's notion of being able to do whatever you set your mind to do is something I believe in." She looked up into the tall blonde's eyes. "You can do it, girl." Avon touched Jennifer's hand.

"Thanks."

"I agree." Both nurses turned to see Ian Williams standing at the nursing station counter, his hand on his IV pole.

"What the hell are you doing here on Peds, Mr. Williams?" Avon spoke as Jennifer simultaneously asked, "What the hell were you doing eavesdropping?" Her voice trailed off as Avon's died. "You aren't even supposed to be out of bed."

He shrugged. "Wondered what happened to my pain medication. It's been nearly a half hour."

Jennifer flushed. "It's my fault, Avon." She raised her eyes heavenward. "Come on. You're going back to your room." She took him by the arm, guiding him down the hall which connected the medical surgical unit with the pediatric unit. "And I will get your pain medication."

The pair walked along in silence for a moment.

"You know, I couldn't help overhearing what you said."

"About what?" Jennifer asked brusquely.

"The *gook*." Ian flushed and corrected himself quickly. "I mean the little girl from the plane crash." He paused. "I was the pilot, remember."

"How could I forget?" Jennifer glared at him. But it wasn't his fault. Ian Williams couldn't have known the impact he had had on her life not once but twice.

He was puzzled. "I don't know what your beef is, Stauton, but I haven't done anything to make you dislike me, have I?"

Jennifer blinked and realized then how she must be coming off. She loosened his arm and slowed her steps. "I guess I have to apologize to you. No. Nothing is your fault . . . except maybe for the crash and that's for the FAA to judge, not me."

"So?"

She shrugged. "Here's your room. Can you get back to your bed on your own, or should I help you?"

Ian glanced at the mussed bed. He knew what he'd like to say, but he knew that if he did, she'd probably punch him out. "No. I'm fine."

"Okay. Great. I'll get your pain medication."

"Wait." He grabbed her arm. "Uh, it looks like I'm going to be hanging around here a while. At least, I'm not flying for a good six months." He indicated the cast on his arm. "I wondered . . . I mean, my girls are already pretty grown. Anyway"—he flushed—"they live with their mother so I don't get to see them that often." He took a deep breath, feeling the pain shoot through him. "What I am trying to say is—if you do decide to go ahead with adopting Angel, I'd be happy to help you with baby sitting and all that."

"Would you?" Jennifer was caught off guard. Then she recalled how prejudiced Ian Williams, the young Army pilot had been when they'd served together. She looked at him with different eyes. People obviously changed. "I'd better go get your pain medication."

CHAPTER 50

Wednesday night, March the fifteenth, the ides of March, Dr. Richard Bell thought, ironically, as the ambulance gurney was wheeled into the ER. Cole was on duty, of course. Hadn't expected it to be anyone else. Glad it wasn't anyone else. He felt comfortable with Cole.

Hell, he'd helped birth the boy and practically raised him. Now that was a good time, when family medicine really took care of the whole family.

Cole used to tell Richard that he'd gone into medicine because of him. Always made him feel good inside, especially since he'd never had kids of his own.

"What is it?" he asked, glancing at the sphygmometer. His speech was surprisingly clear. As a doctor, Richard Bell knew his body was making a final supreme effort.

"It's okay," Cole said.

"Bullshit! It's over, boy. Don't fool an old hand like me."

"No, really . . ." Cole tried keeping his voice from choking. "Listen, I'm going to have Fred come in and do the admission workup." He turned away from his old friend.

Richard Bell reached out and patted the younger man. "Why don't you tell Emma I want to say goodbye."

*   *   *

It didn't take long for the admitting office to find a private room for their former chief of staff.

Within moments of him being settled into bed, Emma Chandler hobbled in with her walker. "Just what do you think you're doing here, Richard? Don't you know this hospital is only big enough for one VIP at a time?"

He gave a hollow laugh. The shakiness had returned to his voice and he knew from the lightheaded feeling that his blood pressure probably had fallen a few notches.

"I am serious, Richard Arnold Bell. You are to get up out of this hospital and walk out that door."

His strength was leaving him. Richard could barely shake his head. "Can't."

"Nonsense." Emma pounded her walker into the floor with such vehemence, Richard thought she was going to break through to the ER below them. "Do you remember how I was a few months ago? Couldn't talk worth a damn, let alone walk and now here I am. If I can do it, Richie, you can, too."

He thought he shook his head. He wasn't sure. Maybe he stretched out his hand instead of, or along with. His hand felt wet. No, they wouldn't be giving him a bath this late at night.

The lightness was penetrating his body. My God, what was happening? He felt like a young man. He felt almost as if he could fly. Then he saw her. His Bonnie. That must mean he was actually going. The suddenness made him shake violently and pulled him back into his mortal body for a moment.

Once more, Richard Bell opened his eyes. He could see and then he couldn't. "You know, Emma, I have always loved you." There he had said it. Bonnie wouldn't be too angry with him. He knew his wife. She'd always been generous to others.

He heard Emma sobbing as he departed. He'd like to have stayed and comforted her, but it was too hard and he was too tired. Yes, it was time for a change.

Richard reached his arm out and felt Bonnie taking his hand, guiding him along. He wasn't going to be alone anymore.

CHAPTER 51

"Lisa, I want to know. Tell me the truth," Sophie screamed at her daughter. Nothing was doing any good. Nothing was breaking through to the girl. Didn't she understand the damage she was doing, not only to herself but to others?

"Fuck it, Mother!" Lisa shouted back. "I am telling you the truth. I have not been helping Ray. I don't care a fuck about him. He's . . . shit." She slammed the door to her room.

"Don't you run away from me, young woman. And I want that language cleaned up." She thought of the whippings she'd received for merely mouthing back to her folks. If they saw Lisa now . . . well, she was just glad that they weren't in the house with her right now. "We are going to hash this out before Cole comes home and before the police return."

The door flung open. "The fucking police are coming here?" Lisa's voice went way up. Sophie was surprised the dining room mirror above the buffet didn't shatter. "I did not do a damn fucking thing." The girl stomped around the room with her boots hitting the hardwood floor like a trotter on a three-gait walk.

Sophie put a hand to her aching head. She thought about taking some of the Darvon pain medication. When had she last had it? Yesterday? And yet Sophie knew that even a day ago, a week ago, or a month ago was too soon. If she was planning on keeping the baby, she shouldn't be having any of that junk, but how much pain could she take? Ken had obviously given her that to test her willpower and push her over the edge. She closed her eyes a moment.

"Lisa?" Sophie tried speaking in a modulated tone, hoping that her daughter would catch on. "Lisa, please. I just want this to be okay." She sank down on the couch and suddenly began a spasm of coughing.

"Mom? Are you all right?" The teen rushed over to Sophie.

Sophie opened her eyes a bit and she blinked. "Yeah. Fine."

"Mommy, are you sure?" The concern in Lisa's voice was evident.

Sophie figured that she must look terrible if Lisa could get out of her mood to talk like that. She stroked her daughter's hair, the same auburn color as Cole's. Lisa hadn't called her "Mommy" in years now. She nodded again.

Before she could ask anything more, the sound of footsteps froze her heart. Voices were outside. It wasn't Cole; it wasn't Frank. It was both of them.

Well, she had tried. Her voice was hoarse. "Lisa, go get the door for your dad."

Lisa nodded.

"Hello, Mr. Willis," Lisa greeted the officer with the polite coolness of a teen. "I hear you've been upsetting my mother." She folded her arms across her chest. "Just what is it you think I've been doing . . ."

Frank Willis had wasted no time telling the parents what he suspected Lisa of participating in.

"Aren't you jumping to a few conclusions, Willis?" Cole Morgan asked. "Granted, Lisa knows the fellow and she has used *in the past,* but she's been clean four months now. Haven't you, honey?" He gave his daughter a long searching look.

Lisa returned her father's gaze. "Yeah. I have. You can even ask Margaret Chandler or John McNamara if you don't believe me." The hurt came through in her voice.

Cole shrugged. "Sweetie, you've lied to us before. And you've overdosed more than once."

The teen sighed. "All right. All right. But I am not lying now." She glared at the officer. "Look, Willis—"

"Lisa—" Cole started correcting her tone.

Frank Willis shook his head. "It's all right, Dr. Morgan. I know how to deal with this element."

Lisa made a face. "Convicted before a trial, I see. I thought we had due process of law in this country."

The cop smiled wanly.

"Look, Willis, I am not using. Okay?" She raised a brow at him. "Ray stopped me at the hospital a few weeks ago when I was up visiting Mom. He wanted me to help him do a few runs with him. I said no."

"Lisa—" Sophie began.

"Honestly, Mom. I did. I was too concerned with you and the horse at Margaret's who was having trouble to want to deal with *his* problems. Besides, he threw me over for Melody."

"An excellent reason not to do drugs," Frank Willis said under his breath.

"Stick it up yours, cop."

The officer's eyes narrowed. "You know I don't have to be so nice. I can bring you down to the station and ask these questions more directly."

"Oh? On what grounds?" Lisa challenged him. "You haven't got a leg to stand on because *I* have not been involved."

Willis tapped his fingers on the antique tabletop. Sophie glared at him. He frowned and stopped. "Okay, if you want *me* to believe you, then you'll be prepared to prove it."

"Sure." The cocky teen threw back her long hair.

"Would you be willing to help bring Roy Warner in? Catch him in the act?"

Lisa sucked in her breath, glancing at first her father and then her mother. Her voice was barely a whisper now. "You want me to betray a friend?" How could the cop say such a thing? Even if Ray was a dirty pig, he had still been her friend.

Frank recognized his advantage and took it. "That's the call, kid. Are you willing to prove to me and your parents that you're not involved with this obnoxious fellow's plan?"

Lisa closed her eyes, trying to keep the dizzy feeling at bay. She hated what Ray Warner represented now. But there was a time when she had willingly gone after him, slept with him, and gotten high with him. Her heart iced over as slowly she nodded.

"Good deal." Frank slapped the table so hard that Sophie worried it might split. "Tonight?"

Lisa shrugged. "Might as well."

She made the phone call to Ray Warner just like the cop told her to do. Ray seemed pretty excited that she was going to be able to get Margaret's helicopter and help him. He hadn't even questioned her about changing her mind. He'd seemed to expect that she'd agree to help him. She hated the smugness in his voice. And would like to sock him one for his assumptions, but she knew she couldn't.

On one hand, Lisa wished she could warn him that she was going to be wired, and on the other, she thought Ray Warner was a stupid son-of-a-bitch who deserved to get caught.

"Darling, you don't know how perfect this is. My

friend Ernest, you remember I told you about Ernie, the 'Nam copter pilot I met at State," Ray said.

"Uh . . . yeah. Ernest Valentino. I remember because Valentino was my great-grandmother's idol. He's here?"

"Yep. Got sprung, I guess." Ray laughed. "Or maybe sprang himself. Anyway, Ernie's got a little pocket change. Wants to go south. Start a little business of his own down there. You know, so we'd be partners."

Lisa shivered as she felt the sweat streaming down her blouse. "Ray, I ain't got no money to help you. And I'm not stealing the helicopter. I was only thinking about borrowing it a little."

"Relax, Leez. My God are you hyped. You taking anything without Ray's knowing it, baby doll?"

"Uh, no." The phone nearly slipped from her hand. "It's just that with Mom sick and all—"

"Oh, yeah. Right. Well, anyway, I want you to tell me when's a good time for us to, uh, borrow the copter. We won't have it more than three, four hours. And all you'd need to do is bring me the keys."

"I can do that. Easy." Lisa let out a relieved sigh that she wouldn't be forced to try and fly the thing herself. After all, Margaret had only given her a couple of lessons. There was no way in hell she could maneuver that thing now.

"Atta girl. Knew you'd come through for me, Leez. Say, you want to come along for the ride?"

"Uh . . . me." She wet her lips. "Uh . . . no . . . I've got a term paper to write. My dad's kinda been down on me, you know. And . . . and besides, I want to be at the Chandlers' distracting Margaret so she doesn't go looking for her copter."

"You'll do your paper there?"

"Yeah, sure. I've become good friends with Margaret ever since I helped her with a sick horse on Christmas."

"Yeah, Leez. I bet you were a good help then. You know, maybe I'll just go find Ernie and see when he can cut loose. I want you to call me at 555-4242 at eight P.M. 'Kay? Tell me what you find out. The sooner we can take a run, the sooner my friend Ernie can get his business started."

"Sure, Ray. I'll call at eight."

Her heart raced so fast she wasn't even aware of having put the receiver down, but she felt her dad's arms around her as he guided her over to the sofa.

Lisa took a sip of the beer Cole offered her. "Do you think I fooled him?" She glanced at her father and then at Chief Willis.

"I'm sure you did, sugar."

Willis just shrugged and smiled. "So, we'll get Ernest Valentino, too. Gonna have a good bonus next Christmas."

The hours ticked by slowly. All Lisa could do was lie down and close her eyes, but she was too nervous to nap. "How are we going to get Margaret to give us her helicopter tonight?"

The police chief merely nodded. "Don't worry. I got the Feds helping me. They can wire it with a long-distance transponder. We'll have couple of trackers flying a long distance away. Ray won't even see them. Then a radio transmitter in the cockpit so we can hear exactly what's going on, and a remote kill switch."

"Shit! You're going to kill them in the air? Forget it." She stood and walked toward the door. "Count me out."

Willis gave her a blank look. "Hey, sister, why don't you watch more cops and robbers' movies. Then you'd know. The kill switch keeps the engine from restarting once Ray and his folks land at their rendezvous. In fact, if we saw a need," Willis gloated, "we could stop the engine midair." He saw the terror in her eyes. "But that's only a last resort. 'Sides we already called Mexico. Got preapproval to follow your boyfriend down there, if need be."

"Oh." Lisa made a face and sat down again. She wasn't being left much of an option.

The call had been made at eight, just like Ray had asked. The phone number had been traced to a pay phone. She could have told them that. She could also have told them that Ray never stayed on any phone call long enough to be traced.

"Okay, baby. Is the copter cool?"

"Uh, yeah. I talked with Margaret and she's going to be helping me with my paper. It's on biology."

He laughed. "You mean you didn't learn enough with me, Leez? Have to give you some more lessons so you can ace this. Sure you don't want to come for a ride with me and get some additional practice?"

Lisa flushed, wondering who else was listening to this conversation. "Uh. No, thanks. I've decided to become a vet and I need to get good grades for that."

"All right then, baby doll. Why don't you meet me at the landing patch at 2100 hours."

"Ray, it's gonna take me nearly a half hour to get over to the Chandlers'. Then I've got to search Margaret's purse for the keys and . . . I . . ."

She saw Willis nodding and swallowed her fear. "Okay, right. I'll get to you as soon as I can."

"Good girl." She could feel his slimy hand on her face. "Don't forget to bring your school books. I wouldn't want you to fail this paper."

A separate wire had been attached to the underside of Lisa's gold cross so that the Feds could hear the conversation between her and Ray before they took off.

She couldn't believe the thing was so tiny and that with such a small piece of metal, the Feds and Willis would be able to pick up anything she or Ray said.

Lisa walked around the helicopter and touched the Circle C painted on the side. She looked for anything unusual, anything that might tell Ray she'd betrayed him. Ray would have no hesitation in killing her if he thought she'd done him dirty.

Shivering, she glanced at the Federal agent walking with her. "What if I get into trouble? I mean, what if he starts to suspect me?" She glanced at her mother and father who'd driven her over to the Chandler estate. "How you gonna know what's going on when they take the helicopter?"

The agent silently showed her the transmitter hidden under the radio.

"He won't, baby," Cole said. "Not if you play it cool. Just don't get flustered."

"But Daddy." Lisa sighed. Willis was probably right. She was chicken shit. It was all right to shoot up and help others to do the same, but to stop this insanity, she was petrified. Of course, none of them knew Ray Warner's temper like she did. The guy could get fierce, especially when he was using. She only hoped that once she was done with this, none of Ray's friends would come gunning for her.

The clouds had drifted toward the moon. Lisa was surprised that Ernie, even with his supposed experience in Vietnam, was planning on making this trip at night. But she guessed the less light, the fewer people.

At eight forty-five P.M. everyone, including her folks, had disappeared into the woods, the house, and anywhere they couldn't be seen. Not even the cars were visible. Where the hell had they gone?

Her heart raced as she walked back and forth. Would

he suspect something because she was out here waiting for him? Would he suspect something if she waited inside the house and came out at the last minute?

Her hands were chapping. Even though Houston days were hot, the nights, especially in the winter, were chilly. Lisa glanced down at the shorts, Grateful Dead T-shirt and knee socks she wore. Great outfit for school, but not for running around in the middle of the night.

A twig snapped near the arbor.

"Hello? Anyone there?" Lisa's voice was so hoarse that she barely heard it.

There was no response.

"Calm down, honey."

Lisa practically jumped into the tree branches. She whirled around.

"Dad, is that you?"

"On your earphone, Lisa."

"Oh. Oh. Right."

"You're doing really good, sweetheart. Take a deep breath and don't act so scared. Remember your part of this will be over right away."

"Right." Lisa did as her father asked and closed her eyes a moment.

She had to just keep calm, she told herself, and everything would be fine.

Lisa had just taken her second deep breath and smelled the night hyacinth, when she felt the arm crook around her neck.

"What the—"

She gasped hard, trying to struggle, turned, and saw it was Ray. "Why the hell did you sneak up on me like that?"

Ray Warner grinned and gave one of his low laughs, the kind that used to send shivers coursing through her veins, the kind that used to give her almost the best high in the world. "Just checking up."

"On what?" *Oh, dear Lord—she wet her lips—he knows. What am I going to do? Molly, I love you.* She thought about the yellow Lab who slept on her bed. Her eyes darted around her.

"Can't be too safe, I say." He tipped her chin up, higher and higher, so that she looked into his eyes. His fingers were tight on her jawbone. "But you wouldn't try doing me in, would you now, honey doll?" He leaned down, parting her lips with his. His tongue swept her mouth as his hands lightly brushed her breasts causing an arousal, but she was almost positive it wasn't sex her ex-boyfriend was after.

Finally she managed to pull away.

"Still the same ol' Leez. Or are you different now? Got some standards, maybe." His eyes twinkled. "Now that you've got a big-time daddy, you don't have to worry much about us peons, huh?"

"That's not true, Ray, and you know it. It's just that . . . it's just that I gotta do this paper for biology. I don't want to fail it again."

"Oh, my, aren't we the smart one now?"

"Ray, stop it. I told you. I'm going to be a vet. I need to study." He nodded and walked around the copter, lightly stroking it as he might a loved one. "How much would you guess this thing costs?"

Lisa shrugged. "Don't know. Few thou, at least. Where's Ernest? You want these keys or not?" She was feeling uneasy with the way he was staring at her from those glassy eyes which held no emotion. "I gotta get going."

"Where's your books?"

She glanced around. Where had she put them? She really did have a paper, but it wasn't due until Monday.

"Go get'm."

Lisa pressed her lips together and shrugged. When Ray spoke in that kind of tone, you did not disobey. Not if you wanted to stay alive. She'd seen him off a couple of people who thought they were bigger than him. She wasn't gonna take that chance.

It actually felt better to be holding her notebook and books close to her chest, like a magical shield of sorts. He was chewing on a toothpick like some Ozark hick as he walked around her. She jumped as his hand touched her ass, stroking it. "Always did have a good one, Leez."

He grinned at her. What type of game was he playing? Did he want the keys or not?

He leaned back against the copter, arms folded, right leg folded for balance and support, as he continued to study her. "Your mom back at the hospital again?" Ray shook his head. "A real glutton for punishment, huh? You'd think that if she had an excuse she'd be just as happy to stay home and watch the soaps. I know my old lady was like that. Loved to call in sick. 'Course all she did was clean houses."

"Look, man, I'm really getting tired and a bit chilly . . ."

Ray took off his sweater and threw it at her. "Put this on, then. Can't have my lady gettin' sick."

Lisa frowned. "Ray, I am not—"

He put his fingers in his mouth and whistled.

From behind the plane an Italian, with a paunch that could make him money playing Santa, emerged. "We about ready, boss."

Ray nodded. " 'Cept we haven't issued any formal invites yet." He gave a sweeping hand to the new arrival. "Lisa Drummond, my good pal, buddy, and cellmate, Ernest Valentino."

Lisa frowned. Somehow she hadn't expected Ernest to look like this. But what did it matter—she was getting out. Now.

"Okay. Here's the keys. I also found a map for you so you don't stray into any military spaces by mistake."

"Good idea, sweetie." Ray rubbed her cheek with his roughened hand. "I'd hate them to be taking target practice and blow you up by mistake."

"Blow me . . . ?" She felt the gun nuzzle her neck. "Ray, please tell . . . your friend . . . to put his weapon down."

"Ain't no weapon, sweetie. Just his natural stiff . . . I mean stuff."

Both men guffawed.

Frantically, Lisa looked around, wondering if she should take a chance and run for it. But Ray saw the look in her eyes and grabbed her arm tighter than he'd ever had before. "I want you to come along, baby. You know. Insurance." It was then she saw the crate of guns near the door to the copter.

She froze, staring. "Jesus," she whispered, hoping it would pick up in the house, "they're trading guns for drugs."

"Nice sight, huh? Bring us a pretty penny. Those Mex bangers don't know what the hell they want. But you do, Leez. You always did. That's why you called me, isn't it?" His hand still encircled her arm. "Fuck your biology paper, Leeza. You're coming with me on this little trip of ours and I will show you some real biology, baby." Ray reached his hand up under her skirt and touched her moist panties. "But if you want some, you have t'beg real pretty, just like you used to do."

Lisa flushed, mortified at what the microphone must be picking up and wondering how they were going to get her out of this. What an attitude! Now the thought of him touching her was gross. But she recalled a time when she had wanted it, craved it, just like she had the coke. Maybe the only thing the Feds could hear were her rapid heartbeats. She closed her eyes. Why hadn't she gone to Sunday school like Mom wanted? She didn't know what to pray, only that she had to do so.

"So." Ray grabbed the notebook and text out of her arms and threw them into the helicopter.

"Say, ain't that Chandler lady gonna miss her?" Ernest asked.

Ray turned to Lisa.

She wanted to speak but she couldn't.

He was waiting.

Shit. Play it cool. Play it cool. "I don't think so. She . . . she had to watch one of her horses giving birth. She . . . didn't have time."

"Excellent." He kissed her cheek, rubbing his rough skin over her face.

No, it is not excellent, Lisa thought. *Why didn't I just get out when I had the chance?* She swore she could hear someone in her mike saying "Shit!" But Lisa knew what her old boyfriend thought: She had always been one to take a "ride" or have "another adventure." If she refused to go with him just because of a paper in school was due, he would suspect something was going on—if he didn't already. Besides, with those guns here, there was something more going on; something, she was certain, that unless she went along, she'd never get the information the Feds would need to close this down.

She dropped the keys in Ray's hand. "Come on, then. Let's go. I don't want to get home too late. Mom's been watching the time."

Ray shook his head and helped her board. As she strapped herself in, Lisa realized that she was trembling all over. God, she could use a good downer now. But nothing would take away the fear she felt.

They rose up over the flat landscape. Lisa realized

how flat and unattractive Texas looked from the air.
"Where we headed?"

"Thirty degrees northeast," Ray said.

"That's it? Thirty degrees northeast? For how long?"

Ray clucked his tongue. "Give me a break, Leez. You
think I'm stupid?"

Oh, God, he knew. She was sure he knew and any
second Ray was going to shoot her in the head. "No. Of
course not." *Shit.* Her voice trembled. *He had to know.*

Ray put his thumb into his vest and stretched it like
a rooster crowing. "Naw. I'm just going to give Ernest
one direction at a time. Got certain landmarks to pass
along the way."

"Okay. Sounds fine to me," Lisa said. But it didn't
sound fine. How were the Feds going to meet them
before they crossed the border if they didn't know
where the helicopter was? Damn it. She prayed that
the transponder picked up, just like the Fed said it did.

Her hand still trembled, almost as bad as Dr. Bell's
Parkinsonian shake. God, she hoped Ray didn't notice.

"Cold?" he asked, putting an arm around her and
squeezing her close to him.

She leaned slightly.

"Hey, cut that out," Ernest said, glancing at them
through the rearview mirror. "You're gonna make me
horny, Ray. We got any *chaquitas* waiting for us?"

"Maybe we do . . . and maybe we don't. You fly right,
my friend, and you'll be rewarded; if you don't . . ."
He whipped one of the guns out from under the seat
and shrugged.

Ernest went pasty and turned his attention back toward
the instruments in front of him.

It seemed to take forever before they turned. This
time due east by forty-five degrees, and shortly after

that, one hundred and eight degrees southeast. It almost felt as if they were going around in a circle.

"Okay," he finally said, "you can set it down anywhere around here."

"Here?" Lisa peered into the landscape. Flat, brown and ugly. It didn't look like they'd even left Fort Bend County, Texas. But then she saw the darkness of the water. "Are we in Mexico?"

"You shitting me, Leez?" Ray laughed. " 'Course we are. Never been down this way, have you?"

She felt the cold metal at her head. "Hey, cool it, Ernesto. What's the big?"

The fat Italian shrugged. "Just checking it out." He grinned and put the revolver into his mouth, spinning the wheel roulette style. "Something don't feel right, Ray. Too quiet, ya know."

Ray glanced at Lisa. "Yeah, I know. You didn't put the cops on us, did you, sweets?" He had gripped her arm nearly to the bone.

Could the Feds still hear them talking? She had no idea if they were still in range or not.

"No one's coming out, Ray. We were supposed t'be met here." He turned around so that the seat belt nearly strangled him. "I think your girlfriend here ain't no girlfriend. And if that's a fact, I wanna piece of her, too." He leaned forward.

Lisa could smell the garlic on his breath and see the oil in his pores.

Ray rapped him with the edge of his gun. "Patience, Ernest. You'll have your turn. Soon as we get our business done." He grinned, an emaciated skull with the skin tight across his face. His hand brushed across Lisa's breasts. she stiffened.

"Time was you use to like that, Leez."

"Still do." She choked, trying to move away.

"You're lying to me, you fuckin' bitch." He slapped her hard.

Her head rang with the pain.

"Where is it, bitch?" Pain went through her teeth as he struck her again. "Where's the mike they put on you? Ernie, how many bugs do you think we have in here?"

Ernest glanced in the rearview mirror. "I don't know but we got one motherfuckin' cockroach on us."

"Shit!" He slapped Lisa again. "You set me up, baby doll and now you are my insurance." He yanked Ernest's greasy hair. "Don't just sit there, boob, start up. Get us out of here."

Lisa could hear the engine grinding.

Ernest turned with tears in his eyes. "I can't. It won't go." He began hitting the canopy. "Ray, I . . ."

The bullhorn behind them told Ray that the Feds were there.

"They can't. We're in Mexico."

Lisa, too, was crying. "Ray, they got special permission."

"I knew it. Bitch. Now you are going to die. No one sets Ray Warner up and lives." He tore open her blouse and pushed up her bra. "Always did think your titties were too small." Ray ripped the undergarment off her.

Lisa shivered.

"You'll be warm soon enough, girlie." Ernest eyed her.

"Stop being a lout and get on that radio." Ray cuffed the other man's ear. "Tell them that we is going to kill this bitch right in front of them if they don't let us go."

"It won't work, Ray. I tol' you." Ernest blubbered like a three-year-old. "I wanna go home. I knew I shouldna trusted you. I . . ."

"Shut the fuck up! For a 'Nam vet you sure are

something else." Ray turned again to Lisa. "Give me that mike, Leez. Now!" His knife was out.

She could barely see with the pain. Damn, why had she ever agreed to this? Why had she thought she could be a hero?

"Fine. Don't give it to me. Your friends think I'm so stupid." He touched his temple and laughed. "But I'm not." His knife cut her skin just enough to let the blood run.

She screamed.

"Don't touch that girl, Warner, or it'll go worse for you." The voice over the bullhorn came.

"So. You are listening, you fags. Right. You want this girl alive, you let us go."

"Can't. Remote kill switch is at the base."

"Fuck you!" Ray shouted loud enough to break their eardrums. "Okay, then we're gonna take a walk."

"A walk, Ray? Where? My feet can't go real far. You know the trouble I have breathing. You know . . . ?"

"Stop being a crybaby, Ernest. Do what I tell you and you'll be fine, or stay here and let them string you up again. Hey, you bozos," he shouted, knowing that they could hear everything with their mikes. "You gonna let us walk or am I carving this young turkey up?"

There was silence. All that could be heard was the hovering of the aircraft.

Finally, the Feds answered. "Go ahead, then. Walk. You're not quite at the border yet. You make it, Webber, and you're a free man. But if you do, you'd better let the girl go."

"Right." Ray laughed and gestured to Ernest to jump down.

His eyes were wide with fear. "Ray, there's scorpions and snakes . . . there's—"

Ray flipped over his gun. "What is it with you, Ernest? Didn't they have snakes and crap in 'Nam?"

"I . . . I . . . guess so, but I . . . I lied t'you." He took a deep breath, waiting for the gun to hit him. "Just took some copter lessons. Flew a tourist group over the Grand Canyon for six months."

"Christ! Two liars. Ernest, stop being a sissy or I'll snake you right here. You heard what they said. Just a bit more to the border." Ray waved his gun menacingly.

Gulping hard, Ernest jumped out, crying as he landed on his bottom. Like a rolling ball, he righted himself and ran for the cover of the rocks.

"Now you." Without another warning, he pushed Lisa out of the helicopter. She screamed as she fell, but realized that she wasn't hurt and rolled backward under the helicopter.

"Good going, girl." The voice whispered in her ear plug.

She nodded, shaking.

Ray paused a moment and then with two of the guns in his hands, one on his belt and one in his shirt, he jumped.

He had just landed when the first shots came. "Christ! Can't a man get a little peace?" He looked around for Lisa and saw that she had tucked herself under the blades. She felt like a hunted animal.

"Stupid idiot. I ain't going there after you." He ran for the cover of the rocks, and paused as the gunfire hit his back.

"You fuckers promised!" Ray screamed out.

Then Lisa realized the shot which had downed Ray hadn't come from the air but from the rocks. An agent led a sobbing Ernest out. They had been there waiting all the time! *Shit!* Lisa thought. *They could've gotten her killed.*

The second federal helicopter landed. Lisa waited in

hiding where she was until she was positive that Ray was in custody and then she ran out to the safety of her father's arms. After that, she recalled nothing.

She was on the sofa at home when she came to. "Am I still in Kansas?" she asked. Cole and Sophie put their arms around Lisa and held her tight. Ray Warner hadn't died, but he was on life-support systems at the hospital, and Ernest was back in jail for having broken his parole. Lisa wondered what would happen now.

CHAPTER 52

The grandson of Julius Ciss was sitting at the old man's bedside, reading to him from the Torah portion of the week, when he noticed his grandfather's roommate spasming and then lying perfectly still.

Alert and trained for such emergencies, Ari jumped up. He immediately felt for the pulse and listened for respirations. "Code blue!" He shouted at the top of his lungs. "Code blue!"

He pulled the young Hispanic onto the floor where he'd have a harder surface for CPR and began doing five thumps to one breath.

Where the hell were the staff here? He'd seen the nurses on duty as he walked in. It wasn't shift change.

Ari checked the carotid again. Still no pulse. "Code blue!" He shouted as he pressed down, being careful to avoid the xyloid process.

"Is something the . . . oh, m'God," Wendy gasped, stunned.

"Get some help! This man's in acidosis. Get me some bicarb. Stat!"

"Oh! Yes, doctor!" She was startled out of her reverie, forgetting that this man was not a physician on staff here. "Code blue!" She ran for the desk. "Call code blue."

Within seconds the announcement had come across the loudspeaker system and then the crew began arriving: respiratory, anesthesia, emergency, nursing, and following them all, Emma Chandler, feeling more spry than she had in weeks, hobbling downstairs so that she could find out what was happening in her own hospital. Of course, she knew better than to get in the way, but as chairperson of the board she wanted to know who had arrested and why.

Mr. Ciss's grandson was more than happy to let the others take over with the ambu bag and the defibrillator paddles. He stepped out of the way, but unfortunately, neither Ari's work, nor those of the code blue crew had managed to save the young man.

Sweating, his arms exhausted, Ari splashed water on his face.

"That was very good, young man. Do I know you?"

Ari looked at the elderly woman moving with a walker. He didn't recall Meredith saying that they had established a psychiatric wing yet, so probably this was one of their OBS—obstructive brain syndrome—usually happening in the aged when the arteries narrowed and not enough oxygen reached the brain.

"No, ma'am." He smiled and sat down again next to his grandfather. They had already moved the body down to the morgue and would notify the family, hoping to get permission for an autopsy so they could find out what exactly had happened to the victim.

"You're a visitor?" She was aghast.

Ari shrugged. "You could say that."

A breathless Meredith hurried into the room. "Ari, what happened? I heard a code blue. I was afraid . . ." She glanced at Julius snoozing.

"It wasn't Papi but his roommate." The young doctor indicated the now-empty bed.

"Oh. *Baruch HaShem*," Meredith said. Blessed Be The Name (of the Lord) was a phrase that she'd heard around the rabbi's a lot and had begun repeating it herself whenever she heard or gave good news. It made her feel . . . well, connected, with the higher power.

Emma spoke up, realizing that Meredith had not even noticed her.

"You know this man, Dr. Fischer?"

Meredith flushed and made the introductions. "You know, Emma, we could stand to add to our family practice group. We're so specialized here that—" She shrugged.

Emma studied Mr. Ciss's grandson for a long moment. She took in the lean frame and crocheted head covering. And, of course, Meredith's new dilemma had not escaped her. She knew her chief of staff must be feeling decidedly awkward with some of the comments floating around. "Yes, Dr. Fischer. I believe you might be right. I don't suppose you'd like to come out here on a regular parttime basis?"

Ari smiled at Meredith and nodded toward Emma. "Actually, I think I would be honored."

CHAPTER 53

There was no reasonable reason why her door should be open, not even ajar. So when she noticed it, Pam halted a moment. She glanced down the hall. Empty, as usual, except when she was bringing a gentleman home. Then, of course, the busybodies were out in full form.

Wishing that she had thought to put the brass knuckles in her purse, cursing that she did not have any weapon with her, Pam wondered if she should risk going in or if she should just call the police.

But did she really want the cops brought in on this? No, she decided, she did not.

"Okay, I'm coming in. But I want you to know I've got a gun," she bluffed, her hand in her pocket looking as weaponlike as she could get it.

"Well, then, by all means, come on in."

"Shit in hell! What the—" Pam kicked the door fully open to see her no-good brother, Randy, lounged out on her sofa. Two empty cans of beer and the remains of some microwave popcorn indicated that he had made himself at home.

Pam slammed the door behind her. "What are you doing here, Randall Overby! You know, I told you *never* to come here." She tried hissing, but she knew that her anger was getting the best of her and that her voice was too loud.

The twenty-two-year-old shrugged and rubbed the stubble of his day-old beard. He picked up the remote and clicked off the television. "Nothing really worth watching on. More fun to watch you squirm."

"What the damnation does that mean?" She popped open a beer for herself. God, she needed something. Stronger than this even, but it was all she had in the house at the moment and it looked as if Randy had nearly cleaned her out of that.

"Yeah, go ahead. Have a seat, sister dear. Make yerself comfy." He popped a pill into his mouth, probably an upper. "Just have a message to deliver personally from me and my partner."

"You and your what?"

Randy grinned. Two of his front teeth were cracked and crooked as a result of poor dental hygiene while growing up and too many fights when he'd become a teen. The yellowing was due, of course, to the tobacco which Randy both smoked and chewed.

"You stink! My God, don't you ever take a bath?" Pam stood, nauseated by her kin's smell.

He laughed. "You are funny, Pam-e-la. I only hope your humor is as good when I give you the message."

Pam's eyes narrowed. She wasn't so sure that she wanted to hear this so-called message. "Randall Overby, you pig, are you the one who's been phoning me at all hours and leaving those stupid notes for me?"

"Oink, oink. Didn't you think it was fun, Pam?" He grinned again. "Frankly, I rather liked the game. But actually, it wasn't me. However, we've decided to step up our actions. Pa is getting impatient and I don't blame him."

"So, you're the one! I had an inkling. Why the hell did you give that bastard my phone number?"

" 'Cause I did, sis. Same reason I do everything else."

"How does tellin' Pa where I am benefit you?" She

knew that Randy, selfish bastard that he was, would never have done anything unless it helped him somehow.

"Don't know that it did. But it certainly didn't hurt."

She closed her eyes and shook her head. "God, you are sick. So, what's this message I'm s'psed to have? And who the hell is your partner?"

"How come you're *so* smart and you haven't guessed?" He made a face.

"Because I've been busy doing other things."

"Like blowin' up Mrs. Martin's car? And Dr. Allister's."

She gave him a puzzled look. "What the hell are you blabbering about, boy?"

The hint of a smile, perfect if he had posed for the Mona Lisa, touched his thin lips. "Well, I won't keep ya guessin' anymore. Nelson's my partner. He and I are getting rather anxious for our share of the Chandler wealth. Hey, Granny Dottie was my gram much as she was yours."

"Yeah and you wouldn't have the brains to think about my plans if I hadn't pulled you in and told you what I was doing; if I hadn't needed some extra help."

"Well, sis, that is just where you made your mistake. Needin' the extry help. 'Cause if you don't cough up one thousand per week now, the police are going to find some concrete evidence of your misdeeds."

"You can't—"

"Can, too. Got you taped asking me to rustle them steer from the Circle C. Got you telling me about putting that drug in the little bitch's place. Got lots of other dope on you, 'cluding your history with men."

Pam flushed angrily. It didn't help to get upset with Randy. That boy would just dig his heels in and become more and more obsessed with what *he* wanted right then and there.

"Once the police hear about these few things, they'll be right happy to have their culprit for these others. And all we have t'do is leave some of that nitrate stuff 'round this house somewhere that you can't find it."

Her mouth hung open. "You wouldn't."

"Would."

Damn Randall. He was being the same obstinate kid he had been when she tried guiding him right. Always took the easy out. "So how the hell does Nelson St. Clair get part of this?"

A quick smile told Pam more than she wanted to know. Nelson was just as much of a con man as he seemed. He'd been Randy's cellmate for a few years at the California Men's Colony in Lompoc. They'd never thought they'd meet up again, but Nelson had remembered all the dirt Randy had given him about his oldest sister. It was only natural that they team up. He was the one who told Randy where Joshua's car had been parked. Too bad the radiologist and his girl, the ugly sister had gotten out in time. Randy hadn't planned on that. He had thought it would be one down and one to go.

Then with Karin, it had been Pam they'd been planning to scare. Only Randy had gotten confused which car was hers. With both of them there, he'd taken a chance. Just the poor lady's luck it had been the wrong one.

"So, Emma Chandler, our Great-aunt Em, has re-made her will in your favor."

"She has?" Pam was shocked. She hadn't heard that and she usually heard everything going on at the hospital. How had Randy?

"Helps to have a partner, sis. Nelson was called in to witness the new will."

Pam blinked hard. This was her worst nightmare. But it was to get worse.

"So what we figure is that you have to find a way to do away with Allison. We'll make another attempt at the older one."

Pam swayed. She was feeling ill. She hadn't really wanted to murder anyone. She'd only wanted what she thought was rightly hers. But Pam knew that once Randall set his mind on something, it was near impossible to talk him out of it.

"Yeah, okay, fine. I'll do what you want. Just get out of my place and don't let me see you skulking around here again. I hate your ornery face."

"Wonderful to have a sweet big sis, huh?"

Pam glared at him as he slowly unfolded his lanky body and walked toward the door.

"Don't you forget now. There are two of us watchin' you, Pam-e-la."

She slammed the door shut after him, chained and double bolted it . . . even though she knew that it wouldn't do any good against her brother.

Now what was she going to do?

CHAPTER 54

The Monday morning morbidity and mortality meeting held both good and bad news.

Emma was healing nicely and had even come down to the meeting, making her way slowly with a walker and nodding to all as staff greeted her. Margaret and Allison helped her into her chair.

Besides Emma's slow recovery, Meredith reported that they had passed the JCH inspection with only a few negative comments and several correctable things which they had to show to the commission within the month.

The audience, most of them at least, broke into spontaneous applause. It was great to have that monkey off their back.

"And—" Meredith glanced at her notes—"Sophie Morgan will be returning to work next week. Tell me, Cole, did she stay out just to avoid JCH?"

Everyone laughed. Cole, of course, denied it.

Ellis noted that Sean and Leroy no longer sat at the maverick table. He wondered if that was because those still there had expressed support for Meredith's work. Not that it mattered a damn bit what religion she chose to be. As long as she was a good, caring doctor, he was on her side. Silly prejudices had always escaped him.

"We also have a new staff member. Ari?"

Ari Micha Mendelson, M.D., stood from his seat.

He was at a table alone. Maybe, Ellis thought, because he had set himself apart by wearing that little crocheted headgear of his.

"Ari is joining our general family practice on a part-time basis. Welcome, Ari." She beamed a smile at him and felt the anger rising from Sean, who sat at the second table from the front.

"The bad news is . . ." Meredith paused and glanced at Rosa who was head of the ethics committee.

Rosa stood. "It seems we are at an impasse regarding a single dialysis machine. We have been using it for Mr. Julius Ciss until a new kidney could be procured for him. However, we have recently admitted twenty-two-year-old Ray Warner, whom I believe many of you in town are probably familiar with. Ray lost use of his kidneys . . ." She paused, not wanting to prejudice the group, and yet wasn't the life of someone who devoted himself to doing good deeds better than someone who sold and used drugs and who had lost the function of his body through his own misuse? "And we now must decide who is to use the machinery. Unfortunately, only one patient can be hooked up to it." She walked among the tables, handing out ballots. "This must seem rather a stupid way to do things, but I've decided that because of some of the issues here—" Rosa glanced up at their chief of staff—"a silent vote is best."

Ken Stevens took his paper and wondered what would these folks do when they had to vote on the winner versus Sophie. Damn, he wished she'd talk to Cole already. He glanced toward his pal. He had promised not to say anything and he wouldn't, not at least for a while.

From the podium, Meredith nodded. "Thank you, Rosa. There is, of course, one more option. And that is one or the other of the patients is transferred by air ambulance to Houston Medical."

Was it her imagination or was the room considerably cooler now. She knew how she would vote. Not only had Julius Ciss's presence made her see her own life more clearly, but in the medical *Halacha* class which she had taken, giving the laws in the Torah regarding medical situations as this, she knew that hard as the decision was, the first person to have the machine would stay on it, no matter how saintly, rich, or debased and unworthy one or the other might be considered. It amazed her how many intricate facets of life the five books of Moses covered. Meredith had thus far not found a single situation in which the Holy Book didn't have an answer or some guidance. Now if she could only get her colleagues to listen.

CHAPTER 55

Dr. Sara McNamara paced up and down outside of ICU where it appeared her sixteen-year-old son might be dying of pneumonia complications.

She was a doctor. A good doctor, she thought. Sara should have known better. Why hadn't she brought him into the hospital when her son had first started wheezing?

Damn it. She'd been so busy taking care of her patients, particularly the Asian girl, whom it now seemed Jennifer Stauton would adopt, to notice what was going on right under her nose. Wasn't that always the case with doctors?

She thought of Ellis Johnston and his misfortune. All the doctors Sara knew, herself included, were so dedicated to the profession of healing that they often ignored their families for the worse. More doctors' wives became hypochondriacs or began a multitude of shopping binges just so they could get some attention, if not from their husbands, then from other doctors and the salespeople.

But she had kept her son, John, with her almost all the time. He worked here at the hospital with her, sorting the mail and helping with odds and ends. If she hadn't noticed, why hadn't Cole or one of the other physicians?

No, Sara thought, as she continued pacing, she couldn't blame anyone but herself.

The antibiotics had worked their magic, but only for so long. Somehow John had developed one of those strains that resisted the medication and fought back against it. She likened the bacteria to a castle under siege. One way or another, it had managed to find reinforcements and hurled hot oil down from the ramparts upon its attackers—the antibiotics and white blood cells.

Even his white count was still higher than it should be. That meant the bacteria was picking them off one by one, and while the white cells fought to be replaced quickly, sometimes it wasn't quick enough. When they returned too quickly, blood anomalies like leukemia started.

"Anything I can do for you, Sara?" Meredith asked as she stopped to console her friend.

Yesterday, Sara had stopped seeing her patients, stopped doing anything but pacing the floor and living in the ICU lounge, just like any other concerned parent.

Dr. Sara McNamara shook her head sadly. "Not unless you can pull up about a dozen new nurses from the air. Everyone in there is too damned busy, and they even have Carrie Harper working there."

While the doctors had very little control over the hiring and firing of nurses, they knew who was competent and who was not. If it hadn't been for their desperate need, Sara knew that Sophie, who had now come back to work part-time, but still looked terrible, would have fired the girl.

"Maybe I should go in and help," the pediatrician said as she started for the door.

Meredith held back the older woman. "You know it's not going to do any good. You'll just become hysterical, read his chart, demand why Ari, who is doing the best he can, isn't doing this treatment and that. He did some specialty work in respiratory diseases and even though he chose to stay in family practice, he knows a lot."

Sara grimaced. "Come with me for some coffee. I want to get my mind on other things. And I'll let you talk about the situation Sean seems to be stirring up."

Meredith debated a moment. She had always thought it best to keep her own counsel on personal matters. But knowing that Bill Martin, their ex-head of radiology, had joined the Irishman in trying to rid the hospital of her, it had become part of the gossip mill.

Inside the hushed sanctum of ICU, Carrie was trying to read one of the drug interaction books. Some things just did not make sense to her, and she saw no reason to dilute the antibiotic when it already came as a liquid. After all, didn't it get diluted when she added it to the IV? So why bother with all the work?

She bit her lower lip nervously. She knew that she was on probation. No one had told her and certainly Sophie had not given her notice to that effect, but she could tell the way the other staff were looking at her and talking about her behind her back. It was just so mortifying.

If it hadn't been so hard to falsify all her documents, Carrie would have left this shit hole of a hospital and gone somewhere else, somewhere they'd appreciate her.

She closed the textbook and wondered where that would be. Pouring herself more of that awful hospital coffee until it was time to put the antibiotic into John's IV, Carrie counted on her fingers the number of hospital she'd been employed at here in Texas. Too many.

'Course, she supposed she could always go and get a job in Louisiana. She'd heard they were pretty damn desperate for nurses—even L.V.N.'s. It should be easy. A snap. She tried clicking her fingers together, but somehow that trick had always escaped Carrie.

Just as it seemed that she was able to make a sound with her fat pudgy fingers, Carrie stopped in midair. She didn't have a license for anywhere but Texas and she wasn't quite sure she could pass their exams, specially with all the math: figurin', converting, and calculating. Never been her strong point. She had paid Ora Sue to take the math part of the Texas exam for her. She didn't know a soul in Louisiana who'd help her.

'Course she wouldn't mind being in the French Quarter, sipping chicory coffee and eating those greasy powdered sweets.

"Carrie, don't you have work to do?" It was Jennifer Stauton, Miss High and Mighty herself. You'd think she was God almighty here the way some of the doctors treated her, and now that she had that Chink kid . . . well, it just was not something Carrie Louise Harper would ever consider doing. Might get some disease or something.

"Sure as shootin'." Carrie smiled, just as pleasant as she could be. One day, she'd like to stick a letter opener in the back of Miss High and Mighty. One day, but not today. Not just yet. "There a law against sittin' for a minute?"

Jennifer glanced upward. "No, Carrie, there is no law, but considering how shorthanded we are, I would think you wouldn't have time to sit."

"Hmm!" Carrie made a motion and slammed the drug book closed. "Just so happens, Miss Stauton, that *I* am giving an IV piggyback of an antibiotic right now."

The way the girl said that it sounded as if she was

having an audience with the Queen herself. Jennifer wanted to laugh, but she didn't.

"All right, Carrie. Once you're done with that, maybe you can help Avon with the dialysis on Mr. Ciss."

"Oh, surely." Carrie almost wanted to curtsey. *Who did the woman think she was? Mother Mary?*

Gosh damn but she hated this job. She hated where people like Jennifer watched over her and . . . glancing at her watch Carrie saw that it was time to give John McNamara the antibiotic.

She held the vial of medication in her hand and considered one more time if she ought to dilute it. But if she diluted it, then he wouldn't get the full strength of the germ fighter, she rationalized. Therefore, Carrie knew that them books just had to be wrong and the pharmacy had probably just gotten the instructions out of the same book.

Smugly, Carrie hurried over to the teen's bedside.

Poor kid. Hooked up to all those damn machines. All because his Mamma didn't take care of him. She really liked John. When he was awake and alert, which he hadn't been much lately, they had some fun conversations. She'd do just about anything to get him well and that's why she didn't want to dilute the medication.

From the corner of her eye, Carrie saw the ICU doors swing open. Mrs. Morgan came in to check on the rounds and make sure that all the floors were covered. Carrie wasn't too crazy about Mrs. Morgan—mostly she tried just to avoid her, because she feared that if the supervisor found out some of the things she'd been accused of, she knew she'd be history.

Once again, Carrie whispered a prayer to herself. *"Lord Jesus, thank you for having not let JCH catch me in somethin' awful. Bad enough they had found what they did. And Lord Jesus, please let me keep this job*

*until such time as I have another. And, oh, P.S. Make
Johnny well again.*" She crossed herself and then injected the antibiotic into the side line for the IV.

There. That and her prayer ought to do him a world
of good. She was just about to wash the pink stain
from around his mouth, when Sophie Morgan stepped
into the cubicle next to Carrie.

"How's it going?"

Like she really cared. "Oh. Fine. Just fine, Mrs. Morgan. You're looking better." Carrie made the comment
without even looking because she was sure the director
of nursing liked stuff like that.

There was a long pause before Sophie spoke again.
"Carrie, maybe you ought to take a sputum sample
of that stuff you're cleaning up. The pink color could
indicate blood."

"Oh. Right. Never thought about that."

"I'll have Rosa write an order to cover it."

Sure was nice when you knew the docs so well you
could order them to do stuff. "Okay, sure." She continued what she was doing, as if Sophie hadn't said a
word.

"When you're finished taking that sample and sending it down to the lab, I'd like to have a word with you."

"All righty." Carrie gave a big smile, feeling none of
the confidence inside.

As soon as Sophie had left, Carrie asked John, "What
do you think she wants t'talk to me about?" Had the
JCH actually told the director whose charts they had
checked and which ones had the most mistakes? Well,
damn it, it wasn't her fault. Not at all. If they hired
enough help here, Carrie wouldn't have to be running
all over tarnation trying to get her work done and then
to get her charting done.

She tucked the covers around John McNamara.

"Well, gotta go see what the boss wants. Be back in a bit."

Carrie could have swore that he'd nodded. Pa always told her that she was seeing stuff. But she wasn't. Carrie knew that she was just a sensitive soul who was attune to things around her.

Sophie, sitting at the station and reading charts, stood as Carrie approached. "Let's go into the lounge," she said, gesturing toward the small room where the nurses working ICU had their own little refrigerator and coffee-maker. This is where they usually heard shift report.

"Sure. No problem."

"Did you send the specimen to the lab?"

"Uh . . . yeah . . . I mean no. I took it and it's on his nightstand. I'll get it later. No big. Maybe I'll run it over to the lab, myself."

Sophie frowned. "Considering how busy you are here, I would think sending one of the orderlies would be best."

"Yeah. You're right. Of course." Just agree with whatever they say. Make them happy. It was how she'd learned to control her pa. And then you could just go on your merry way and forget it.

"Carrie." Sophie called the girl's attention to her. "Are you all right?"

Carrie nodded.

"Do you have a lot of personal problems on your mind?"

The L.V.N. shrugged. "No more than anyone else, I would guess."

"I see." Sophie wet her lips. This part of her job was always the most distasteful. From the folder she carried, she pulled out a pink paper.

A pretty pink, Carrie thought. Was she getting some sort of award, or what?

There was a strain in the air, like when you had t'move your bowels and couldn't, like someone wanted t'do something and was being held back. Yes, that was how Carrie would best describe it.

"Carrie—" Sophie's voice was soft—"I'm sorry to tell you this, but I don't think you're working out well here at CMC. I was hoping that there might be something temporary that you could work out, but it seems. . . ."

Carrie's mouth dropped open. Three hundred flies could jump in for all she cared. "You mean, I'm fired?" The shock hit the L.V.N. like a tsunami. "But what have I done wrong? I've helped everyone and worked with everyone . . . I . . . You can't just fire me. You just can't. My pa . . . my pa . . ." Carrie burst into horrendous sobs.

Avon ducked her head into the lounge. "Everything all right?"

"Fine, Avon. Why don't you close the door, okay?"

"Uh, yeah. Sure." The black nurse hurried out.

Carrie continued her sobbing. It sounded like an elephant with a cold. She flung open the door separating the lounge from the nursing station. She didn't care if anyone stared at her. She didn't care. They did it anyway so what did it matter.

Sophie held out the pink paper. Not so pretty anymore.

"Here, you need to present this to the cashier. She'll give you the equivalent of two weeks' pay."

Carrie wiped her eyes with her dirty sleeve. She grabbed the paper and tore it in half. "Keep your stupid money. Carrie Harper doesn't take handouts."

With those words, Carrie stormed out of the ICU, slamming the glass doors behind her.

She was so danged mad that she nearly forgot her

purse. And so she had to screw up her courage to go
back in. She did so, running by Jennifer and Avon, who
were staring at her. Probably having a good ol' laugh.

"You all ain't heard the last of Carrie Louise Harper.
No siree."

Carrie, and on the floor. Screw up her courage to go back to. She did so, running by Jennifer and yeah, the little Strong, earlier. Probably bundle a good at lunch. Would and be robbed her to Carrie Louise Harper, No one.

CHAPTER 56

Her apartment was cold when Carrie returned, but that was probably because she hadn't gone home from being fired at the hospital and she hadn't turned on the heat. But by this time, Carrie was beyond caring.

First she had driven around awhile and then she'd gone into the bar and had a few drinks. Rob Roys. What her pa liked drinking when he had the money. 'Course that weren't often. But it seemed fitting that she should drink her pa's favorite, seeing as how he called the shots. How much had he paid that stupid bitch of a doctor's wife to fire her?

Carrie was sure that that's what had happened to the other jobs she had. Made only sense 'cuz she knew she hadn't done anything wrong. Certainly not wrong enough to fire her.

She sank down on the sofa she'd gotten from the Salvation Army. Not too bad for fifty bucks.

The tears were all gone. Numbly, she stared at the crack in her ceiling. "What the hell are you going to do now, Carrie Louise Harper?" Then she giggled.

A picture of Jesus on the cross which she'd torn out from some magazine was pasted on the wall. Carrie began wagging her finger at the painting. "You were sup'osed t'take care of me. I asked you special, didn't I? Well, didn't I?"

There was no answer from the photo. Normally, Carrie would not have expected one, but tonight she did. Tonight she felt Jesus had really screwed up. She remembered the omen that had come to her just before she'd seen the job ad. A car license plate that had said "CMC."

Why had He told her to answer the ad for CMC if he wasn't going to give her a good job? Why had he helped her with the stupid licensing people to change her name? Just to play around with her?

"Hell, no." She glared at the picture. "No one fucks up with Carrie Harper, L.V.N. D'ye hear that?" She stood up to her full height of five feet, eight inches. She really wasn't short, just a bit on the dumpy side.

From under the sofa, Carrie removed her father's shotgun. She didn't know why she'd gone and done that, but she'd seen the butt sticking out from under the skirt of the sofa. Like another omen.

Firing at the picture, she blasted the wall. With tears in her eyes, Carrie cried, "That's what I think of you, Jesus. You and all your big promises . . . You're nothing to me. And neither is that fucking hospital!"

She was shouting at the top of her lungs, but obviously she wasn't really doing it, because none of the neighbors were banging on the walls or ceiling like when she did speak real loud. From this Carrie concluded that this was a dream she was in. And if it was a dream, then she was going to have a happy ending.

The idea came to her, just like magic. She wasn't quite sure. Maybe Jesus was sorry. Maybe he'd put the idea there. But it was a good one. No, it was a great one.

Carrie laughed out loud. Pleased with herself and with her thoughts.

"Okay you motherfucking Stauton and you pig's eye Sophie, I'm gonna get you now. If I don't have no job, then you folks don't either!"

Without her coat, without her shoes, Carrie strode out the door of her apartment and headed toward CMC's ICU.

Yeah, they were going to see they couldn't mess with Carrie Louise.